The Timber Stone

···

Dave Abare

Hear Our Voice LLC

"To Lenore. Your love and support of me in whatever I wish or imagine is selfless and beautiful, as are you. I love you."

The Timber Stone

A novel by David Abare

CHAPTER 1

S he must have recognized me. She was in that garden for an hour and had looked over her shoulder thirty, maybe forty times. Half of her glances included a smile. One was followed by the dropping of her gloves, moving as if she might come say hello. She didn't. Instead, she wiped sweat from her forehead and sipped blush wine from a glass with ice cubes. Finally, she waved. Rock on.

We were in Central Vermont. The East Village may boast celebrities on every corner, but not here. So, when a guy with my history moves in, you're going to notice. She had, but was playing coy. For the moment, I was alright with that.

The early June sun and scurrying breeze had most of the cul-de-sac tending to their lawns, pools, and landscaping. Mowers roared, weed whackers whined, and dogs barked as they chased sweaty humans around their lawns. My canine pal, Pickle—a twenty-pound pug with the energy of a world champion tumbling squad—surveyed the neighborhood and its inhabitants, hoping to soon drench them in slobber. He was most interested, as was I, in the gardening beauty a hundred yards away.

"We just got here, buddy. Let's soak it in for a bit," I told him. He tilted his head, and one-third of his tongue stuck through his crooked little choppers.

I should have been inside writing instead of gawking. Half the reason I migrated here was "the book". But, the weather was sublime and my motivation had dwindled from paltry to zero percent. It didn't need to be on paper yet anyway. It was all safely tucked away in the noggin', ready to be unleashed soon enough. I'm no writer, but a hefty advance and my name on something other than a bunch of crappy songs written years ago sounded appealing. Plus, after everything that happened, time to get the hell out of L.A..

Los Angeles gets a bad rap, so I won't pile on, but I was more than ready for a change. There are few natives there—everyone is from someplace else. Half the people you bump into on the street are more famous than you. The ones that aren't want to know how you can help them be. Eh, I said I wouldn't pile on. Vermont's nice. There's a familial quality to it, all New England really. That certainly doesn't exist in Southern California.

I could have brought my laptop outside, busted out pages as the mowers whirred, sipping on an IPA, all the while glancing across the street like some creep. She hadn't been shy about staying in my eyeline, so it wouldn't be *that* creepy. Pathetic, yes. Pickle sure wanted to say hello. He whimpered and wiggled his curly tail every time she looked over, which he noticed despite the distance. The dog could spot a pinto bean atop Mount Everest, and I could barely read my driver's license from a foot away.

"Soon enough, Pick," I told him, which sent his wrinkled, apple-sized head tilting in the opposite direction and his tongue back into his mouth.

It was always possible that she didn't know me and was just being curiously friendly. The previous owner of the house, Bob, lived there for twenty-five years from what I heard at the closing. Anyone new in the neighborhood would draw stares. Maybe she heard about "the incident" on the TV show and was concerned her tranquil cul-de-sac would be turned into a den of debauchery, sending property values into the dumper. I had no such plan, so those fears would be unfounded. Of course, my relationship with booze left the door of possibility open.

Her house was smaller than mine, but the exquisite landscaping made it look a lot more impressive. I paid a couple fellas from Craigslist to plant a few bushes and tune up the lawn before I moved in, but there was no comparison. She had rose bushes, rhododendrons, and begonias all exploding with pinks, reds and yellows. And her grass was greener than one of those awful smoothies I used to drink at the L.A. gym.

Little Miss-Yellow-Sundress-Pulling-Weeds caught me staring and smiled. I waved to her as my other hand stroked Pickle's head. He whimpered, still wondering why we weren't frolicking with the beautiful woman across the road. It'd be douchey if I didn't go say hello soon, but I also didn't want to go in guns blazing. Central Vermont, with its clean air, quiet streets, forthright people, and relaxed pace was dead nut opposite of Los Angeles. I wasn't about to muck up the flow. Plus, I'm not a kid anymore and my body has serious objections to standing up too fast.

This was the second time I'd seen her outside since I moved in, and so far, no sign of other life. No lover, no children, no pets. They might all be playing Xbox inside and chewing rawhides and whatnot, but early indications were that she lived in the quaint little shack all by herself. If the book I was supposed to be writing were a novel, and not whatever it's yet to be and was paid too much money to scribble, I could pen some fiery thriller—*The Woman in the Yellow Dress* -- she lures people into her picturesque home with sultry smiles, boxed wine, and pleasantries, only to poison them and use their remains as garden fertilizer. That was probably already a book. Had to be. And that was precisely why I was writing a memoir and not a novel. The only original idea I'd had in years was to up and leave L.A. almost overnight.

Shit, *that* wasn't even original.

I chose Vermont because I'd always loved it as a child. I grew up in Connecticut, and at Christmas my mother would take us to see cousins in Rutland. I loved the powdery quality of the snow and the way it clung to the trees, covering nearly every visible surface. Snowmobiles filled the streets and nobody was ever yelling. People smiled, knew each other by name, even shook hands out of respect. Those winter days were filled with us kids drinking hot cocoa and sledding. The adults tipped small bottles into their coffees, laughing loudly around a wood stove.

I found the house by sheer luck. One of my band roadies mentioned his father was selling his Vermont property. I looked at the pictures online and did a quick video tour. It was just what I wanted, so I made the deal through email and flew in for the closing. I probably should've cased the neighborhood a bit because who the hell knew what kind of backwoods loons might be living next door. *Forensic Files* reruns occasionally flitted through my head, but so far it seemed safe enough. Then again, how would I know? Pickle was no help because Charlie Manson could walk up to the front door with a Satanic Bible, a battleax, and a flame thrower and he'd still lick the dude's skin off as his tail went in two hundred−mile−per−hour circles atop his wiggly butt.

I decided to head over and say hello. What's the worst that could happen? A whole hell of a lot, especially if you had read that awful, *The Woman in the Yellow Dress*. I tied Pickle to his run, because he can be a lot to take in at first if you're not a dog person. He'd climb straight into your mouth if you weren't careful.

The little bugger looked at me like I'd just strapped him into the electric chair when I clipped his run onto his collar. "Holy smokes, and I thought I was pathetic. Well, you know what, pal? We're a package deal. If she's got a problem with you then she has one with me. Let's go," I instructed, unclipping the tether, sending him into spastic circles.

Pickle bounded across the lawn, careful not to travel more than a few feet ahead of me, as always. He relished outdoor adventures but wanted me close by to experience them with him.

"She may be more of a cat person, buddy," I told the panting pooch. He looked up at me but continued prancing forward, tongue stuck out like an Olympic ski jump.

Man, I love that dog.

CHAPTER 2

We're living in a time now where walking right up to a woman, even if you're smiling and look somewhat pleasant like me, could be viewed as hostile. I understand, I get it—absolutely. For years women were supposed to just accept these Neanderthals grinning at them for a few seconds before their eyes fell to their chest and then had to listen to, "Looking good, honey," and "Daaaaaaamn!" while wondering if the staring and verbal dysentery meant the moron was now also going to be *a problem*, as many were. I like to believe that I was never that overt. That I wasn't some hulking, leather–jacket–wearing sack of testosterone with lips, but the truth is—especially in the band years—I probably was. I convinced myself as I grew older that because I was on the other side of the coin for so long, with women clamoring to meet me after a gig or on the streets when that horrible TV show aired, that I was *clean*. That I couldn't be labeled a womanizer because all I was doing was responding to their advances. In truth, however, I'm certain that most of the women I met would have been just as happy talking about the show or one of our albums instead of being objectified and then abandoned backstage somewhere like Grand Rapids, Michigan.

I was never hostile or dangerous, but I'd had many moments of female schmuckery in days past.

I tend to wander with words, which you'll notice, so I apologize. I also speak colorfully a lot, but I assure you it's not an attempt to be cool. It's just a by-product of the life I've lived. In my early days with the band, I tried to be more refined, choose softer language, etc., but after a couple months hanging out with roadies, even the Queen of England would start dropping some F bombs. I was rather adept at assimilating to my environment, so I usually didn't scare anyone off, at least with language. Almost forgot why I'm even talking about this, but it's because I was headed across the street to introduce myself to that neighbor of mine. I didn't come in hot, don't worry. Not carrying a bottle of whiskey or pulling in the driveway on a Harley or wearing a tool belt or some idiocy; just sauntered over casually like an early autumn leaf floating down onto your potato salad at a Labor Day picnic.

"Hey there," I said. Classic opening.

She looked at me and grinned, taking off her gardening gloves and dropping them at her feet. "How are you? All settled in over there?" she asked while Pickle made a beeline for her shins.

"Pickle, dial it down, buddy," I said, shaking my head. "I'm sorry, he's nuts about meeting new people."

"Oh, it's fine. He's adorable," she said, squatting down to meet him on his level. "What did you say his name was, Pickle?"

"Indeed. Not sure why, but yes," I answered.

"Oh, aren't you just precious, you little stinker. Look at that face," she said as his tongue shot out like a frog on cocaine, dabbing and slopping her cheek and neck.

"Pickle, let her breathe, nutjob," I said, scooping up the maniacal mutt and holding him against my leg while I crouched down.

"He's a sweetheart. No bother," she said, wiping the slop from her neck and face onto her arm.

"He's something, alright. So, yes, I think I'm mostly settled in over there, finally. Hopefully, the noise some of those nights wasn't too loud, moving things around and whatnot. I'm the proverbial bull in a china shop," I replied.

"Oh gosh no, not at all. I have an eight-year-old boy, so most of my waking hours involve high decibels. I'm Laurel, by the way, Laurel Mayes," she said, waving her hand at me, which was insanely adorable.

Ixnay on the living alone.

"Pleasure to meet you, Laurel," I said, extending my hand.

"Oh, jeez, I've been working out here all morning. I don't want to get your hand all gross," she told me, before letting out an overzealous laugh.

"If you saw what I pulled out of the disposal in my place when I moved in, you'd have no fear about soiling my hands," I said, her eyes widening.

"Wow, I'm surprised because Bob—he was the gentleman who used to live there—was very meticulous. Can't imagine him leaving the place in anything but perfect order."

"I was half joking. Bit of a hairball was all it was, and the place was immaculate, absolutely. Had a chance to meet Bob, at the closing, seemed like a nice fella. Any idea why he was selling? Didn't want to ask him because it seemed invasive, but it's so beautiful here. Life inside my own Norman Rockwell. Can't imagine why anyone would leave."

She shrugged her shoulders and dipped her head, which was also adorable. She was pleasant, demure, had kind eyes, and even with the likely terror an eight-year-old could bring to a neighborhood, it seemed doubtful she was scaring anyone away.

"He'd lived here a long time, but I know he had family down in North Carolina he wished he could see more. We knew each other, but not that well," she said, her eyes wandering around like a meth head following a housefly.

The sneeze that followed explained the stroke I thought she was having. "Bless you. Holy smokes, that was a production."

She chuckled. "Thank you. I know, it's crazy. This sunlight makes me sneeze a lot, and when I feel them coming, I'm all over the place," she replied.

"It's cute. I didn't know eyeballs could move that quickly."

She chortled, and her face turned rosy. Pickle sat tight against my thigh, his chest firm into my palm, waiting to explode forward if I loosened my grip.

"Well, Bob's loss is my gain," I said, smiling at her, and immediately regretting it as the redness in her face deepened. Not in the "Awww, that's so incredibly sweet" way, but instead the, "Oh, here we go...another idiot trying to mount me" way.

"I'm Josh Traxon, and I apologize for that horrific sentence, and more so that I was actually looking at you when I said it. I might've got away with it had I been scanning the landscape versus right into your eyes like some lunatic. Can we just erase these last fifteen seconds and—"

My rambling pseudo apology was cut short by a small human moving at cat-like speed across the deep, rustic white front porch and down the wooden steps, sneakers clapping and clomping. "Who are you?" the boy inquired at full volume.

"Ethan be polite. This is our new neighbor, Mister..."

"Traxon. Josh Traxon," I interjected, watching her search for my forgotten surname.

"Oh jeez, I'm so sorry. I'm terrible with names, but you only told me a second ago," she offered, her head turning away toward the boy at the top of the porch.

He stood there staring at me, his left hand clutching what looked like a fluorescent green Ninja throwing star with rounded edges. His chestnut hair was cropped tight, almost a buzz cut, undoubtedly a mom Special.

"What's that you got in your hand there, Ethan?" I asked him, Pickle whimpering and wiggling. He pulled the doodad up close to his chest, just covering the fuzzy face of one of those *Pokemon* critters the little folks were all into.

"It's my fidget spinner," he answered, twirling it around on his pinky for a couple seconds before it fell to the porch with a *wap-clink.*

"Ethan, why don't you go back inside for a minute, see if Gram is okay?"

"I just talked to her. She asked me who the man mommy was talking to is, so I runned outside to ask you," Ethan replied.

Laurel's face reddened again. "I'm sorry. My mother lives here with us and..."

"No worries," I assured her, grinning back up at the kid, tempted to correct his grammar but remembering that at eight I usually had my hand in my pants and was afraid to speak, never mind form proper sentences.

"And it's *ran* outside, Ethan, not *runned*. You know that. Don't be lazy with your words," his mother admonished.

Ethan said nothing, continuing to stare at me and Pickle while he rolled the toy around between his fingers. I could feel his grandmother gazing at me disapprovingly from one of the large front windows as well, though I had no evidence of this, other than a sudden spine-tingling chill.

"Well, I don't want to be a bother, just figured I'd formally introduce myself. It was nice meeting you both, and I'm sure I'll see you around."

Of course you will, dummy, you live directly across the street.

10

"It was nice meeting you too," Laurel said, shielding her eyes from the sun with her forearm.

"Would you like some cashews, either of you?" I asked, fumbling for them in the left front pocket of my jeans, sending Pickle up onto my knee to scope out the situation.

"Cashews?" Laurel questioned, her face scrunching up in the middle.

"I know, it sounded ridiculous before I even finished saying it. Offering you pocket nuts. Ouch, now that sounds even worse," I said, running my hand over the back of my neck.

"I actually love them, but I think I'm going to pass on the cashews in your pocket for now."

"Good call. Wow, yeah. Sorry."

She was silently laughing—cracking up but making no sound, as Ethan stood watching our curious interplay, twirling his gizmo.

"I'm sure Pickle will adore you, Ethan. So, if your mom is okay with it, I'll bring him by again soon and you two can chase each other around the yard."

Ethan giggled or coughed or something I couldn't quite decipher, so I winked and made a silly face. He whipped around, bolting back into the house, shouting, "Nana, it's the neighbor man! It's the neighbor man!"

"I'm sorry," Laurel offered, shaking her head, watching her boy dash off. "He's been a little excited seeing you move in...and I think he and my mother were discussing it earlier. He's generally a pretty mellow kid but this has been a lot I guess."

"The world's a fascinating place at that age. Every new person you meet is an adventure. He'll soon discover that I'm about as fun as a box full of dirt, though. Will break the poor kid's heart."

She scrunched up her face again. "Can I assume you don't have any kids yourself?"

I shook my head no.

"Ah, well, if you *did,* you'd know that a box of dirt is about as exciting as it gets at eight years old," she said, a sly grin painted the left side of her face.

"Well, I can tell you that my intellectual capacity and vocabulary are right there at his level, so add the box of dirt thing in, and I guess we're gonna be besties, as they say."

"Who says that?" she asked, furrowing her brow.

I smirked and then nodded my head a couple times before mumbling to myself.

"It was nice meeting you, Mr. Traxon—great name by the way—and if you need anything as you're getting set up over there—tools, duct tape, you name it—we have it all here. My mother bought up every ounce of survival gear in existence when the Y2K thing was happening. Don't think ninety percent of it was ever touched."

"First of all, call me Josh, please. Secondly, let your mom, who's apparently MacGuyver, know that I'll definitely take her up on that. I'm fairly handy, but I have nothing more than a couple screwdrivers, a pair of plyers, and a crappy hammer."

"I guess I'll be seeing you soon, then."

Don't do it. Don't do it. Don't do it.

"Indeed. You guys enjoy the rest of your day," I said, avoiding a trillion obvious, pathetic comebacks as I scooped up the pooch and held him to my chest.

"Oh, and Josh," she yelled over as I left her yard, "Were you a weatherman on TV at some point, or on the radio? I can't tell if it's your voice or face that's familiar?"

A weatherman? Hmmpf. I love Al Roker as much as the next guy, but do I really look like a guy who points out occluded fronts and cumulonimbus clouds in front of a green screen? Could be in jest, though. Trying to play coy, while in truth she'd recorded every episode of my awful show and had my band's tattoo on her lower back.

"Nope on the weatherman and radio. You're on to something, but let's save that for another time," I suggested.

"Sounds good. Take care," she said, and then smiled and turned back toward her house.

I'm not going to lie and say I didn't check her out from that angle, nor will I pretend that what I saw filling out the lower half of that yellow, flower-infused sundress wasn't spectacular. I'm a weak, flawed, generally pathetic man that once stepped into a sewer drain because a woman smiled at me for more than three seconds. I was seventeen and probably huffing Raid, leave me alone.

I walked back to my place, popped a cashew into my mouth, grinding it up nice, and then took a deep breath in through my nose and let it resonate before pushing back out through my mouth. It was an influx of pine, cut grass, lemon rind, and stagnant water, with a hint of the nut I'd been chewing. I'd had far worse things up my nose and in my mouth in the past, including all kinds of nightmares sourced by the chubby pup I was cradling.

The daylight had stretched itself over the landscape of my front yard, bending off the bright white corners of the outside trim and spilling into pockets that had been dark an hour earlier. A lone beam ricocheted off one of the white gutters that hung from the piece of roofing that covered my front porch, illuminating a patch of grass that was withered and amber in color. In L.A. ninety percent of the grass looked that way, and if you were lucky, you'd get a patch of hunter green, shaggy growth here and there on your lawn, which in total was no bigger than a card table. This particular patch, however, wasn't the result of poor soil or climate, but instead, the ball of wrinkles and eyeballs I was carrying.

When I lived out west, one of the roadies and guitar techs for my band, Jeremiah Stoven—what a name on that guy—showed up at my place with this nine-week-old puppy. It was wiggling and whining to get out of his arms, dead staring me, so he let it go and the dog was about to stroke out trying to climb up my leg. I sat down on the floor, and his wrinkled, smushed-in face released this maniacal tongue that wiped across every inch of my cheeks and chin as Jeremiah told me their dog had four puppies and this was the last one. He knew I was a dog nut and said he wanted me to have it. Ballsy move, just showing up with it, aware that I'd always been enamored with the critters. I hadn't had a dog in ages, so Jeremiah said, "It's time, dude," and just left the two-pound hairball with me, almost four years ago now. Have to say, it was a near genius move on Jeremiah's part, arriving pup in hand, never letting me get a word in, and then vanishing as the canine was pissing on my Fender jazz bass. The little bugger had some accidents early on, but he was a quick study to housebreaking.

Pickle had decided, for reasons that only his tiny, deranged mind could know, that when he peed in the front yard of his new place, it would only happen on this one, now brownish spot of turf. He'd storm out of the house, perform his ritualistic dance of what I'd always called "devil circles," where he'd speed in figure eights confined to a small stretch of earth, then explode into random darts and weaves with his tongue dangling and flopping like an uncooked slice of bacon out of the side of his mouth. Then, without warning, he'd make a beeline to 'the spot' and take a leak. I guess this lunatic expulsion of energy was formally called "the zoomies," according to whatever experts' study dogs going batshit nuts, and it was completely normal, but a sight to behold. He'd always done the frantic running, zoomy whatever it is, but the peeing on that specific patch was new behavior. Of course, I had just taken a small animal that had known the same home for his entire life across the country and plopped him in a place that looked entirely different than anything he'd experienced. There was one dainty tree in our backyard in L.A. that wasn't any taller than the fence that bordered our property, and now he's surrounded by hundreds that dwarf most of the houses we had on our old block.

Go ahead and take a leak wherever you want, buddy.

As I walked onto my lawn and Pickle shot into the grass, flames nearly coming off his paws as he did his thing, I heard the distinctive rumble of a classic muscle car approaching. In L.A. they were everywhere—an all-day event rolling down the block, one after the next—but this was the first I'd heard here since I'd arrived. Sounded like a Chevy, but I was miserable at discerning the difference anymore, having defected to German cars long ago. I sat on the top step of my porch, watched Pickle lose his mind for a moment, then caught the first sight of the black Pontiac GTO as it entered my eyeline. Not a Chevy, but still a General Motors product, so not a total fail.

The car pulled into Laurel's driveway. She slid off her gloves and made her way over to the vibrating machine, the driver still inside. The engine cut, and Pickle was squatting on his spot, taking a leak. He was all boy, as evidenced by the massive set of nuts I'd removed years earlier and the oversized schwang he had between his legs, which, in full glory, looked like a lipstick for a hippo. Regardless, he chose to squat and pee versus lifting his leg at least ninety percent of the time. Maybe dogs, along with humans, were beginning to allow gender lines to blur, at least when it came to bathroom concerns. Or perhaps he'd watched me sit on the toilet to pee for the duration of his life and, like me, he'll pee anywhere he pleases. Damn, I love that dog.

The driver of the car stepped out, and I watched Laurel's little boy fly out onto the porch and then do an about face and run back inside, Laurel saying something inaudible to him as he ran away. My guess was that in mere moments this guy would be looking my way, which was customary for any man driving a high horsepower car and catching a whiff of new testosterone in the area. Pickle was barking at the new visitor across the road, little farts coming out of his tiny butt as he forced air out from his lungs, which often confused and frightened him, so he'd turn his head back and stare at his own butt, bewildered. I knew dogs had moments of brilliance, but there were times when I felt like sweet little Pickle would lose an argument with a jellybean.

GTO guy did, in fact, start peering over at me. Laurel grabbed his arm and held him back from heading in my direction, which was odd because, other than being delightfully handsome, he'd have no reason to be angry with me. Maybe she told him about the pathetic flirtation and he was jealous, or maybe he was just an asshole and wanted to come pee on my lawn too, mark his territory and whatnot. Either way, Pickle was the only one that would be doing any marking around here, and if three-hundred-seventy horsepower guy wanted to tangle, he was walking into more than he expected.

I heard that in my mind and sure, it sounded douchey, but it wasn't untrue. There are a few surprises with me if you follow along, none of which involve modesty, apparently. One is that I'm insanely good at chess for no discernable reason other than luck, and had an online tournament starting in ten minutes.

"Pickle, come on buddy!" I yelled, snapping him out of his barking fit and sending him scurrying under my legs and into the house.

Laurel and the man with the car made their way into her place, him taking one more peek over at me. If he knew who I was, he'd lose his shit. Who the hell wanted that moving in across the street from your girlfriend?

My eyes met his right before shutting the front door.

Josh moves e4. Black GTO counters e5. Josh moves d4. Black GTO counters queenside Knight to C6.

Just some chess geekery. I'll explain later.

CHAPTER 3

‑‑‑

N o matter what you may think, and regardless of what you've read, heard in movies, or what some stoned, aging hipster told you at a barbecue right after he shamed you for not liking David Bowie enough—being famous kicks a fair amount of ass.

Sure, I know where your mind's going. The endless "Yeah, buts..." and anecdotal examples of this celebrity or the next, the cautionary tales of rock stars and artists, and the poor lottery winner who ended up living in a dishwasher box behind a pizza place—*I know*. No point in disputing any of those examples as they're all true, and for each instance you can name as being an awful price paid, I can probably name three more that were far worse. One very famous writer friend of mine didn't really die of "natural causes," but in fact expired because he got hammered on seven-dollar merlot, passed out with peanut butter on his no—no place, and his iguana bit into his scrotum and the poor guy bled out. *He died after a large green lizard—albeit a beloved pet—tore into his man purse, causing him to bleed to death.* Read that sentence as many times as you need to, let it sink in, and then realize that this writer friend of mine likely died with a gargantuan smile on his face because he went belly-up with over nine hundred thousand Twitter followers.

Undoubtedly, some of you will now scour the Internet and figure out who I'm talking about when you find a picture of the poor sap with a lizard on his shoulder, smoking a pipe or something that writers do. It won't matter because if we could reanimate my old friend and ask him, he'd still say he loved being famous even if the entire world found out that a mini Godzilla noshed on his giggle berries and killed him.

I, too, am famous, as you may have gathered by now. Not upper echelon, household name level, but famous enough where you'd likely recognize my face, and undoubtedly my voice, with its milky baritone notes cradled in whispers. The voice served me well in my years with a band, and before I offer up the big reveal in favor of a long, drawn-out, anti-climactic tease, let me mention that I wasn't a front man or lead singer in some legendary rock outfit, but instead a backing voice. Played the bass. Was on a popular TV show for five seasons. Dated an LA Laker girl.

Nothing? Shit. Come on.

Just Google me—you already know the name—but for those of you in your late twenties up through your fifties, there's no way you don't know who I am. Normally bass players in moderately successful alternative rock bands don't leave much of an imprint on society, or even on the fans of the bands they're in, but I was able to elevate myself through a combination of writing intriguing, if not ostentatious, lyrics and never shutting my mouth when there was a camera nearby. My bass playing was atrocious—still not even sure if I know how to play the damn thing—but with the nice pipes I was able to add a colorful layer to the band's sound, and we managed to crank out a few hits on Alt-Rock radio over seven years and change.

Even if you don't have all four albums from Shaky Bones—don't ask, I didn't pick the name—and you can't recall any of our songs, you certainly recall the television show *Melting Pot* on The Artists Channel. Remember that horrible, MTV/VH1 rip-off station that lasted about ten years and was all anyone talked about for five? Yeah, that one. Well, their most popular show, *Melting Pot*, was where I ended up for five seasons after the band folded, likely because I was usually hammered and never shut up, and something about that screams great TV, I guess.

Before I get into why I moved to Vermont after living in Los Angeles for more than fifteen years, let me just clear the air on that one notable incident on the show. One needn't be Stephen Hawking to know that if you put several monster egos together in a house—musicians, actors, athletes—there's going to be drama. Not Shakespeare or Lifetime movie kind of drama; I mean full-fledged, batshit Springer-esque drama. An unrivaled flurry of yelling, screaming, hand gestures, self-importance, and indulgence. *Melting Pot* was that and then some, but audiences loved it, and so did I. For a while. I'm not ashamed to admit I became caught up in the spectacle of it all, and yes—flying too close to the sun on wings made of Agave, I made love to a potholder on national television during my final season. In my defense, the producer was very aware of my relationship with tequila and took no precautionary measures prior to our "Very Special *Live* Season Finale," keeping the home where we all resided during taping well stocked with my Mexican kryptonite. Not to mention, it was a beautiful potholder—soft pastel colors and fabric as gentle as a dewdrop falling from a dandelion.

I don't have regrets about it, and I'm not just saying that like every dolt who gets busted doing something ridiculous does. Five days later, they're sobbing to a late-night talk show host, or even worse, in a self-produced video they post to YouTube or Twitter that will exist for endless lifetimes, giving douche chills to anyone with functional retinas and eardrums. That never happened in my case, nor will it, because as I said when I first started rambling, being famous is great. Greater still when you're not remembered as a cowering, blubbering fool because you screwed up—and they blocked out most of the potholder party anyway.

I know, some of you who watched the show or have just searched me are saying, "Heeey, waaaaiiit, what about that *other* incident?" Fair enough. That was an awful time in my life, but that's not why I ran across the country to Vermont. I moved here because the money I was miraculously able to hold on to from the days in the band and the TV show goes a lot further in Vermont's serene woods than in La La Land. I sold my thirteen-hundred-square-foot house nestled between Valley Park and Hermosa Beach for enough to buy an entire town in upper New England, but settled on a twenty-two-hundred-square-foot Colonial and some mid-life-crisis-machines with four wheels and stuck the rest into a couple mutual funds this nerd in Rutland advised me to when I got there. Seemed like a nice guy; smart, successful. But when I asked him who his favorite band was, he giggled and said, "I'm more of a Top 40 fella" and I nearly had an aneurysm. If he wasn't driving the six-figure sports sedan parked out front, I probably would have just left and put all my cash in a pillowcase because I can't have a professional relationship with someone I have *nothing* in common with, you know?

The other reason I traveled east was to write. Not a pathetic novel or some collection of dreadful poems like so many actors and musicians do, but a memoir, or whatever I want it to be, really. My agent told me there was a hundred-thousand-dollar advance and decent royalties if I would put something together, so I started scribbling some pages. Beginning a project like that, I imagined, would be a lot easier in the tranquil surroundings of Vermont versus the lunacy of Los Angeles, where even a has-been like me can't walk down the street without TMZ jamming a camera in your face.

Yeah, yeah, I know, I said fame is great. Settle down.

CHAPTER 4

"**H**oly crap, you're...that guy, from the show! Justin, or..."
One of the side effects of C-list level fame was the "I know I know you" stare. I would be standing in line at McDonalds or washing my car or just looking up at the sky like a lunatic—whatever—and someone nearby would keep looking at me with a terrifying, clown-like grin until I acknowledged them. If they figured out *why* they knew me before they engaged, it was even worse. This one just did, and she was headed right for me.

"Joshua. How are you?" I asked, super psyched.

"This is so cool! Terry, get over here," she said, summoning a severely disinterested, rotund man about ten years her senior, holding a greasy white paper bag full of French fries. "This guy was on TV, that show I used to watch with all the celebrities. I can't believe it."

This happens a lot in L.A. and other big cities, but I have to say I'm dumbfounded that my first real trip out of the house and into a town with about seven hundred residents found me ensnared in such a scenario.

"Thanks for watching. Always nice to meet fans," I offered, which sounded even more pathetic and disingenuous than it appears on the page.

"Oh, I adoooooored you on that show, didn't I, babe?" she asked fry guy. He waved, then wiped a three-inch strip of grease across his gray T-shirt before staring at the ass of a woman getting into a Dodge Neon. "Seriously, I had them all taped. Loved you and the whole gang."

"Much appreciated," I responded, nodding.

"I read on the Internet that there was going to be a reunion show," she said, simultaneously striking her bulbous life partner for gazing at the caboose fifteen feet away.

"Well, there's always a lot of rumors about that, but I think the show's done. The network's gone, and I can't imagine it would have traction anywhere else. Was fun at the time, though. Hey, it was great to meet you, but I need to run to the hardware store," I replied.

"Terry," the woman snapped, whacking her fella on the shoulder. "Take a picture with your phone of me and Josh here. You don't mind, right?"

Ahh, the "assumptive close." They gear up for the picture but slide in at the end that they have concerns about "if you mind" or not. At that point, they're already leaning into me, smelling like cigarettes, butter, or cat pee (the three most common scents of random street pic requests) and some other nut is snapping the picture. If I protest or run off before it's taken, I'm cursed out, and five stories show up online that I'm awful to my fans. I rarely balk on the pictures, but there's no question I'm frostier to the fans of the TV show than I am to those who loved the band.

The music fans, for the most part, want to talk about our songs, concerts they went to and other bands they adore. The initial star struck phase quickly dissipates into musical nerd-vana, and

24

I can hang with that a lot longer than these two who, if pressed, will admit they went to a mall and waited an hour to get JWow's autograph.

"I still can't believe it," she shouted, inches from my ear. "So, are you like, living here now?"

"Indeed," I said, knowing what was coming next.

"Cool! We should all hang sometime. Terry has a poker game at the house every other Friday, and we're always around. Terry, give him your business card," she yelled to him as he stood on the curb, less interested in me than a cat would be in anything you're doing that doesn't involve string.

"I'm sure I'll see you around. It was great to meet you. Have a good day, guys," I said, scurrying down the block.

She smiled at me, but it was a defeated smile. She stood there, in a shabby green dress, pink flip flops, and dyed blonde hair fluttering in the breeze, watching me go down the sidewalk towards the hardware store, and as always, I felt bad. Not despondent, not wrecked, but a smidge of guilt. I never had the star struck gene myself, and it's hard to exist in the mind of those who have it. I admired talented musicians and artists and have had some engaging conversations over the years with many of them, but even before I was famous, I never gushed over the luminaries and idols. I understood why others might, on some level, but my utter disdain for small talk made it virtually impossible to entertain anyone for too long in these situations. If I looked back, offered one last smile and a nod, she'd likely still be staring, lips downturned and face sullen, or she'd instantly snap out of it and shout something else, hopeful for one last engagement.

Don't turn around. Don't turn around. Don't do it, dummy!

"Nice meeting you, Josh! Oh, and hey, whatever happened with that car accident?"

DAVE ABARE

Sweet fancy fucknuggets.

Therein lies the danger of allowing guilt and empathy to cloud reason, because most of these folks will shout something from fifty feet away that's not a simple answer I can give while trying to leave. I stopped and turned around, running my right hand across the back of my head. "I'm fine, yeah. Long time ago now, but thanks for asking. You take care."

She said something I couldn't hear, so I waved, turned around, and huffed it toward the hardware store before Terry started offering me fries.

The street was Small Town Americana 101. Cracked sidewalks bordered by maples, elms, and vibrant flowering plants in weathered wooden boxes. Hand drawn signs hung in most windows, advertising sale items, business hours, or the potluck being held at the VFW Friday night. Across the road, a man painted the street on canvas as locals stopped to say hello and compliment his work. The Dodge Neon, piloted by Terry's ass obsession, pulled away from the block, and its exhaust leak scared a handful of feasting sparrows from their sidewalk-crumbs up into the trees. As the green leaves shuffled and intermingled above my head in the May breeze, a familiar, smirking face, clad in a yellow T-shirt and baseball hat, appeared directly in my path.

"Hey, I know you. You're the guy who delivers my oil, right?" I asked.

His face contorted, staring straight up at me, the fidget spinner twirling in his left hand.

"Okay, wait, maybe I'm mistaken. You're the guy who changes the oil in my *car*, that's it."

He fought back a laugh.

"Oh, waaaaaiiit a second. Now I remember. You're the little guy from across the street, Ethan. I'm sorry, but I'm new around here, so everyone kind of looks the same," I said, eliciting a shaking head from the child. "Where's your mom?"

"She's in the hardware store with Nana and Barry, getting a hose for the washer machine."

Kinda loved that he said 'washer' machine there.

"Ah, gotcha," I said, right as Laurel came flying out of the store in a panic, calling Ethan's name.

"Ethan, honey, what did I tell you about running off like that? You scared me half to death," she said, crouching down to Ethan's eyeline and pulling him against her. "Just 'cause we live in a small town doesn't mean you can wander off. That's dangerous, you know that."

"Your mom's right, dude. Luckily, you ran into me and not these two loons I bumped into down the block. Lotta crazies out there," I said, winking at Laurel, and immediately hating myself for it.

"Hey, Josh," she offered, still visibly shaken. "I'm sorry to come out of there yelling like that, but he tends to disappear sometimes, and I get—"

"Don't worry about it," I interrupted. "I freak out when I can't find my keys; can't begin to imagine if I couldn't find my offspring. We were having a cool chat, though, weren't we, buddy?"

His face reddened, and he pulled up tight against his mother.

Laurel wrapped her arm around his torso and squeezed, smiling down at him. "That's probably why he ran out here. He saw you through the window, and he's a little obsessed with your car, I think. Watched you leaving in it this morning and was all he could talk about," she said.

"Ahh. So, are you a Porsche fan, or just love things that are loud?" I questioned.

"We could hear your car even when you went far away!" Ethan shouted.

I laughed, then smiled at Laurel, who made the "Well, it *is* pretty loud" face.

"You know, I was thinking I might need to take that exhaust off the car and put the stock one back on," I said, nodding my head. "Fine for noisy Los Angeles, but less so for idyllic backwoods New England towns. Sorry if I disturbed you guys."

"Oh, jeez no, it's fine, and he loves it, really. He saw a documentary on Porsche on Netflix—the kid watches everything, so I suppose I should feel blessed—so when he saw it in the driveway this morning he about freaked out," Laurel said.

"I liked the black car, too, but the Porsche is cooler," Ethan explained, somewhat murdering the brand name, but not bad for eight. "I would have traded it for that one but got red."

"Oh, the BMW, right. Well, good news is that I still have both cars, little dude. Didn't have to trade anything. I had the Porsche delivered on a truck, and it's been in my garage since before I got here. Going to need to get a pickup truck soon, too, I'm thinking. Gets snowy up here," I answered.

Ethan looked up at his mother, wide-eyed.

"Well, I'll let you go, and thanks again for looking after him for a minute, I appreciate—"

"You'll have *three* cars, just for yourself?" Ethan questioned at full volume.

Laurel rolled her eyes and smiled while an older woman and my Boris Spassky (just look it up) came up behind them. He dead stared me, then rubbed his right hand across the top of Ethan's head like he was trying to detach a vampire bat, nearly dislodging his ball cap.

"Hey, guys," Laurel said, turning toward them. "This is Mr. Traxon. He just moved in across the street."

"Right. The guy with more German metal than a Panzer division. Heard the Porsche this morning. What, you pull the cats off that thing?" the man in the strategically trimmed facial scruff inquired.

Notice how he had to mention he heard it *this morning*? That's dick measuring. Making me aware that he was there early this morning, knowing I also saw him last night. Translation: I am way up inside this woman, and you're not. Problem is, numb nuts, that declaration is like bringing your queen out right away. You've already revealed your weakness is making bold, reckless moves in the hopes it scares off your opponent, but I'm not some chess coach at the YMCA with a stained, knit tie and horn-rimmed glasses. I'm a walking, living, breathing Deep Blue with just enough Bobby Fischer to turn your lights out before you even realize you're playing.

That may have been a bit over the top. I came in third in my last online tournament, barely, and I make a buttload of mistakes even at my level, but it's fun inflating myself in my head.

"No, still got 'em. It's a BBi system a friend in L.A. stuck on for me. Lotta bite, but all legal. I'm Josh, by the way," I answered, extending my hand out toward his. It often twisted up these testosterone bombs when you hit them with kindness right out of the gate. He glared at me but returned the handshake, careful to make sure he applied enough pressure to crack an avocado pit.

"Josh, this is my mother, Helen. Mom, this is—"

"I know who he is. I'm not an idiot, Laurel. Hello. You moved into a beautiful home. Robert always took care of it, and I hope you'll do the same. He didn't have pets. They can wreck a place in no time," the silver haired woman interrupted.

29

Hulk handshaker smirked, Laurel shouted out a "Ma," and I looked into the tiny woman's eyes like Kasparov that first moment Magnus Carlsen sat in front of him at the chess board at the age of thirteen, uncertain of what to expect going forward while simultaneously knowing everything.

"Pleasure to meet you, ma'am, and I assure you that I'll keep my place looking immaculate, inside and out. Plus, Pickle—that's my dog—he's housebroken and well behaved."

"An Akita is a dog, a Mastiff, Bloodhound. Whatever that is, ain't canine. Probably easy to carry around though, in a backpack, or those tiny fake seats in the back of your car," my new best friend Barry said.

"Barry, stop," Laurel chimed in, as her mother laughed. Ethan squirmed, feeling Barry squeezing his pepperoni stick sized fingers into his shoulder.

Barry looked like Boomer Esiason, the ex-football player now commentator, though Barry's hair was a thinning, dirty blonde buzz cut. Both times I'd seen him now, he was wearing black jeans and a tattered T-shirt, this one navy blue with the sleeves pulled up enough to reveal tribal tattoos creeping down each of his arms. His chin was too small for his face, which widened and flared out as it went up from the neck, and his eyes were at the far end of the dark blue spectrum, closer to black.

Laurel's mother looked like the woman that may sell you the best bread you've ever eaten at a local Polish bakery. Tiny in stature, but no BS, wearing little makeup and only silver dot earrings to compliment her hair of the same shade.

"Hey, it was nice meeting you all, and I'm sure neighborhood picnics are going to be a blast. Need to zip into the hardware store, so I'll see you around," I said, keeping the sarcasm light though evident.

Laurel frowned as her mother and Barry walked past me, Ethan clutching her hand and staring up at my left ear.

"Nana and Barry said that earrings are for girls," Ethan reported.

"Honey, stop that! That's not—"

"It's fine, Laurel, really," I assured her. "You know what, Ethan? Lots of people have different things they like and opinions on how to dress, and that's okay. Boys *and* girls sometimes wear earrings, and I think that's cool. It's the same with cars, as some people like cars that can go really fast in a straight line, use a lot of gas, and weigh more than an aircraft carrier, while others like well-engineered cars that can go even faster and turn like a jet plane."

The obvious jab was lost on Ethan, though he listened intently. Laurel knew it was a dig at Barry and smirked but left it at that.

"I'll see you around, Josh, and sorry for the...well, just sorry for them," Laurel said, rolling her eyes.

"Nice seeing you, and don't worry about it. Small town, I'm the new guy—I get it. I'm sure mom and Brutus over there will adore me in no time. If not, I've always wanted to check out Alaska," I quipped.

"There's big bears there!" Ethan shouted up at me.

"Sure are, bud. Some around here, too, though less likely to eat us from what I hear," I replied.

Ethan's eyes stretched open, and Laurel chuckled.

"Take care, Josh," she said, pulling Ethan around and toward the other two, who'd just stopped on the sidewalk, looking back at us.

Fifty yards away, Barry eyeballed me, then whispered something in the tiny woman's ear, causing her to nod. I wanted to believe it was, "You know that guy has a bigger meat hammer than me," though I assumed it was more likely,

"Look at that earring-wearing wuss with the fancy little dog."
Whatever it was, it was a bold, if not reckless, move across the
board, and I would adjust my pieces accordingly. Laurel was
a kind-hearted, warm-tempered, gorgeous woman who, for a
currently inexplicable reason, was shacking up with a baboon.
Her mother, Helen, well, she was icy but not a lost cause.

I abandoned my analysis of the situation and walked over
to the hardware store, hopeful to find a decent shower head.
The current one in the master bedroom, no matter how many
different directions I turned it, provided nothing more than a
weak, dribbling tinkle. It's one of those items you forget so often
when buying a new home. I always check the water pressure
by running a few faucets on the main floor but fail to inspect
the showers, which are crucial. I'd almost rather skip bathing
altogether than have a half-assed stream of water pee all over
me. Baths are out because, at six-foot-four and two hundred
and twenty-five pounds, I feel like a rhino in a thimble full of
water.

Down the road, I heard the familiar rumble of Barry's
American muscle fire up. He probably got a stiffy knowing I
heard it. I hate to be so cynical and assumptive with people
sometimes, but after a while, like playing the same opponent in
chess time and time again, you start to see patterns emerge.

When someone shows you who they are, believe them.

No idea who said that, but even if it was Charlie Brown, the
shit is deep.

I couldn't shake Laurel. That shimmer in her eyes, smiling
like she knew it cut me at the knees. Maybe Barry was her
second cousin, just in town for a while. Maybe he was dating her
mom—hey, it's possible. Or maybe...*she actually liked the guy.*

It didn't matter, as I had bigger problems. Another online chess
tournament started in an hour and some yoyo with a sideways

baseball cap just followed me into the hardware store, grinning. I considered getting some peanut butter and a lizard.

CHAPTER 5

T he game of chess as we know it today began to take shape
in Europe in the late fifteenth century, though it had its
origins—as a slightly different game—in India hundreds of years
earlier. This is a fact, of course, that any dunderhead can find in
chess books or on Wikipedia. The only reason I'm telling you is
because if I'm going to converse in chess moves here and there,
real cool like, then you may want to have a basic understanding
of the game. Plus, you might enjoy having a few little factoids
at the ready if you're with your new girlfriend at her boss's New
Year's Eve party.

*"Yes, I did see the chess board. Beautiful. Looks like the pieces
may be marble, alabaster even. 'The sport of kings,' they call it.
Had its birth in India somewhere in the ninth century, and by the
time it made its way through Europe, it evolved into the modern
game of international chess we know today."*

Feel free to rework this with your own nuances and
inflections, but either way it's got just enough pompous
nerdiness and cocksure bravado to it that you'll leave her and
others in the room somewhat awestruck. Or they'll immediately
despise you, and her boss will turn out to be rated over nineteen

hundred and insist you play him in the living room where your soon-to-be-ex-girlfriend will watch you be eviscerated by the guy as he sips on a Moscow Mule as Steely Dan's "Aja" plays in the background.

I didn't learn how to play chess by accident, and it's not really luck, as I'd suggested. I'm also not some gifted idiot savant that looked at the board one morning and deconstructed the game in thirty minutes either—my father taught me at eight years old. The old man taught me little else, other than the difference between belts. Not how they looked, what purpose they served, or which colors best suited certain outfits, but how each type felt different striking my skin at over a hundred miles per hour. Chess was part reward for surviving the beatings and part penance for whatever insolence he'd invented in his head.

The first month I sat at that board, I was almost more terrified than when the belts came off, and he knew it. He'd get this grin on his face, sinister and satisfied, as I stared at the letters and numbers framing the natural brown and off-white squares on the pine board, perplexed. He'd wrap his meaty sausage fingers around my frail hand, dragging it onto a bishop, then slide the piece across the wooden surface, shouting about its role in the game. He'd illustrate the power of the knight, slapping the miniature white horse onto spots on the board in little L's, avoiding the sides. Railing on about the explosive power of the pawn in middle and end games, he'd veer into longwinded, drunken rants about overvaluing the queen. Incessantly, he'd align "Scholar's Mate"— one of the quickest potential checkmates in the game, built on the bishop and queen—hoping to catch me off guard, which he often did.

For about five weeks.

Something happened at that point. I'm not claiming anything supernatural, and I have no sensible explanation—but I could *see* the game. Not see it the way Magnus Carlsen sees it, playing games in his head blindfolded against ten freakin' Rhodes Scholars, the brilliant bastard, but see it enough that I was beating the old man handily in just months. That fact put the belt on me more frequently for a while, but then, abruptly, that dissipated with no explanation. Drinking bourbon until you're cross eyed and beating the snot out of your kid, well, that's some evil shit that you pay for on the inside as much as the outside, no question. But, when that same little kid annihilates you at a game *you* taught him months earlier, I'd imagine the embarrassment must be gargantuan.

The old man was gone by the time I was ten, but I'll always be grateful that he turned me on to the game. Now I sat staring at a screen with my nineteen hundred and seventy-four rating, munching cashews, about to start a tournament. Pickle stared up at me with a red, stuffed crab toy in his chops, his black ears flopped down beside his eyes, head tilted about twenty degrees to the right. He wore an expression communicating utter disgust. After all, how dare I choose to look at the computer instead of chasing him and wrestling the toy from his jaws.

"Go sit over there. You know I can't play well when you're staring at me,". In response to my request, he increased his head tilt and a sliver of his tongue peeked through his teeth. The next move would be wrapping in between my legs, occasionally looking up at me, waiting as long as it took for me to return eye contact. The curly, golden-brown tail would wiggle in a clunky circle until my gaze went back to the computer, and his wrinkled apple head would softly thump back onto the wood floor in defeat. Sometimes, at the old place, the sheer sappiness of his expression would shatter my resolve. I'd resign from the tournament early and chase him around the carpeted house. The entire main floor was cherry hardwood here. Not exactly the optimal setup for a running, twenty-pound beastie with unclipped claws.

Pickle wasn't the primary distraction from the tournament though. There was also the beautiful, engaging woman in a turquoise summer dress who recently walked inside her house with a probably-makes-his-own-fishing-lures-and-chews-tobacco looking oaf. Sicilian Openings and *en passants* were being clouded by moon-sized eyes and dirty blonde hair caressing tan shoulders. There was no question that I hoped to meet someone when I came back east. Eventually. Start dating again, settle down—all that grown up junk. I just didn't expect that the first object of my desire would live a hundred something yards away and smell like sunshine and unicorns.

"Fuckballs," I said out loud, raising one of Pickle's brows.

Oh, and about the chess move notations, it's easy enough to understand. A chess board has sixty-four squares, eight horizontal and eight vertical. We call the horizonal spaces A through H, and the vertical spaces 1 through 8. If a piece rests on the F3 space and then moves to the E5 location, say a Knight, which is the horsey, then we note it, "Knight F3 to E5." I'm not going to name and explain all the rest of the pieces for you because if you're interested, which is doubtful, you'll take the time to learn that on your own.

The first game began. "PugChess69" versus "DaHypeIsReal." You can guess which one I was. I had to change my username years earlier because I blurted it out on a radio show and a couple kooks started messaging me, incessantly requesting games. The lengths some will go to walk amongst the famous is mind—boggling, especially considering this celebrity right here usually plays wearing boxers, black socks, and no shirt while a drooling, flatulent, cat-sized canine gnaw a rancid, stuffed crustacean between his hairy legs.

White to E4, as always.

CHAPTER 6

I'm not ignoring the accident. I'll get around to it. My attention, however, is focused on a long stretch of elastic band hanging halfway out my pug's ass, entwined in dog crap and strands of hair.

It's not earth-shattering news to mention that dogs will eat anything, and if you've never owned a pug, then you've yet to experience a living Roomba. These stubby-legged, infinitely famished little critters will lick and chew carpets until every crumb of the footlong sub that didn't end up in your mouth finds its way into theirs. They'll drag their sloppy tongues across wood floors—a soft, fleshy pink magnet, depositing trails of drool as it slides over the surface and takes every forgotten morsel with it—for hours unless you stop them. They'll find week old, sun-dried hamburger tidbits in the grass from a recent BBQ that ants are attempting to crawl away with and lap them up like it was commanded by God. In this process of unsanitary gluttony, every fiber or hair that has also found its way to the ground will hop on for the ride and take the trip down the GI highway and end up at the other side.

That's where you come in.

It's not that I'm squeamish to the idea of tugging the poop strands out of the poor little guy's butt. Not at all. It's the vocalizations, and eye contact, made during the act that make me uncomfortable. In the last couple years—and keep in mind this happens at least twice a month—Pickle started making this off-putting groan/humming noise as I pulled his business out, while also deciding he wanted to look at me during the procedure. Hey, I took his balls away, so he doesn't have much at this point, but if he's somehow getting off on this, at least have the decency to look at a squirrel up a tree, for Pete's sake.

It was done. This time he'd spared me the deep stare, but the noises were still cringeworthy. The elastic band was a new touch; not sure where he scooped that up. I tried to keep the area free of anything that could harm the little freak. Feeling better, he barrel-assed out into the backyard and started his zoomies.

The rear of the house is a solid acre of open land, bordered primarily by sugar and red maple trees, with a few tamaracks and white pine's mixed in. The leaves were in full bloom, with the calendar and temperature nestled precisely where the native hard and softwoods thrived best. The maroon leaves of the red maple's fought their way for light and audience, overpowered in the explosion of green. The previous owner, Bob, had cut down a couple trees at the back edge of the yard and made a trail into the woods with a natural, inviting archway at the front. The day after I moved in, I took a walk out, heading through the man-made gap with Pickle in tow, panting like Sisyphus pushing that rock up the hill. At one point, his flat face burrowed into some sort of mysterious ground nugget he shouldn't be eating. After I snapped at him, his face popped up, curly tail vibrating for a moment, and then he went right back in. Gotta love the little bugger. It's the same thing I'd do.

The enormity of his surroundings put Pickle in a state of stupefied euphoria throughout the day. Sometime around dusk, we both discovered something forgotten. For Pickle, it was moths fluttering about. Losing his mind chasing the small airborne critters, always as if it were the first time. And me, those lost years in smoggy L.A. made me forget the verdant orchestra of wooded nature.

The green, red, and brown leaves scratched against one another in the breeze, their white noise providing background hum for the rest of the symphony players. Creaking trees, worn from years of obliging the wind, hummed intermittently between the lulls of the leaves. The crickets and katydids teased their rhythmic chirping in triplets, sound checking their performance that would be the dominant melody as night fell. An angry squirrel screeched warnings to unseen foes from a distant branch, unknowingly adding his version of the wooden guiro to the sonic architecture. From every direction, feathered critters whistled and squawked like stuttering wind instruments, while the long grasses that mat the dirt floor ebbed and flowed in the invisible current, adding breathy whispers. You get the idea—it sounded cool.

As a young boy, when I wasn't at the chess board, I'd spend hours in the woods climbing trees. I'd learned a trick from a neighborhood kid, Raoul Seviana—will never forget that kid's name—he called "parachuting." You seek out small, thin trees, saplings for the most part, and shimmy up their slender trunks until you feel your body weight bending the tree. Then push your legs out, letting them dangle while your hands hold the trunk firm, and gravity does the rest. If you find the right tree—pliant yet formidable—and align your body and hands perfectly, you'll float down to the earth like a feather, with the wood stretching and creaking in pleasant harmony. If you climb too high, too fast, or choose a tree without the requisite support frame, you're likely to crash violently to the ground as the trunk explodes with a *crrraaaaaaack!* and the few leaves that rest on its branches shake loose in anger. There were many sprained ankles in the years between seven and ten, when my tree-parachuting was most active. On one occasion, I landed on my back in a mound of rotted, saturated wood that was the chosen domicile of a spotted salamander. Totally pancaked the poor little fella, just like you see in the cartoons. I was broken up about that accidental murder for weeks. Far longer than over any human relationship that had ended abruptly, which meant I was either a borderline sociopath or way too fond of salamanders.

"Pick, come on," I chirped, knowing there was zero chance he'd comply on the first request. He was in the froggy sit, where his hind legs were flat against the ground and front legs were sprawled out in front of him, panting and staring back at me after my command. It had become a game, him knowing the initial order was more of just an alert and that future instructions would follow. "Come on, nutjob."

This time he shot straight up and ran toward me, passing between my legs and scooping up a raunchy, chewed-to-shit plastic bone toy that had been out in the yard since we'd moved in. Bugs, bird droppings, dirt caked all over it, but he still dove on the thing and started munching as though it was a slab of baby back ribs.

Right as I was about to dry heave, I heard a door slam shut across the street and a familiar voice yell, "You're being ridiculous."

Laurel.

A male voice mumbled. It sounded like my hero Barry, but I wasn't certain until his car started up and tore into the street, likely leaving a patch of tread forty feet long. Nothing like having the tranquil Vermont woodlands shredded to bits by a shrieking muscle car driven by a neanderthal with 'roid rage.

"Let's go inside, Pick," I said, smacking my hand on my leg in the universal sign for, "*Okay, now I really mean get over here.*" He complied, then trotted out in front of me, up onto the back deck, and in through his doggy door, twirly tail wiggling. Once he was inside, I secured the safety gate that confined him to the deck. As much as I adored the little fella, sometimes I preferred to immerse myself in the wooded symphony without worrying about whether he was eating mud or trying to dig a hole to Guam. Or, in this case, interrupting.

I walked around the house to the front and saw Laurel sitting on her front steps, her white and blue floral dress fluttering at her ankles, her face resting in her palms. The smell of burnt rubber clung to the tepid air, and a smoky residue slid across the landscape in front of me. I contemplated going in my front door and not getting involved, but then I remembered I was an idiot and infatuated with her.

"Hey...all good over there?" I shouted across the road before stepping off my lawn.

"Nothing some Pinot Noir and a bath won't fix," she hollered back.

"That combo could solve ninety-five percent of the woes of the world," I replied, walking across her yard toward her, avoiding eye contact in a dreadful attempt to be coy and nonchalant. The strategy went down in flames when I tripped on a sprinkler head and toppled forward, almost hitting the ground.

"Oh my God, are you alright?" Laurel asked, hopping up from the porch and slipping into laughter she disguised with her hand over her face.

"Bruised ego, a bit of an underwear check, but otherwise all good," I said, straightening myself up, and brushing off the front of my jeans, continuing forward. "Genius idea though, the booby traps. Never know who may be slinking up onto your property in this raucous town of fourteen people."

She was still silently laughing, her palm covering her mouth, though a spattering of squeaks and howls crept through.

"I realize I barely know you, but I get the sense that if I *had* fallen and my arm was severed, flopping around on its own for a moment as I bled out, that you'd likely be doing the same thing," I jabbed.

"Oh jeez. Seriously, I'm so sorry," Laurel said, her face amber and wrinkled, fighting back an onslaught of guffaws. "Though you may be right. What a way to finish that stumble, with a dismemberment."

I looked at her from twenty feet away, the floral print dress clinging to her bronze shins in the steady breeze. Her hair was up in a ponytail, and her pouty lips were colored in a warm, soft red, glossless hue. The skin on her face, gently tanned and now smooth as the laughter abated, was relucent in the light of the day's sky. Her lips softened when she smiled, the left side higher in a near smirk as I closed in, stopping in front of her.

"You know, one of my secondary goals, aside from escaping the noise, pollution, insanity, and duplicitous underbelly of Los Angeles, was to come back east and sue someone. Make a few bucks," I said, swiveling my neck around, scanning her front lawn. "I was expecting it to take me at least a year, but your sinister yard hazard here has done the trick in only days. How is your last name spelled again?"

"Huh," she replied, peering over at my house with her neck extended. "Well, I'm no Warren Buffett, but I'd venture a guess that with the cars you're driving that my kid won't shut up about, you're doing all right over there across the road. But if you really want my last forty bucks, it will have to be in a check you'll need to hold until Friday."

I chortled. "Problems with the fella? I heard him race out of here, though I suppose most of New England did."

She sighed, then shimmied to her left. "Here, have a seat, no need to stand there in pain. Might as well sit and be in agony."

I squinted my eyes, then obliged, easing my way down, my ankle still throbbing.

"You want me to grab some ice for that?" she asked, staring down at my foot.

"No, really, it's fine. One of those deals that will ache for ten minutes then disappear forever. I sit on the toilet to pee at this point, so this shouldn't jam me up too bad."

"Sure, we can overshare," Laurel deadpanned. "No wonder Barry is so threatened by you."

Jackpot. Come on, if she's going to toss that out there already, admitting that my dear friend Barry is agitated by my presence, then that must mean something. It's as good as telling me she loves the way my eyes look in the warm light of dusk. Kinda.

"Threatened? He said that? Why? He doesn't even know me. I barely know you. Had only a couple brief conversations," I said, playing dumb, and tossing a few cashews in my mouth that I'd just pulled from my pocket. Sure, he was threatened by me. I'm in the ballpark of sexy, a barrel of laughs, and I had a cool dog.

"No, he didn't say it in so many words, but he made it pretty clear. A couple weeks before you moved in, we were having a talk about 'us,' his role in Ethan's life, where he wanted to be career wise—all the typical adult stuff—and he got pissy and stormed out of here like he did today. Later, I mentioned I needed a 'man and not a man-child' or something, and he rattled off a list of a few men from town, how I should be with them, blah blah blah. Really mature dialogue. And then when you showed up, he had to hear about your cars from Ethan, so I think it just sent him over the edge. He's not a terrible person. He had an awful upbringing like everyone else, and has trouble managing his anger, but he tries. Usually."

"Hey, listen, I'm the living embodiment of a man-child, so you can squash that argument with him tonight. Plus, I've no designs on you. You're a neighbor-harmer with that freakin' sprinkler, and you live right across the street, so you'd always be bothering me to fix things and borrow eggs. And, frankly, I sort of have my eye on your mom. We had a moment back there in town. Cashew?"

She laughed, shaking her head no. "I see. Well, she's been sort of sweet on Barry for a while now, so you may need to step up your game. Trade in one of those foreign cars for a bulldozer or something."

When she finished her sentences, especially ones filled with levity and humor, she did this almost imperceptible set of tiny nods with her head, three in a row usually. It was a tick that would be lost on most of the population but glared liked a neon sign to the obsessed.

"So, I gotta ask, are you going to be okay if he comes back? Meaning, does his anger ever cross the line into..."

She turned her head away, looking off into the sky above the trees. "If he's been drinking, he can get a little ornery, but he's never hit me or Ethan. I can't say it would shock me if he did, honestly. I'm not saying that to be dramatic, but—"

"I'm just the new guy across the street, and I don't want to complicate your life here," I interjected, "but I hope that if that does become a concern, you won't hesitate to give me a call or stop over. I'm sure there's police around, but sometimes they—"

"Sometimes they happen to be the cousin of the idiot you let yourself get involved with," she replied, cutting me off.

"Oh, fuckballs. Seriously?"

She laughed and flipped her hair back over her shoulder with her right hand. "Fuckballs. I like that. And yeah, Barry's cousin is a state trooper. He's more level-headed than Barry, but blood is tight here. I'm not worried about the violence, though. I'm more concerned about the fact I'm wasting precious days with a moron."

Hard not to chuckle at that one, so I did.

"Well, like I said, if you need anything."

"I don't want to drag you into this, Josh. It's embarrassing, frankly," Laurel said. "I'm sure it will be fine. He just needs to cool off a bit and stop being so blockheaded. We're not married. We don't say 'I love you.' It's been a fling at best, and now it's circling the drain."

"Sounds like a great time," I replied.

She smacked my shoulder and let her face fall into her hands, groaning.

"I'm sure the drama will increase exponentially if he comes back and finds me sitting here on the porch with you," I suggested, standing up.

"Screw it, and you can hear that dumb car almost as far away from here as yours. If you want to scurry back home when we hear it, I won't think any less of you," she said, souring her face in mock disgust.

Quite possibly was in love already. Ninety-three percent chance.

"I would only do that to avoid discomfort for you, not out of fear. You have noticed my size, right? I'm rather huge, and I have a vicious attack dog who, when not licking the floor or himself, is at the ready to kill on command."

"I'm not entirely sure he's not a cat, and I don't want anyone fighting. That's ridiculous. Let's change the subject because I still

47

know that I know you from somewhere, and I'm thinking I may know where from."

"I'll let the brutal insult on my dog go, for now, in the interest of moving forward. So sure, enlighten me. Where have you've seen me?"

A smirk built across her face as she slid her phone up against her right thigh and peeked down at it. "You were in Shankbone! And on a TV show," she blurted out.

"Does Wikipedia really say 'Shankbone,' or do you just need glasses?" I asked, in playful disgust.

"Oh no, I meant, *Shaky Bones*" she said, pulling the phone onto her lap and reading it from the screen. "I can't say I know the band, but I *do* remember you on that show. I think I only saw it a couple times, though. There was a cute hockey player, no?"

"Yeah, yeah, Luke. Freakin' guy used to stare at his calves in the mirror for fifteen minutes at a clip. He was insufferable."

Her eyes widened as a half-smile filled up her face. "Hmmm, a little jealous I see."

"No, jealous...what? Of that numb nut? Absurd."

"Aww, I understand," she said, patting my leg.

I snickered then looked away, back toward my house, wondering how much of the deck Pickle had licked already and pondering the size of the hairball I'd be tugging out of his butthole in a few hours.

"Somewhere in this blurb I read, it mentioned a car accident. There was a woman. Was she...your wife, girlfriend? Do you mind that I'm asking this?"

Ugh. Like I'd said earlier, I wasn't running away from this, and it wasn't difficult to find the details if one dug a little, but I was hoping I could avoid delving into it so quickly with her. She'd been candid and open with me though, so I didn't want to come off like some typical asshat who was buttoned up tight about all his own garbage. Tough call.

"Yeah, there was an accident," I said after sitting quietly a moment. "Wouldn't you rather hear about the debauchery that went on backstage after a rock concert or behind-the-scenes insanity of a TV show comprised of C-and D-list celebrities living together?"

She stared at me, blinking once, her chin in her palm, elbow resting on her knee. The woman could have asked me to peel my own skin off with a spoon and I'd have done it.

"All right, fine. So, it wasn't my wife. It was a woman I'd known for a while, and yeah, we were dating. I suppose you'd call it that, for almost a year prior to the accident. It was a turbulent time, though also invigorating in some ways. Real co-dependent, unhealthy stuff."

"How so?"

I looked over at her, then turned away and stared back at my house for a few seconds. "What's the closest you've ever come to death?"

"A lot closer than you'd probably guess," she answered without hesitation. "Go on."

CHAPTER 7

S he opened the door, letting her head fall back to her left shoulder, smiling wide, just as her eyes squinted at him.

"I told you I'd show up," he said, sliding his right hand down around her waist as he pushed through the half-opened doorway.

"Well, I'm the one always telling you I believe in miracles," she replied, wrapping both her hands around his neck and pushing herself up onto her toes.

He towered over her five-foot four-inch frame. The wavy strands of her dirty blonde hair were almost longer than her arms, gathering in the center of her chest while she looked up at him. Through the hair, he could see the bright red lips of the Rolling Stones T-shirt, cut strategically and intentionally at the neck to reveal ample cleavage.

"You're my little miracle, no doubt," he told her before leaning down to kiss her forehead.

"Oh, come on. You know I don't like that band. Why do you have to ruin something sweet by saying that?" she asked, pulling back from his kiss.

"What's curious to me is that every band you don't like happens to have a female lead singer, and the ones you love, including Mick's there, hugging your knockers, are fronted by these egotistical male sex-on-a-stick dudes. Why do you think that is?"

"Well, you know that's bullshit because I can't stand your singer, Marty, and he's as full of himself as they come."

He smirked and shrugged his shoulders, having no answer for her well documented disdain for lead singer Martin Wyles.

"Okay, so you've got one exception, but you know I'm right. Plus, Gwen is a sweetheart, and if you met her—"

"Oh right, a sweetheart. Just because you love her ass doesn't mean she's making soup at an orphanage," she interrupted, pulling away from him and walking into the kitchen.

"Where do you come up with this shit," he said, shaking his head and watching her walk her snug faux leather pants into the other room. "And speaking of asses, I don't think you should worry too much in that department. I show yours much love."

She turned around, flipping him the middle finger and sticking her tongue out before grabbing a bottle of whiskey off the poorly stained wooden island in the kitchen. She took three large gulps, placed it back on the red-orange granite countertop with a *plink!* and then sauntered back toward him.

"I know you love mine," she said, grabbing it from behind with both hands. "Who wouldn't? All I'm saying is that I saw you check hers out, sitting there at the Grammy's all cool and disinterested like you were Sid Vicious or something, and as soon as she got up and walked down that aisle to the stage, your face lit up like a damn Christmas tree, following her every gyration down the carpet. I have the tape. You wanna watch it?"

"So, is this what we're going to do all night? Rehash stupid moments from years ago, or are we heading out?"

She sneered, then turned and went back into the kitchen and grabbed the whiskey bottle. He followed.

"Easy babe," he cautioned her, putting his hand on the neck of the bottle as she brought it to her lips. He pulled the whiskey from her clenched hand, downing a few ounces then placing it behind her on the kitchen island. On top of the worn and rust-covered refrigerator behind the island, he noticed several empty bottles of the same whiskey in addition to a dozen or so brown beer bottles, some on their sides, the rest empty and standing.

"Don't start your shit, okay? What I do when you're not around is none of your business, I've told you—"

"Sasha, easy, all right?" he interjected, looking away from the fridge and down at her sunken brown eyes. "I'm not judging you or prying into your business, I'm just concerned is all. I worry about you, after the..."

"After the fall? You can say it, jackass, I was there. I remember. You think I give a crap what those country club phonies think about me? I don't. With their designer pills and coke pit stops every fifteen minutes, but I get lit up on margaritas and slip down some stairs, and suddenly I'm a damn junkie because I'm not one of the beautiful people. Fuuuck them. I hate every one of those scumbags. Monsters in fancy clothes, just like him," she shouted, her words slurring.

"Who? Me?" he asked her, but she ignored him.

He stared down at her, her face rosy and brushed with sweat across her forehead, her fingers clenched and tight against her palms. She was wearing new earrings, ones he'd sent her from the road. Tiny silver cowboy boots, each wrapped in a snake, dangling from each earlobe about two inches down. She'd seen them at an outdoor music festival they'd attended months prior, the crafter explaining they were her last pair and only for display, so he sought her out and bought some weeks later. When they arrived, she texted a pic of herself, topless, wearing them and a crooked smile.

"I don't want this night to turn ugly. How 'bout some love instead?" she said, running the tips of her fingers under his chin. Her hands smelled like cigarettes and lemons, he observed. The apartment itself more like an ashtray filled with old wine and cough drops.

"Sweetheart, all I have is love for you, you know that. It's what keeps me awake at night when I don't hear back from you for days. I worry, though..."

"I'm sure whatever her name is in Chicago or who-the-fuck-ever in New York takes the edge off. Don't pretend we both don't know most of your nights aren't spent alone."

He sighed, then turned toward the bathroom, brushing past her. "Heeey, stop," she said, pulling at the arm of his leather coat. "Don't get all pissy. Just...just have a drink with me, all right," she asked, then nuzzled herself up against his chest.

He moved his right hand through the hair on the top of her head, then gently pulled her chin up, looking down at her. "One drink, then we head out and have some dinner. Enjoy ourselves without getting crazy?"

"Pinky swear," she said, offering her outstretched pinky up at him. He locked his own into hers, wrapping around it tightly before shaking his hand up and down.

"I've missed you, gorgeous."

"You better have," she said, before pulling away from him and heading for the whiskey bottle behind her.

CHAPTER 8

"Huh. Seems there's some rock star stories in your past that we need to explore, too," I alluded, wondering how such a youthful, angelic beauty like her might brush against death at such an early age.

"Nah, nothing like that, but stop stalling. I want to hear this," she replied.

I resisted the urge for more jabby comebacks and continued. "So, this woman I was seeing—"

My story was interrupted by the faint, yet distinct rumble of a muscle car intermittently accelerating and decelerating in the distance, its exhaust popping like gunfire. Laurel picked up the sound and leaned in toward its origin. "Oh, crap," she said, standing abruptly.

"Your drain-circling life partner. Has to be," I suggested. Her return glance revealed nauseated anger.

"You need to leave. I don't want this to turn into something ugly, especially with Ethan inside," she said.

"Of course, no problem," I said, standing up and walking toward my place. "Are you *sure* he won't get out of control?"

"I'll be fine. Just go," she urged, waving her hands in my direction, shooing me off.

The sound of Barry's car grew louder, accelerating on the final stretch, and the rear end broke loose as he made the turn onto our street. He hesitated on the throttle, his gaze finding me leaving Laurel's yard, then hammered the gas and made his way up the rest of the road. I watched him slide at forty-five degrees into the driveway, partially onto the lawn. Laurel remained motionless on the front porch, her arms folded at her chest, slivers of her hair fluttering in the warm breeze.

Barry got out of the car, and a bottle of something hit the driveway, bouncing twice then rolling up against the mailbox post. "Hey, fuckstain. Why don't you come back over here?" Barry yelled from the driveway, slamming the car door.

"Barry, stop," Laurel shouted, rushing toward him at the end of the driveway while he crossed the road, headed for me.

When I was twelve years old, a husky, obnoxious moron named Billy Grift—another epic name—called me a "turd brain" before crossing the street, several of his minions in tow, threatening to beat my face in. I recalled the way my breath felt, quickening, watching him and his cronies approach, how my teeth felt clenched hard against themselves in my mouth. It was mid-summer, dusk, and the crickets were making a racket. A few scattered fireflies began testing their love signals across the hazy landscape in green, yellow, and red pulses. My neck had begun to tighten and sweat leaked down from the center of my chest to the front of my stomach, right as Billy and the gang reached where I'd been standing.

I'd love to tell you that when Grift started pummeling me, I deflected the blows like an adolescent Bruce Lee, ducking, parrying, defending, and then pouncing on top of him like Ralphie from *A Christmas Story*. That I rained furious blows down onto his chubby, grinning face while he cried out for mercy, right before I let him up and taunted the others in his shithead crew, making them scurry off like mice into the summer grass. I'd love to tell you that, but it would be a gargantuan lie. That maniacal, lumpy jerk face beat the tar out of me that day. Knocked out a tooth, cut up my lips and cheeks, and one of his idiot sidekicks even stole my sneakers. Stole my freakin' shoes, which were at least three sizes too big for him.

Today wasn't going to be Grift 2.0.

"I'd like to applaud your use of the word fuckstain. It's vastly underutilized. At least for my tastes," I said to Barry, his formidable frame barreling toward me with a sloppy zig zag gait, hinting at his recent infusion of distilled spirits. It was a smoky bourbon, I determined, when his ample noggin made its way into my airspace. "Whoa, Barry, listen, I don't want to—"

The swing at my jaw missed. A too slow, blatantly telegraphed poke, even for a drunk.

"Hey now, let's not do that," I said, sliding off to the side of his center, keeping him firmly in my eyeline while I moved near the edge of the curb. Laurel came flying up behind him, her flip flops clip-clapping against the asphalt.

"Barry, stop it!" she shouted at him, though his gaze was still fixed on me.

"Laurel, it's all right. Barry and I are just going to have a quick little chat. It's okay," I assured her, but she wasn't listening. She grabbed Barry's arm, attempting to spin him toward her and away from me.

"Stay the hell out of this," Barry yelled, yanking his arm from her grasp, the recoil causing Laurel's hand to smack up into her mouth, startling her.

Now Barry had fucked around, and he was about to find out. I mean, I know he didn't haul off and pop her one right in the chops on purpose but watching her cower after that hand whacked her...only so long I could be a pacifist.

"Hey, Barry, now why'd you have to go and do that? Whatever problem you have is with me, not her so—"

This time it was an uppercut, a second or two after he let his chin fall and eyes avert. It was easier to spot this punch coming than a water buffalo in a cubicle.

"No, no. Come on, man," I said, after ducking to the left and sidestepping in the same direction. He wasn't in a listening mood and decided to lunge at my throat, so it was time to button this fella up.

I slid behind him, grabbed his approaching wrist and pulled it down toward the street. Rotating it counterclockwise, my other hand grabbed hold of his elbow and turned his arm over. Driving it through him like pole, I sent him onto the grass of my front yard. Thankfully, Pickle wasn't outside, or he'd be losing his mind with excitement and then start licking the poor guy's face while on the ground. Can't imagine it could get much worse than getting your ass kicked by the new guy in town, in front of your squeeze, and then having a cat-sized dog with a boner licking your grass-stained face.

"Stay down," I told squirming Barry, kneeling on his back with one leg, applying pressure to his wrist and hand that I still held firmly. It happened so quickly that Laurel hadn't had time to even process the events and was simply standing in the road, mouth slightly agape.

"If I let you up, are you going to knock it off? Talk to me and not start swinging again?" I asked him. He said nothing, but Laurel was now at my side.

"You can let him up," she said, leaning over him.

"Fuck you. I can handle my own business, Laur," Barry yelled, clearly handling his business, face down in the grass, dirt, and bugs.

"Josh, just let him up. He's drunk. He won't be any trouble once I get some coffee into him," Laurel said.

"I told you I can—"

Barry's shouting was clipped by me applying more rotation to his wrist, which was in no way me trying to be a tough guy. If I was going to impress a woman like Laurel, I realized, it certainly wasn't going to be with badassery, chess moves, or rock star pedigree. I might have to invent something or levitate.

"Okay, I'm going to let you up," I told Barry, reducing the pressure. "Are you going to be cool?"

Barry made a grumbling, snorty noise and then pulled himself up onto his hands and knees when I let go. He stayed in the pushup ready position for ten seconds, looking as though he might puke, but then pulled it together and stood up, wobbling.

Barry's dark gray T-shirt with indecipherable screen print was streaked with grass, and his face was beaded with sweat. He stabilized, brushed off his shirt and black jeans, before hobbling back to his car.

"Hang on a second, Barry. I can't let you drive."

Laurel walked over to him, leaned into his right side, acting as a crutch, and started walking him across the road to her front porch. She turned and smiled at me. A defeated, forlorn smirk is really all it was. I understood.

The commotion in the street was enough to get Laurel's mother and Ethan out onto the porch. They stood at the top step, staring at Laurel while she shuffled Barry in their direction, glancing at me before making their way toward the two of them. Laurel's mother was wearing an oversized black and white Kentucky Derby-like hat and sipping on what may have been a mint julep. Though her bright, lime green Walmart pants were a dead giveaway she wasn't horse money royalty.

"What happened, Mr. Josh?" Ethan shouted to me, after stopping in the grass, halfway to his mother and Barry.

"Nothing, little buddy. No worries," I yelled back. I wasn't sure what she'd tell him, but I had no desire to complicate the already messy situation.

Laurel sat Barry down on the lowest step of the front porch. The rest of them gathered around talking, though I couldn't hear what they were saying. Ethan kept popping his head sideways out of the pack, looking over at me. After a few peeks, I realized me standing there staring was creepy, so I went to check on Pickle.

It wasn't my plan to emasculate the douchebag. He came at *me* and was an obvious danger to Laurel, not to mention the danger of him driving in that condition. I was only protecting myself and others, not puffing up my chest and showing my feathers to the woman who was now nursing the wounds of said A hole.

Hmmpfh.

Pickle will understand. He always understands.

****

The back of my house is thickly bordered by the trees, as I mentioned earlier. There's just enough gap between the roofline and the treetops to view a nice slice of the evening sky. Tonight, it was speckled with about two hundred stars from my count. I gazed up, hoping to see a shooting star or an asteroid or Quasar or some sort of spacey thing that Carl Sagan would get off on. Pickle was out cold next to me on the deck, the result of an hour-long trek through the woods after the Barry debacle. His little legs splayed out behind him frog-like, his breath jagged and snorty—typical with pugs since they have elongated palates and short snouts. When the day finally ends,

59

Pickle always sleeps in the bed with me. Like clockwork, as soon as I settle on my back, he's in my right armpit. He'll wiggle his curly pseudo-tail, anticipating the jump into the bed, hop on up once I began to sit back, and scoot right into his nook, nuzzling and fidgeting until he's on his side, facing away from me. The finale involves him turning his head upwards, looking up at me, licking the roof of his mouth in this slow, cartoonish manner as if he has peanut butter stuck up there, then plopping his head down and conking out. That routine was more reliable than the sun's setting. Every single night.

Sounds adorable, and it is, but I have a strict "all bets are off" policy once I fall asleep. I can't be responsible for Pickle's location in the bed when I'm out. I'll often wake up to take a leak hours later to find him at my feet, on my other side, behind my head on the pillow, or occasionally, and much to his disdain, next to the bed on the floor. Apparently, being woken by a thrashing idiot who sent you careening over a mattress cliff and onto the floor saps all requisite energy for hopping back up into bed.

Pickle's current slumber was interrupted by the familiar *clip clop clip clop* of flip flops making their way around the side of the house. His head shot up, tilted, and then his stubby legs Fred-Flintstoned him over to the slats in the deck, barking furiously at about four decibels.

"Heeeey," Laurel said, approaching the back of the deck, a bottle in her hand I couldn't make out in the dim evening light. "I wanted to bring you a little something...for having to deal with that mess. I'm just so—"

"No apologies. Seriously," I chimed in. "Shit happens. I've had a mountain of my own drama."

"I'm just mortified. You should never have had to deal with that. You just moved in here and it's so..." She let her words trail off, sitting on the second step of the deck stairs. I stepped down to the grass, facing her.

"If I told you how many drunken dustups I've been involved in, sometimes being the offender, most times, thankfully, being the diffuser—it's no big deal, Laurel. I mean it. My only concern is that you guys are safe. Tonight, and going forward," I assured her.

"I appreciate that. I think we'll be fine, but it's so embarrassing."

"Is he still there?" I asked cautiously, not wanting to dig.

"No. His cousin came by to get him after I called, much to my mother's disapproval. She wanted him to just sleep it off and then have me drive him home later. Moms of the year over here, both of us. I bring the degenerate into my kid's life; she wants to keep him there."

I chortled, right when Pickle decided he wanted to be in Laurel's lap, which surprised me only in the time it took him to make the move.

"Hey, easy little bugger. Give her some space," I told the vibrating canine, who was licking her furiously, causing her to place the unidentified bottle onto the ground next to her.

"Oh, aren't you just too precious," she told the pathetic pug, rubbing his ears and leaning her forehead down toward him so he could lick there instead of her lips and eyes and every other spot on her face that wasn't already drenched.

"Come on, dude," I said, scooping him up and placing him back on the deck before snapping the gate shut.

"It's no bother, Josh. I love dogs. Just don't have the time with all the insanity I have going on over there. But look how adorable little Pickle is," she said, letting her voice raise a couple octaves at the end, directing it to the dog, turning him into a wiggling, sappy mess. Her massive, hypnotic eyes stared at him, but their power went peripheral and had me woozy.

"As much as we all judge one another on the idiotic moves we make in relationships and chastise each other for pathetic choices or staying too long, every one of us are hypocrites and liars. We all do the same shit. If any human walking this earth could sort out why we're drawn to one person versus the next, stay with another when we bolted on the one before, and every deranged nuance in between, they'd be a trillionaire. They'd probably be banging their sociopathic ex and crying themselves to sleep like the rest of us, but at least they'd be doing it in a solid gold castle on two-thousand-thread-count sheets."

Laurel leaned forward into her hands, coming apart with laughter in that hushed way that she did. Pickle tilted his wrinkly noggin, hearing her curious whisper-giggling, then went right back to licking his foot. "You're too funny," she said. "Should have been a comedian instead of a guitar player, I think."

I scrunched up my face. "I learned a long time ago that my humor only resonates with the inebriated and insane, which describes most of the patrons of a comedy club, so maybe you're right."

Laurel smirked, standing up on the step. "Well, I can't do anything to fix the sanity issue, but we can solve the sobriety problem if you have a corkscrew in the house."

I returned the smirk and looked over at Pickle, who had a keen sense of knowing exactly when I was staring at him, regardless of where he was or direction he was facing. He stopped licking his foot, stuck his tongue out, panted for a few seconds, and then fixated on Laurel.

"That was the first thing I unpacked. I'll be right back."

CHAPTER 9

I once had a hangover, the morning after a show in San Francisco, where I wasn't sure I still had a tongue. My mouth was so dry that when I became conscious again, somewhere approaching one in the afternoon, my tongue was fused to the roof and felt like it wasn't there. I tried puckering my lips, gathering some saliva, and then, in a move illustrating the amount of brain cells the previous night's Stoli had eradicated, I attempted to use my non-existent tongue to find my tongue. I was "lifting" the muscles in my mouth where the tongue once was to find the actual one that was glued up above. It makes sense if you've ever been that tanked.

This morning's hangover wasn't as brutal, but the cottonmouth and throbbing temples were both raging. I remembered sitting on the back deck until past midnight, right before Laurel's mother sent her a text. I think I commented something like, "Who does she think she is?" and both of us laughed far too vigorously. I know I walked her to the street and watched her get safely inside. Then I leaned against my mailbox, swaying like a sapling in a forty-mile-an-hour crosswind, for at least ten minutes. I let Pickle take a quick leak, before flopping down on the couch face first, still sound of mind. The problem is, I awoke in my bed. In addition to the empty industrial-sized bottle of red wine that Laurel brought over, there was an empty bottle of anejo tequila on my nightstand. The bottle looked good. Sculpted, angular lines and vibrant hand painted, amber sunburst label on cloudy glass, contrasted with the black faux granite top, but the image immediately forced up a quick dry heave.

I ran to the bathroom, Pickle at my heels, and vomited like a pledging freshman at Kappa Delta Holyshita. The puking noise always freaked Pickle out. I think he assumed I was dying, which wasn't fully inaccurate, but had no idea how to help. So, instead of barking, charging at the toilet, or scurrying frantically, he flattened his curled pig tail out against his butt and ambled away, depressed. I gave him a quick wink as I wiped my mouth and reached for the toilet paper, but he didn't wink back. He never does.

After two rounds of tummy cleansing, I washed up and shuffled into the kitchen to survey the damage: one empty tequila bottle, a half-eaten box of crackers, and some hard cheese I'd left out. The floor was dry, the counters weren't sticky, and nothing was broken or knocked over. As a slob, I was tidy in my chaos.

I know the question you're asking, at least those of you who aren't malcontents or alcoholics, and that's, "How come you finished off a bottle of tequila on your own if you were already drunk?" and it's a great question. Not one I'm going to answer, you nosy pricks, but it's valid. I know there's another question that looms, and it involves what may or may not have happened with Laurel, but on that one I will gladly answer. Nothing. I behaved. I didn't swoon. I didn't creep. I didn't paw. And, we enjoyed nothing more than the simple pleasures of two adults getting shitfaced on a jug of wine, laughing at the absurdity of life. At some point, I know I farted, far too loudly than one would ever want to in front of someone as lovely as Laurel, especially in jeans on the hard wood of a deck. She was rolling. Pickle was licking her neck as she leaned over losing her mind. I assured her through stuttered laughter that, "I never do that," as she flipped me off, laying on her side, gasping air for multiple reasons.

Speaking of my repugnance, I've had a maid much of my adult life. I realize this fact doesn't endear me to most people, knowing it's a luxury and often thought to be lazy and snooty and all, but my reasons are born from necessity and not affectedness. I'm actually a wonderful cleaner. I put countless hours and detail into washing my cars when I want to. But when it comes to the space I live in, for some reason, I don't see the apparent filth in which I allow myself to exist. Every woman I've dated for longer than a week has commented on my sloppiness, either outright or dropping clues like, "Uh, is that a piece of spaghetti on the wall?" or "I don't think counter tops are supposed to make that noise when you pull a glass off them." I only mention the maid because I was surprised at how clean my place was after the previous night. In days past, especially with empty tequila bottles afoot, I'd have needed a Hazmat team and fire.

As for my current domicile, it's a colonial style. Typical New England variety from the outside, with an open breezeway and lots of hardwood when you walk in. The entire place has a nice "open" feel, which I always hear on those goofy home shows is heavily sought after by these late twenties couples who work as a baker and crossing guard but somehow have a six-hundred-thousand-dollar budget for their first home. The bathrooms feature purples and blues, tile floors and—

Brump brump brump.

There was a knock at the door.

Maybe Laurel, hopeful to pick up where we left off, minus the flatulence. I scooped up the yapping, four-legged freak at my feet and went to the door.

"Good morning," I said, disappointed and startled to see Laurel's mother standing on my porch.

"It's afternoon, but judging from the smell, I'm surprised you're even awake," she jabbed.

I put Pickle on the ground, hoping he'd morph into an Akita and show her all the pleasures of what a "real dog" could do.

"Sadly, I am very much alive, yes," I quipped.

She blasted right past me, into my house, and turned around to face me as I stood in the doorway. "So, what's your plan?" she asked, folding her arms in an exaggerated fashion over her mint green polyester shirt.

"Can I get you anything, Miss...?"

"I'm fine. Call me Helen. I'm not your elementary school teacher," she snapped. "What's your plan with my daughter?"

I hesitated, not a function of being uncertain of the answer, but because Pickle was sniffing her calf while jumping on her leg. She wasn't acknowledging it in the slightest. It was fascinating.

"Pickle get off of her," I told the pooch. He ignored me, as did she.

"I really don't feel like asking you a third time, Mr. Traxon," she replied, Pickle now on to her other leg, his scratching suggesting he was attempting to start a fire.

"Pickle," I yelled, this time sending him off the leg and to my side. "Sorry about that. It's hard to focus on what you're saying with him doing that. Here, why don't you have a seat—"

"I'm fine where I am," she said, dead staring me.

I wondered if her refusal to comment on the dog, who had to be annoying the hell out of her, was because it was her way of failing to recognize him as an actual dog. Her long game of making a surprise move. Chess's *Zwischenzug* if you will. Had to be, because there's not a human being on Earth that would want little Pickle's frantic hyperventilating scratch-a-palooza on their leg. She ignored it like it was a vacuum salesman knocking at the door during the season finale of *The Bachelor*.

"Hmmm, well, Helen, I'm not sure how to answer that other than I'm glad I met her and hope to see her again. She a wonderful woman, as are you, I imagine, and—"

"Cut the crap, guy," she interrupted, uncrossing her arms, and pointing at me with her right index finger, which was bent about thirty degrees at the end. "You think I didn't look you up after Laurel told me who you were? Reality TV star and rock and roller. I'm sure you've had your mitts all over every floozy from here to Oxnard. So now you take a little break and think you're going to add my daughter to the list? My daughter, who has a little boy to worry about, among other things, and doesn't need some flake that couldn't give a crap about her, putting ideas in her head and getting her all turned around. Not to mention she's seeing someone."

"Helen, listen—and nice Oxnard shout out, by the way," I said before she moved a few inches closer, wiggling the horrible bent finger in a jagged circle. "I'm not going to deny that my past life was full of a certain amount of debauchery, but—"

"Ha," she yelped. "I watched videos of you on the you tubes. That stupid show with the other imbeciles. You were either drunk, talking about how many woman you've bedded, *in* bed with some woman, or getting loaded and doing something I don't know how I'd even explain."

The potholder. Not big in mom circles.

"Helen, I hear what you're—"

"Listen, Dick Jagger," she steamrolled over me. "You want to live across the street, be a good neighbor, smile and wave—you won't hear a peep from me. You want to borrow something or come by for some aspirin after one of your benders, or even toss a ball around with Ethan sometimes, you go right ahead. I'm not saying you're a monster. But any designs you have about turning my daughter into one of your bed buddies, or worse—letting her think you want something more than that—well, you can forget it."

Dick Jagger. I think I fell in love with her right at that moment.

"Do I get to talk now? Dick Jagger. Gotta say, Helen, that was epic. I'm not saying that to curry favor, as you've made it clear you're not looking to add yourself to the groupie list. I'm saying it because it genuinely gave me a chuckle," I said, using my fingers to manually turn up the sides of my mouth. "I won't deny what my life once was and the crimes I'm guilty of, and I won't pretend I'm not embarrassed by much of it, but I can promise you my interest in Laurel isn't to 'add her to my list.' I barely know her, but what I do know I'm fond of and would like to know more. You don't have to believe that if you don't want, but it's the truth."

She wrinkled her eyes and tightened her lips, saying nothing.

"As for that potholder, it never even returned my calls. So, I think it's over."

She nodded her head, moving in closer, her brownish-gray hair barely at my nipples. "Mister Funny Guy, always with the jokes. Same way you were on that dreadful show. Life isn't a joke. My daughter isn't a joke, and neither is her little boy. I hope you show some class and respect what I've said. Laurel has enough on her plate to deal with. She doesn't need you adding unnecessary emotions and complicating everything."

I rubbed my hand over my chin and mouth, as if contemplating something, when in fact I was still trying not to laugh at Dick Jagger.

"I'll see myself out," she said, walking toward the porch.

"Hey, wait a second," I said, sliding past her. The light of the early afternoon nearly bowled me over, and I instantly had fourteen migraines. "I hope Laurel and I can be *friends*. That's what I want, alright? She was here much of last night, as I know you know, and *nothing* happened. I'm not looking for a medal for that, but, yeah, Laurel is a beautiful woman. Of course I'm attracted to her. But I know she has a little boy and other complications in her life. Any relationship we choose—and yes that's *we* choose, not you—to engage ourselves in is not really your business. We're both adults. I'd like to think you'd respect that, and if you have any specific problems, in addition to apparently everything, that you'd take the time to discuss them with me. In the meantime, however, as I said initially, I barely know Laurel. I don't even know if I *like* like her yet. And, as much as I'm somewhat hunky, I suppose there's always a chance she isn't smitten with me. An exceedingly small chance, sure, but a chance. Not to mention, Barry there has a lot to offer, which I know you're aware."

If I were any kind of a real writer, I'd be able to adequately describe the look Helen gave me after that comment, probably with just a word or two, but I'm just some dope, so I can't. I will say, however, that it was not one of reverence.

"Some people have real problems, Mr. Traxon, and they can't all be washed away in bottles of wine, cute anecdotes, and cash. Respect what I've said, and we won't have a problem," she demanded, pointing with the cockeyed finger as she exited. Pickle gingerly emerged from the living room floor.

69

"I know, buddy," I told him, rubbing his ears with my thumb and forefinger, causing him to moan and grunt. "Not our biggest fan, but we grow on people."

He ignored me, continuing to moan from the eargasms, while I watched Laurel's mother make her way into the house. Laurel peeked out, waving at me, before she was pulled sideways and the door slammed shut.

The thing about chess—which you know by now—is how I relate everything in life. What else would we use, Candy Land? There are often moments when novice players *think* they're about to checkmate the opposing player, but in fact aren't even close. In many of those cases, if they're playing a stronger foe, they'll soon be mated themselves. Laurel's mother had a strong opening, but I'd yet to see her middle and end game. My suspicion was she'd double up her pawns and box herself in. This would make for a quick, painless death from the hands of the pseudo-man with the cat-sized dog and an eye for her daughter. This was what I was speculating, acutely aware my opposing queen was five-feet-and-change of sheer terror, with a heinous, crooked, wagging finger and less fear than Leonidas at Thermopylae.

CHAPTER 10

"Nooooooo way, pal. This is my car," the woman said, snatching the keys from his hand and scampering over to the driver's side of the yellow convertible Mustang.

"Babe, come on. I want to make it to the restaurant in one piece. Give me back the keys or I'm not getting in the car with you," he snapped back.

She stopped at the driver's side door and stuck her tongue out. "Are you serious? I'm feeling good, but I'm fine to drive. Stop trying to be my old man. He was a shithead, and so far, I still kinda like you."

"Toss back the keys, or I'll be calling the cops on your cute ass the moment you drive out of here."

"What the hell, Josh? You used to be fun. What a freakin' wet blanket."

"I'm still fun. A lot more fun when I'm breathing."

She rolled her eyes and tossed the keys over the car toward him, avoiding his face by a foot as he reached up and grabbed them. "Fine, but you better not drive like a wuss. It's beautiful out, and I want to have a good time. Otherwise, I could have stayed here and drank with the cat. She doesn't tell me what to do."

Josh reached his hand toward her stomach, stopping her when she reached the passenger's side door where he stood. "Can we dial this back and just go enjoy ourselves? It's like walking on eggshells with you sometimes. Seriously."

She laughed out loud, pulling away from him and plopping herself into the passenger's seat. "Nice touch, Josh. You know that's the name of the book about me. Such a freakin' comedian."

"Just because some half-ass online shrink told you he thinks you may have Borderline Personality Disorder doesn't mean you do, Sasha. Two thirds of the world are fucked up with bad history, drugs, and other garbage. Not everyone needs a label, babe," he replied, jumping into the driver's seat of her Mustang and firing up the engine.

She looked over at him, slid her hand over the crotch of his jeans, and leaned in toward his face. "The crazy ones are more fun. Isn't that what you told me once? Now take this crazy broad somewhere before I dump your ass."

He leaned into her, kissing her lips, right as her hand started massaging between his legs. As he hardened, her fingers pulled away abruptly. "That's for later. Right now, I need another drink, and you need to get us out of here."

Sasha opened the glove box and pulled a silver and black flask from inside. She unscrewed the cap while Josh backed out. "Don't say it. Just drive."

Josh smirked. She took two gulps from the flask and wiped her mouth before screwing the cap back on and dropping it into her lap. He shook his head, then slammed the pedal to the floor, sending dirt and gravel flying behind them. The rear end cut loose, sliding left, but Josh corrected the line and surged ahead on the blacktop, Sasha shouting into the open air with hands raised to the sky.

CHAPTER 11

I f you're someone who drinks, you'll hear the phrase "hair of the dog that bit you" at some point. It will likely be uttered by a dude that resembles your elementary school janitor if he'd aged forty years overnight under sunlamps while soaking in bourbon. The idea is that, should you have indulged in too many beers, shots of whiskey, et cetera, that the best way to "cure" your hangover is to go right back to the same poison that put you in the living hell. It's a stupid plan, but one I engage in regularly because, despite what I tell you, I'm not that bright.

The tequila shot I downed after Laurel's mother left wasn't sitting well. I'd cracked another bottle, while digesting our discussion. Although the headache shredding gray matter in my skull earlier had abated, the tequila was now burning its way through my stomach and looking for other fun tissue and organs to chew while singing "El Son De La Negra."

Despite my agave flu, I needed to head into town to see my accountant. He apparently had a check for me for an unknown something or other. I also needed to make another stop at the hardware store for miscellaneous household whatnots. I decided the accountant would be first. As I sat waiting in his deliciously appointed mauve and green eighties-like lobby, I discovered a small child attempting an enthusiastic game of peek-a-boo that I'd been unintentionally ignoring for several minutes.

"Are you hiding on me?" I asked, sending the dual pigtailed, miniature blonde behind her mother's legs across from me.

"Oh, it's her favorite game. She'll do this for an hour with anyone willing," the mother explained as the little girl popped her face between mom's calves.

I leaned forward, widening my eyes. She ducked and rolled underneath the chair her mother was sitting in. "You're quick, but I can still seeeee youuuu."

There was a squeak and a giggle.

"Brianna, come up on mommy's lap before you bonk your head again—she's always doing that when she plays this—come up here, babe," the woman said, scooping her daughter up from under the chair, causing squirms and more laughter.

The girl's mother was late twenties, brunette, beautiful. Several years prior, I'd likely have creeped her the hell out by moving into the next chair, making sure my arm sleeve tattoos were visible before asking about her three favorite bands. You're not supposed to give yourself douche chills, but it's become more frequent as I recollect days past.

"She's adorable," I told her before scrunching up my face and sending the smirking daughter into her armpit. "If Captain Calculator in there recommends any music to you, as he's prone to do, I'd ignore it. His taste is straight dumpster fire, just FYI."

The mom chortled, sliding little Brianna over to her left leg. "This is the first time I've come here. Need to get my taxes filed as I'm already on an extension. Music, like what, polka?"

I popped up in the chair. "Wow, polka. I'm not sure I've even heard that term in all the years you've been alive, so no. That would at least be interesting. He's a 'whatever's on the radio guy,' which, as I say this, realize you could be too and that I sound like a pretentious moron."

She laughed again before sliding Brianna back to the other leg. Her amber bangs slid down in front of her left eye and she blew them away with her upturned lips. "Well, with her in the car, I suppose you could say it's mostly radio stuff. She likes to belt out whatever melody sounds good that day. Way out of tune, of course, but it's cute."

Not long ago, I would have shifted gears and made the conversation about whatever greased the wheels best for a potential mattress party. I can't say there was a definitive moment when I forced myself to stop sexualizing these younger women, or at what hour of what day I began to understand there was value in simple, honest conversation and not simply skin on skin in a tour bus or Motel 6 shower, but there *was* a moment. I know what you're thinking, and of course she's part of that equation too. If I hadn't been transfixed by the angelic Laurel, there was at least a nineteen percent chance I may have regressed and moved in on mom here.

"Hello, Mr. Traxon. Come on in," my accountant said, dressed in the familiar charcoal suit and rocking a black bow tie.

"Looking sharp, buddy. That's why I come here—your fashion sense is second to none." I winked at the little girl and nodded goodbye to the mom, who returned a smile that could knock over a train. "Hey, wait, she was here before me."

"Oh no, I'm really early," the mom assured me. "She loves to come to these offices. She has a blast. You go ahead."

I nodded at her again, following my accountant in through the door.

"This won't take but a minute. Thanks for coming down. I know you're busy with the writing and getting acclimated here, but I wanted to make sure I got you this check. I also wanted to discuss options with you since we haven't fortified a financial plan yet," he said, motioning for me to sit in the chair across from his desk, which I did.

"I wasn't expecting any checks that wouldn't have just been mailed. What are we talking about?" I asked him as I pulled a few cashews from the pack I'd opened before coming in.

He fidgeted with papers on his desk while I cringed at the awful droning coming from a small radio in the back corner. The same line repeated over and over on top of pre-programmed beats, the shrill voice making tinnitus seem like a blessing.

"So, the parent company of the network that owned your television show was bought out, and whoever structured your contract had some foresight, as they included a clause where, should that happen, you'd get a flat percentage payout. This is in addition to any ongoing residuals going forward, should they re-air it or sell it again. I can't speak to what percentage your castmates may have received, or if they even had any ownership of the show at all, but your share is rather significant."

I leaned into his desk. "Significant? I wasn't aware I owned any part of that show, and how on earth is there any money in buying the rights? It's not *Cheers*. It only gets replayed on that lousy network sometimes, and I get tiny checks from—"

"You'll have to take all that up with your attorney, who, as I see from my notes here, also got a little slice of the pie. Needless to say, he put together a nice payday for you in the event what happened...happened," he interrupted. Bold move for the nerd. I liked it. The music was still an abomination though.

I chuckled. "Well, no shit, ol' Tony grabbed himself a piece, of course. That guy was responsible for more millionaires in L.A. than the nineties sitcom boom. I'm happy to give him his share of something I didn't know existed. So, what are we looking at here?"

He slid the check over to me in a dramatic fashion, slow and deliberate, nodding his head gently and peering at me over his glasses.

"Three hundred and eighty grand?"

"Yes, three hundred and eighty thousand dollars."

Listen, I'm not trying to be a dope here. I know it's a lot of money, and I was as happy as Pickle rubbing his ass across the carpet at three miles an hour to get it, but he built it up like I was getting five mill or something.

"Cool. Thank you. Should I just sign it, have you deposit into my money market account, or what were you thinking? Maybe buy my own plane?"

Discerning my sarcasm, he pulled the check back and stopped grinning. "Mr. Traxon, this is a significant amount of money. From what you described, it's also 'found' money, so I'd think you'd be thrilled."

"Absolutely, of course—hey, you want a cashew?" I asked him. He shook his head no. "But I'm curious if you've looked at my accounts lately, because from my recollection, I should have a good deal more than that amount in total, unless you've been skimming. Flying the globe first class, following Maroon 5 around, have you, Lyle? If I see Katy Perry driving around in your Bimmer, I'm gonna be pissed."

He blushed and shook his head. "Of course not, don't be ridiculous Mr. Traxon, I—"

"I'm just busting you. My money is still all there though, right?" I jammed in, playfully.

"Of course. However, that's one of the other reasons I wanted you to come down here, as I feel some diversification makes sense. I have a colleague in town who's a certified financial planner and could assist in turning your sizable assets into, well, significantly more sizable."

These money guys have tunnel vision. They can never see anything other than cash turning into more cash. The larger the piles and more creative places they can stuff those piles, the bigger the boner they get. My pal here was nearly salivating when he slid that check over to me. I almost wanted to let him have it just to see the look on his face, imagining all the write offs and compounding interest he could fantasize about as he ran his fingers over the paper.

"You don't have all my cash in a sock drawer, right? I'm sure I'm *diversified* enough for now, but yeah, we can set up another time to talk if you want. For now, how about you deposit that into whatever account makes the most sense and doesn't get both of us indicted. Then bring in that girl who's waiting out there and help her out. I need to run to the hardware store and get to the pooch," I said.

"Fair enough, Mr. Traxon. If you could sign the check here for me," he said, handing me a silver pen with his full name, followed by CPA, on it. Got to be impressed by a guy with his name on a sweet pen.

"How 'bout you call me Josh? You've got access to all my cash, we both like BMWs, and I'm a sucker for a dude in a bow tie. I think it only makes sense to be on a first name basis."

He ruffled some papers on the desk and stood up. "Perhaps you're right. Thank you for stopping in, Josh."

"There you go. I feel better already."

"One last thing, Mr. Trax—Joshua, excuse me. I also received a call from your agent, about money for the book you're working on. Almost got the sense he was fishing for information on your progress. Have you two been in touch?"

I rubbed the side of my neck, tension shooting between my shoulders and up through the back of my head. "Uh, yeah, I probably should give him a ring back. Talk to your money guru there and set up a meeting late next week. Call me with the time. Cool?"

"Cool," he replied, his face flushed, likely realizing that nothing a bow tie wearing man listening to a "Macarena" remix on a single speaker radio said could truly be cool.

"Take care," I replied, extending my hand to his, which he shook firmly.

While I walked out, I heard commotion in the small bathroom of the waiting area. It sounded like the little girl and her mom—I mean who else could it be? They were laughing as the water ran. I considered waiting for a minute and saying goodbye but thought better of it. Our moment was over.

The street outside was speckled with patrons weaving their way in and out of the town's shops. I scanned the distance between my accountant's office and the hardware store, looking for signs of Vermont's thriving paparazzi scene. The coast was clear. I strolled down the sixteenth of a mile, give or take, to the destination, wondering how Lyle would trash me to his buddy about my near ambivalence to the fat check.

"Almost four hundred thousand dollars, Joe! The guy almost tore it up in my face, like he was offended it was so small!"

Accountants, money managers, agents, lawyers—they always have a better plan for your dough. A smarter place to put it, a method to pay less tax, or some form of mathematical hocus pocus. I understand they're just trying to help, and of course they're right about all of it—I mean, what the hell do I know? But I've found myself at that place in life where I have enough. Enough to play a little, and enough to give some away. If I can save on taxes because Lyle wants to jam most of my cash in some tax differed annuity or Roth IRA or any of those other egghead deals out there, awesome, but no matter what, I'm still going to end up okay. Sort of odd that a guy who is good at chess is such a dunderhead when it comes to money, right? Conversely, when I asked Lyle if he played the day we met, he said *"Oh jeez, no. Don't think I've ever even tried."* I'm not one to embolden stereotypes, but if there was ever a fella that looked like he should be a chess freaking master, it's Lyle.

"Hi, Mr. Traxon!" a voice shouted as I arrived at the front of Town Hardware. It was Timothy, one of the hired hands, wearing his green smock and grinning ear to ear, as always.

"Hey there, Timmy. You look happier than any man should be allowed. Whatcha got for me today, my friend?"

"Wanna come see the new leaf blowers?" he asked, leading the way quicker than I could keep up.

The owner of the store, Dan Toggins, was with a customer at the front counter. He nodded and smiled before continuing to answer the woman's questions about tile grout. Fella was always pleasant enough, amenable to anything I inquired about, and I had no reason to suspect he disliked me other than the fact that, from time to time, I can rub people the wrong way. Shocker, right? But I'd noticed he'd toss me a bit of a stink eye now and again. It was nothing blatant, and it was quite possible I was overreaching, though I'd lay odds I was more right than wrong.

He was a tall son-of-a-bitch, Mr. Toggins, with a Ned Flanders mustache. He always wears an American flag pin on his overalls. One day I asked him about it, real casual like, nothing douchey. He squinted his eyes a smidge and then asked, "Did you serve?" I told him no, and then he paused for a minute before answering that someone made him the pin. I smiled, nodded, and then inquired where I might find two-stroke oil. I thought I heard him sigh as I walked away. Half of my old roadies were ex-military.

Some were still active-duty reserve. My neighbor in L.A., Alex, was in Vietnam and the first Iraq war. They all gave me similar looks sometimes. I can't say I blame them. It's a brotherhood of selfless, brave, dedicated folks who choose loyalty to a country and its people, wherein I've always been a dunderhead with few priorities outside my own world. I've long wished I'd joined the Air Force though, as I'd been obsessed with aviation from a time shortly after the chess affinity, and some structure and discipline wouldn't have been the worst thing for me. Oh, and I'm working on the selfishness thing, but I'm doing it at my own pace.

"Here they are," Timmy said, grabbing hold of a backpack leaf blower hanging on the wall. It was a gas-powered pull start, bright green plastic, black tubing, and priced about fifty dollars more than it would be at the big box home improvement store twenty miles away.

"Looks good, Tim," I told him. "I don't need one right now, but I promise you that when I do, I'll come see you, okay?"

He smiled wide, then slid both his hands into the huge front pocket on his overalls.

"So, can you help me with sockets, buddy? I'm missing a few. Probably happened during my move, and I need to mess around with one of the cars over the weekend," I said.

"Are you working on the Porsche or the Bimmer, Mr. Traxon?" Timmy asked.

"Wow, you know your cars. Which one's your favorite?"

"I like the Porsche because it looks like a race car."

"Indeed, it does. You ever been in a race car?"

Timmy shook his head no, back and forth, grinning. Dan Toggins had just finished up with the customer at the front and made his way over to the two of us.

"Holy smokes, Timmy. Looks like we need to get you out on the road soon. Get some RPMs cranking and wind hitting your face," I said right as Dan put his arm on Tim's back.

"What's happening over here?" Toggins asked.

"Mr. Traxon said I can go for a ride in his race car," Timmy shouted, his hands grabbing onto Dan's forearm, tugging at it.

"Well, I don't think anyone in town has a race car, but why don't you go out back and bring in a few stacks of that potting soil. We can talk about it later, OK," Dan said.

Tim let go of his arm and let his head droop down before shuffling off toward the back of the store. "Bye, Mr. Traxon," he said, offering one quick grin when he peeked back at me.

"You call me Josh, okay?" I told him. He didn't hear me and continued out the back door.

"Is there anything else you need? Did I hear you ask about sockets?" Dan asked, peering down from two inches above and six inches too close.

"Yeah, I can poke around and find what I need. No problem. Timmy's a great kid, isn't he?" I asked, knowing it would provoke whatever was lurking behind his dark brown, untrusting peepers.

"My nephew's a sweet kid, yeah. That sweetness invites trouble, though. I do what I can to look out for him, with his dad being gone. He enjoys his days at the store, talking to customers, helping his uncle, having his lunch every day right at noon. I don't like to upset that routine, and I'd ask that you didn't, either."

I looked up at him, his gaze taut and concentrated, the slightest veiled smile barely peeking through his lips. "I'm not trying to cause problems for anyone. Timmy has just made it clear he likes fast cars, and I have a couple, that's all. We talk about them, he laughs, smiles, and gets excited. I can't say I see any harm in that. You?"

He nodded his head, pursing his lips. "The sockets are in aisle five. Everything you need should be there."

"Hey, I appreciate that," I told him, lying. "You have a good afternoon, Dan."

He glared but didn't jab me for the casual use of his first name without the requisite introduction to do so. I wasn't trying to be a numb nut. Well, maybe part of me was, but from my first visit to the store it had been a battle with this guy every time I talked to Timmy. The young man had Down Syndrome; he wasn't an invalid or incapable in any way I could discern, and he loved social interaction. I wouldn't pretend to know all the particulars and nuances of caring for someone with said condition. What I did know was everyone entering that store was greeted by the happiest, most loveable, kind-hearted dude in the state. Most of the time, those greetings were stifled by Dan, who sent him off on a store errand, or two doors down for a coffee. Timmy's "routine" was being the coolest motherfucker in Vermont, and, from my observations, big Dan there was stamping out his mojo.

Speaking of mojo, when I walked out of the hardware store, I was surprised to see Laurel step out of her car and head for the market. I practically sprinted across the road, prompting an unnecessary beep from a distant pickup truck. Unless death is imminent in less than three seconds if I don't move, beeping is bullshit.

"Laurel," I shouted, as she scooped up a small wicker basket outside the market, her mouth erupting in teeth whiter than the Andes as our eyes met.

"Heeeeey, neighbor. Any interesting visits lately from busybody locals?" Laurel inquired, before grimacing and rolling her eyes.

"Come to think of it, I did have a pint-sized woman stop by and verbally beat the snot out of me, yeah. She seemed less than enthusiastic about my relationship with her daughter, who, of course, I have no relationship with, other than being pals," I answered.

"Pals, huh?"

"Yup."

"I see."

I scrunched up my face. "So, where's that adorable, petite housemate of yours, anyway? And what about Ethan? Is he safe alone with her?"

Laurel chortled and wrenched her head to the left when someone slid up next to her. A woman in her late thirties holding a bag full of groceries was giving me "the look."

"Can I help you, or..." Laurel asked, letting her words trail off.

"Oh, I'm so sorry. It's just that, are you... Josh Traxon? From Shaky Bones?" the excited woman asked.

Laurel looked at me with her best non-verbal "Really?" face and then back at the woman.

"I suppose I am," I answered.

"Holy crap, I thought so! My ex-boyfriend was wicked into you guys. He turned me on to you, too. Then I got hooked on that show. Oh em gee, I can't believe it's you," the woman proclaimed.

Laurel laughed and made a move that would go down as one of the most magnanimous, sexy moves I'd ever been a party to. "Hey, Josh, we better get going, babe, if we're going to get this shopping done before we head to Trish and John's place," she said, sliding her hand into mine and tugging me forward.

"Oh right, of course," I said, looking down at her. "It was very nice meeting you and thanks for being a fan."

"Would you mind if I snapped a quick pic? I'm sorry. It's just that if I send this to my ex, it will totally torture him, and I'm all about torturing that idiot these days."

I peered over at Laurel, who still had a firm grip on my hand. She nodded while offering the faintest of eye rolls. "Absolutely. Anything I can do to enable the misery of an ex."

The woman pushed in next to my right side, angling her camera from above, careful to turn it so Laurel wasn't in the picture. I felt Laurel's hand tighten on mine when she observed the woman's maneuver.

"Seriously, thank you so much. I can't tell you how much this is going to piss him off," the woman exclaimed, staring at the pic on her phone.

"Glad I could help out. Nice meeting you..." I said, leaning my head, prompting her for her name.

"Oh, yes, you too, and it's Ashlynne. Thanks again," she said, before scurrying off down the sidewalk.

"Of course, it's Ashlynne. What else could her name be," Laurel suggested, still holding my hand.

"Hey, anyone who wants to use my image to annoy an ex has my blessing. It's good for the soul," I replied, my hand still locked onto hers, leading her into the market.

"So, when I dump you in three weeks and start sending you pics of me and Rob Delaney outside a café in London, you'll be supportive?"

I slowed my pace and looked over at her, stopping right in front of the zucchinis. "If I can stand you for three whole weeks, it will be a miracle to rival life itself. And Rob Delaney, seriously? That awkwardly tall, smarmy comedian slash actor? He has a sweater on even when he's naked."

Laurel let go of my hand and tugged on my T-shirt. "Well, at least he'd be naked."

I squinted my eyes halfway before reaching for her hand again. "Okay, settle down. I'm just here to get some apples and bread, wasn't planning on hearing about all your twisted sexual fantasies."

She gripped my hand tighter, pulling herself closer to me. "Don't be jealous. I'm sure we can find a spot for you somewhere in the mix," she said, before letting go of my hand and sauntering down the end of the produce aisle.

Game on.

CHAPTER 12

"That's what you call dinner? Gnawing on a couple chicken wings and pounding four Jack and Cokes? One of which they wouldn't have served you had they not known me," Josh said, trailing her back to the car.

She raised her right hand, extending her middle finger.

"Sasha, come on. Let's get some coffee and hang out for a while. It's a beautiful spot, and we rushed through the whole—"

"Some frickin'...some damn rock stah you are, Josss. I mean, geez dude," Sasha answered, her words wobbling along with her gait.

Josh accelerated his pace and met her at the driver's side door, her fingers latched onto the handle. "Whooooa. Yeah, we're not doing this again. Get your ass over to the other side, or do I need to stuff you in there myself?"

She snickered and smacked him with her right hand while still facing the car. "Such a goddam prick and a busskill. What the hell happen to you, Trax?" Her words were interrupted by a hiccup. "What the...serioushhhly."

Josh reached underneath her, scooped her up, and carried her to the passenger's side of the car, her legs and arms flailing as she traveled. "Put me dow, you mothafucka!"

Josh ignored her pleading, plopping her down into the passenger's seat, then reaching across her body to secure the safety belt while she slapped at his back and neck. He crouched down to her eye level next to the car, securing her wrists with his hands before he spoke. "I don't wanna do this. Can you calm down so we can head back to your place without another scene? If I let your arms go, will you stay in your seat and let me get us out of here?"

She smirked at him, nodding her head until he released. "You better nah drive like a pushy, or you can forget abow havin' this one," she said, running her hand between her legs.

Josh let go of her hands and scurried back to the driver's side, trying to get the car started and moving before she undid the seat belt and got out. She remained still, only leaning in his direction when he sat in the seat and started the engine.

"I love you, but I hate you too," she said, before pursing her lips for a kiss. Josh leaned in and planted a tiny peck on her mouth and then drove the car out onto the street.

"Lame," Sasha shouted, as the car sped off and she straightened up in her seat. "That was frickin lame, asssshole."

He ignored her and continued driving.

"Why you gotta be like this? You were fun when we met, annnow...and now you're like, just lame as hell," Sasha proclaimed, glaring at him as he drove. "I bet you ffffuck like, like ten women a month more screwed up than me...but all a sudden I'm the loser. Screw you," she shouted, kicking her foot over toward his right leg.

"Hey, I'm driving!" he yelled over the wind noise. "Calm down. If you want to have a tantrum, wait until we get back to your place."

Sasha scowled and thumped herself back into her chair. She continued that, leaning forward and then slamming herself against the backrest repeatedly.

"Hey, I'm asking you to stop. I know you're pissed, and I know you want another drink, but—"

"Oh, fuck you," she screamed, leaning toward him as he shifted the car into fifth gear. "Don't start preachin' about my drinking again, asshole! You think I dunno how much you party when I'm not aroun? Mister high and mighty, like you ain't all fucked up yourself. Just because you can dial it down for me, prolly juss so that overused dick of yours will work, you think I dunno you're a damn lush. Pleeaasse."

Josh ignored her, hoping a lack of engagement might induce calm.

Sasha continued staring at him while he drove for another mile, then leaned back in her chair and sifted through her purse for her phone. When she found it, she scrolled through pictures in her camera roll, eventually finding the one she wanted and turning the phone to face Josh, He continued driving, unfazed.

"Come on, look at it. You know you want to," Sasha said, wiggling the phone back in forth in his periphery. "I don have to even tell you what pic this is cuz I know you know, baby."

Josh signaled right, hoping a turn down a less populated road might get them back to her place sooner.

"Cooooomee on, Trax. I knooooow you wanna take a peek," Sasha said, pressing the cold glass of the phone against his cheek.

"We'll be back to your house in less than ten minutes. Can you just sit still and stop trying to put this car into a ditch?" Josh shouted over the rush of air across the open cabin.

Sasha relented, slamming herself back into her seat before hiccupping repeatedly and then tossing a gum wrapper from her pocket into the air. Josh considered making a comment but chose to accelerate and hope the speed lulled her inebriated self into a temporary trance. While the car moved over the broken road at seventy-plus miles an hour, Sasha slid herself toward the car door, resting her head against it. Josh eased off the accelerator, not wanting to disturb the snooze she was taking, but still motoring ahead quicker than the lumpy pavement called for. Sasha's head rattled against the mustang's door, jostling her awake briefly, before she nuzzled herself back down against it.

"Three more miles," Josh whispered to himself, watching an RV whiz past him in the opposite direction, its roof loaded with all the trimmings of a family's summer vacation at the beach.

Sasha shot up from her slumber, kicking her legs and feet against the footwell of the car. "What the hell, Traxon, where are we?" she screamed, before leaning into him. "I need to peeee."

"We're only a few miles—"

"I wanna see if thissh thing will work for me," Sasha interrupted, reaching between his legs.

"Hey, come on, stop it. I'm fucking driving here! We're almost home," Josh snapped back as he pulled her hand out of his crotch. Sasha grunted and reached inside the pocket of her leather coat.

"What the hell is that?" he asked, leaning towards her as she turned to face the car door. She dumped a small heap of cocaine on her hand and snorted it. "Sasha, are you fucking kidding me right now? What the hell is it with you? Every damn day can't be playtime," he shouted over the warm air swirling around the cabin. "I mean, seriously, it's time to talk about getting you some help or some—"

"Oh, shut the fuck uuuup, you lame ass dickweed," she screamed back at him. "You get yourself some help asshole. Right now, I'm bout to help myself to this, which is the only thing about you I even freakin' like anymore. Why don't you take me down to that lil' river near here and fuck me you ashhhole, or would you rather go fly fishing? I bet you would, you sick fuck. Want me to put my hair into pigtails. That make you hard, asshhhole?" Sasha reached down between his legs before unbuckling her belt and climbing into the driver's seat, hitting the steering wheel with her shoulder, sending the car veering to the left.

"Stop it!" Josh screamed, pushing her away while trying to regain control of the car. It straightened out just as she thrust herself back on top of him. The sudden force and friction of her body against the wheel sent the car shooting leftward again, and Josh overcorrected in panic, sending Sasha back into the passenger's seat, laughing. When he began to steady the Mustang's travel, Sasha leapt at him once again, pulling herself up onto him, kissing him wildly on the neck and face. He tried to nudge her off himself as he maintained the wheel with his legs, but she resisted, and her lower back caught the steering wheel, turning it and sending the car's rear end into a violent spin to the left. Josh tried to correct the line, furiously spinning the wheel in the other direction. The car fishtailed while Josh mashed the brake and clutch simultaneously, eventually heading to the right and catching a stretch of curbing, sending the rear end bucking skywards and down an incline toward some trees at forty miles per hour.

Smoke. Glass. Dirt. Dust. Death.

CHAPTER 13

S unlight sneaking through cracks in window covers has a
GPS set for drunks. The heinous, blinding rays will angle
and contort themselves in a clever hunt for your corneas, with
their accuracy measured by how shit-housed you got the night
before. I'd been on a whiskey jamboree, and my lips were rolled
backward, up inside my mouth, while my head was pulsing like
one of those cacti full of scorpions, so the light was boiling my
pupils as I lay motionless.

Pickle was laying on the couch next to me, his tail rotating in
clockwise, syncopated motion when he noticed my squinting
eyes meet his. Anyone who ever questions if dogs are truly a
man's best friend need only watch the selfless, benevolent way
that Pickle behaves when he knows I've torn one off. He stays
close by but never whines. He waits silently while I breathe and
gurgle and drool off the side of the couch or bed, or at least I
assume he does because in all these years he's never woken me,
and I know from exes that my drunken slumber is far from silent.
He won't even lap at his water dish while I'm out, cautious not to
wake me, I imagine, because he's usually a thirsty little bugger.
I've had women I was involved with blast my own awful music to

get me up after a knockaround—which is pure evil—and little Pickle won't even get a drink of water until I'm up. Makes me want to cry, but so did most everything of late.

"Hey, buddy," I said, which was the signal for "all clear," and Pickle shot to life and raced at me full balls, jumping onto the couch, licking my face like it was a spiral ham bone. "Ohhhkaaaaay, let me sit up."

The pooch licked me a few more times, his tail spinning furiously, and then flattened out on the couch awaiting the next move. I sunk my face into my hands before dragging them across my skin and summoning the strength to stand and find a shirt.

Shirtless.

Laurel was here late the night before. I recalled sitting on the couch for most of that time, but there was no recollection of either of us being topless. There was a gigaton of whiskey, some exuberant laughter at the absurdity of her relationship with Barry, and a little at the expense of her mother, some messin' around, and then she watched me play chess. That's where I got fuzzy. Most of the time I'm playing chess, or doing almost anything, I'm topless, so no shocker there. But after the groove we were in, how'd it end up with her leaning over me at a computer?

Pukefest.

Laurel threw up on me, covering most of my shirt and part of the throw rug near the kitchen. The memory popped in as I cracked the door open to let Pickle zip out and finally take a leak. Laurel had followed me for two whiskeys, but then stopped drinking for at least an hour. We didn't smoke any weed, there was nothing but nibbles on snack food, but she abruptly threw up while watching me play. Normally I wouldn't question a woman heaving on me, especially after having to listen to me drone on about whatever bullshit I was spewing, but this was sudden and unprovoked. Had to be a stomach bug or the like, and hopefully I wasn't too much of a dope when she left because I was flyin' by that time.

"I'll give her a call and check on her soon," I told Pickle, who only cared about burying his face in his water bowl, the poor bastard. If only I could train him to not be subservient to my revelry.

There's a moment we've all had with a soon-to-be lover when the conversation slows, the pauses expand, and the eyes meet in a less casual, intermittent way, finally locking. The few seconds feel like minutes, heart rates climb, and sensations in dangerous places come alive. Immediately you're kissing, and then hands are exploring those dangerous places. Laurel and I had that moment last night, though it was cut short abruptly. Not by the puking, which came later, but by an unknown interloper.

I'm fully aware of how my past endeavors, her "relationship" with Barry, the short time we've known one another, and being a single mom may dissuade a woman as bright and sensible as Laurel from engaging with me physically, but she was all hands on deck last night for a while. We mauled one another like teenagers in a Judy Blume book for several minutes, but then she extricated herself from my enthusiastic grasp and clumsy lips. She played it off with the usual, "Whoa, things are moving pretty fast here," rap, though she's no Meryl Streep, so that was a bust. After the awkwardness subsided, we moved on, and I didn't bother to probe. She had her reasons, all of which I'm sure were valid, and there was no expiration date on the courtship—it didn't have to reach its apex at that instant.

The conversation moved into my fascination with chess, at her prompting, and it was a stellar topic to dial the heat back because, let's face it, it's not exactly salacious. She seemed genuinely interested, if not a little distracted by what I now assume were her churning insides. In all the years on the road with the band and during my time on that dumb TV show, I had hundreds of conversations with women. Some—okay, *most*—were, for me, verbal foreplay and no more substantive than a Twinkie, but that was only because in most every case I redirected anything authentic or profound back to the primal and sophomoric. There was a discussion I had with a media consultant on the TV show, Jessica was her name, that was one of the most captivating and engrossing experiences of my adult years. It began as my typical shithead come-ons, though she masterfully diverted it into philosophy, theology, and art. We ended up speaking for over two hours without a stitch of clothes being removed or a shred of DNA being exchanged. I lost touch with her, which was a good thing, as she was eons more evolved. She didn't deserve the human wrecking ball that I was in her life.

Thinking back, there were far more genuine conversations than I might have initially guessed, but many had been buried in alcohol and shame, not to mention the occasional trauma. I told myself for years that my wandering eyes and frat boy behaviors were a result of lack of time to focus on anything specific, and my environment. Of course, that's bullshit.

With Laurel, before the vomitorium, I listened to her candidly discuss her fears, missteps, and apprehensions. She also offered astute observations on world history, the current political climate, and geography. That last bit was an odd detour, but the fact she was so well-versed on New Zealand's topography was amusing. Although this may sound like, "Wow, can you believe this *woman* is so smart," I assure you no such implication is true. Instead, talking with Laurel reminded me of the many brilliant and formidable women I've known. Although those personality facets were filtered through a distilled spirits lens, extracting only a fleshy plaything. And last night Laurel looked so damn beautiful, so sexy and alluring sitting across from me on that couch. What gave me the biggest boner, though, was her jubilation at finding water on Mars.

A knock on the door interrupted my recollection. Pickle's ears pricked up, but before he raced to the entryway, yapping and farting as he went, he watched to see what I'd do. Maybe all he heard was a *house sound*—some random, unexplained creak—why bother burning calories and expending energy when he could remain cozy in his body-warmed utopia? However, if what he heard *was* the front door, and I got up to check things out, he needed to be there immediately because new friends and unlicked skin awaited.

I leaned forward, sliding my butt a few inches off the couch. Pickle's eyes were glued to mine.

The faint knock returned, this time a decibel or two louder. Pickle's head rotated thirty degrees to his left, though keeping his eyes fixed on me. I started to utter, "Who is it, buddy?" but only got to the first vowel sound. He was hauling ass to the door, barking as ferociously as a twenty-pound canine with a smushed mouth could.

"Who is it, Pick? I bet it's that tiny woman from across the street and she's going to tear me a new one." Pickle looked up at me briefly, far more interested in what existed on the other side of that door than my words.

"Hello, Josh. I...uh, well my mom said maybe I could see, or you would let me see, I mean, your cars. If that's okay?" the meek voice asked, as Pickle shot out, full sprint, to greet Ethan with hops, jumps, and way too many sloppy licks.

"Pickle, come on man. Let him breathe," I said, but that dog was on full autopilot. Ethan crouched down, making Pickle more insane. There was little that dog loved more than small humans willing to meet him at his level. He would whimper in ways only heard in said scenario The tail rotation would increase fifty percent, licks by twofold. Ethan giggled and snorted in response carefully adjusting his position to provide Pickle the most advantageous position. This sloppy, ridiculous dance continued for many minutes.

"Let him up, Pick. I know you think everyone comes here for you, but we have cars to check out," I said, prompting Ethan to stand up and the puppy to freeze, tongue hanging out, wondering what was next.

"If you're busy...I could come back," Ethan suggested, gazing down at the dog, which sent the tail going again. He was wearing a T-shirt that was just a picture of some generic red cartoon race car with the words, "The only speed I know is *faster*!" which was awesome, of course.

"Not at all, little man. I have nothing going on. Your mom definitely said it's okay to come over, though?" I asked, peering across the road, seeing Laurel in the kitchen window waving to me.

"Um, well yeah. She said I had to ask you, but..." his words trailed off as he looked back down at the dog. I waved to Laurel, scooping Pickle up with my other arm to put him back inside, which was tantamount to lifetime imprisonment in his puppy mind.

"Let me just toss the pup back in the house, K? There's lots of things in the garage that can jostle around and hurt the little fella. That means you need to be careful too," I said. Ethan nodded, fidgeting with his white baseball cap. "Just for a little bit, Pick. I'll come get you soon."

I closed the door, watching the dog's eyes go lifeless. He was now an abandoned pug, shot out of a spaceship in a capsule to float around the universe for eternity.

"I like that shirt you have on there. Is that from a TV show or something?" I asked Ethan on our way to the garage.

He looked up me and smiled but said nothing. Good for him. Let him wear his rad shirt without having to answer to me.

I punched the code into the garage keypad, and the door lifted with a metallic clanking and high-pitched croak. "Thing is pretty loud, right? I need to grease it up or something. Would wake you and your mom out of a sound sleep, I bet."

Ethan looked up at me and smirked before stuffing his hands in his front pockets.

"Here they are," I said, walking into the garage, Ethan right at my heels. The space was set up for four cars, though I only had two inside currently. The bays were set back to front, requiring only two doors, and allowing cars to line up one behind the other. At present, the spaces in front were empty. The Porsche and BMW were backed against a workbench covered in cardboard boxes. On the walls I'd hung a few racing posters and marketing items from various car manufactures, along with a few pieces of rock band memorabilia. The rest of the space was neat, organized, and far tidier than inside the house.

Ethan walked over to the jet-black Porsche first, sliding his hand from the rear quarter panel up over the roof line. "First thing I ever did when I saw a 911, slide my hand right over it in the same place," I said, startling Ethan. He pulled his hand away and looked back at me.

"Don't be shy. Touch her all you want. She needs another wash soon anyway, so it's okay if you get fingerprints on her," I explained walking up to the car's posterior. "Cars look pretty when they're clean, but you can't have any fun if you don't get them dirty sometimes, right?"

Ethan snorted and then went back to touching the car. This time caressing the front side panels and over the hood. His eyes were fixed on the shape, following the lines as his hand slid over the smooth surface. I watched him, grinning, as he crouched at the front wheel, admiring the massive yellow brake caliper, poking at it with his index finger.

"Do you know what those are?" I asked him.

He turned toward me, wide eyed. "The brakes. I like the color."

"Me too, and very good. You know cars, dude, no question there. I had a choice of red or yellow for the brakes and liked the yellow better. What color would you have got?"

"I like red but, hmmm, uh, prolly yellow too," he answered.

"So, do you know what part of the brakes those are?" I asked, feeling the return of hangover number six thousand forty-five announcing itself inside my cranium.

He shrugged his shoulders.

"These are called calipers. They grab on to this big brake disc here," I said, crouching next to him, resulting in a fart that reverberated off the garage walls and sent Ethan into mad hysterics. "Whooopsie. Too many cashews last night or something."

"Mom farts all the time when she gets up in the morning," Ethan declared at full volume through his laughter.

"Holy smokes! Not sure I wanted to know that," I exclaimed, which only bolstered his laughter. I could see Laurel's mother firing off any number of putrid hot air bullets, probably as she smiled with pride, but not her daughter. She was too ethereal, too demure, too classy. Apparently, I was wrong. Ethan, here, just sold her out as some middle school bully with IBS. "Let's pretend the last thirty seconds never happened, shall we? Take a look at the engine."

Ethan was still giggling but stood up and walked to the back of the car while I popped the engine cover through the open driver window. If he wanted me to start it, which would be ludicrous if he didn't want me to, I'd need to toss back three or four aspirin or risk a full cranial implosion. The relative darkness inside the garage was at least filtering out the vile sunlight.

"This is called a boxer engine. Have you heard that before?" I asked. His eyes, however, had moved away from the car. They now focused on a marble chess set resting on a small wooden tabletop set against the garage wall. My mouth curled up into half a smile, staring at this miniature version of myself, minus the alcoholism and flatulence.

"Whatcha looking at, bud? The chess set?" I asked.

He nodded. "Mom tried to teach me how to play the other day, but she was sick."

"She did, huh?" I questioned. "Well, I know she wasn't feeling that great yesterday either, so hopefully you don't catch whatever she's got. Did she show you how the pieces move, where they go and all?"

"Um, a little bit, but I think she was mixed up."

I laughed. "Mixed up? Well, it's a crazy game," I said, heading over to grab the board and pieces. "How about we take a break from the cars, sit on the porch and play for a while?"

Ethan smiled. "Okay, but can we see the cars more after that, too?"

"Of course, and if your mom is alright with it, I will take you for a ride. Maybe see if she wants to come along."

"Umm, she was kinda pukey this morning, so I dunno if she would like to, but we can ask her if you want."

"She wasn't feeling good this morning? Like how?"

Ethan stopped walking, almost at the porch. "She was throwing up sometimes a little bit."

It was one thing to put myself in hell with hangovers but taking someone like Laurel down with me wasn't cool. Sure as shit Momma Laurel would be telling me off about it. It was somewhat shocking it wasn't her at the door instead of Ethan.

"Would it be okay if Pickle came out while we played?" Ethan asked.

"That little troublemaker?" I replied, mock angry.

"He'd probably knock over the pieces and stuff, huh?"

He would too, the little mental case. Though there was an easy solution to that problem.

"Alright, well, I'll let him out to sit on the porch, but the thing is, we need to get him nice and tuckered out so he won't be a loon. Do you think you can run around with him and tire him out?" I knew what I was asking was equivalent to me asking a cheetah if he'd enjoy chasing a wounded gazelle after a ten-day fast, but it was fun to watch the little dude's eyes.

"Sure!" he shouted, leaping onto the porch. "But before we play, can you remind me the rules a little? Cause I think mom was maybe cheating. She said the horse moves kinda funny and jumps people, but she was laughing."

I chuckled before placing the board onto the porch. "You're right, it does sound silly, doesn't it? But she's right. It's the only piece on the board that can do that, though. So, it makes it unique, beautiful, and wicked valuable."

Kind of like your mother, who is no longer watching in the window, but that part I didn't say out loud.

CHAPTER 14

The kid wasn't half bad at chess. He understood the piece movement basics and had a rudimentary idea of strategy, but of course—like everyone who first begins to grasp the power of the more intriguing pieces—he wanted to zoom his queen all over the board right away. It's intoxicating, that queen, with all her might and majesty. But, for all her power, she's as vulnerable as a wet paper trampoline holding cinder blocks when she's in the wrong place. She can explode across the board in a fury, dazzling onlookers, taking prey, yet fall victim to elementary traps laid by clever suitors if the environment is not respected.

Ethan had been gone an hour and Pickle had a full belly, so I saddled myself up to my laptop to write. The last page that appeared on the screen was the same one that'd been there for a couple weeks:

That's the thing about drinking. It doesn't know your name or care

who you are, where you've come from, or where you're going.

It only cares about continuing. The relentless pursuit of the next open bottle and the next suppressed memory, as you ferry your fears into false

bravado and revelry until morning's light and its unvanquished demons

demand their wage.

"What a load of shit," I said before snapping the laptop cover down.

Lyle, the bow-tied number cruncher, suggested I check in with my agent about progress on "the book," but at my current pace, that dumpster fire wouldn't be finished until Pickle evolved opposable thumbs. Calling agents, having that awful conversation about banal nothingness, knowing the entire time they're only concerned about when they're going to get paid was an excruciating endeavor. Of course, I couldn't fault agents or managers for wanting to make a buck. Some of them managed to pull miracles out of their asses for clients that should be rolling pretzel dough in salt at the mall and not on TV or writing books. They all seemed to have the same personality too; hyper enthusiastic and positive when you first get them on the phone, but two minutes in, they're miserable explaining they can't book you as a community theater usher, or whatever project you're working on must be done in a week or they're going to be waterboarded by imaginary entertainment terrorists. I'd get back to the book soon, but first I needed a shower, some protein, and an IPA.

The search for a hoppy beverage was cut short by another knock on the door. I figured this time *had* to be Laurel's mother. No way she would dial it all back after the case she laid out the other day. If anything, she would double down. If Laurel was nineteen or twenty, I'd get it, but she was a grown woman with a child and home. I guess if she were my daughter, though, I'd probably be telling the asshole former rock star across the street to choke on a T-Bone.

Surprised again. Laurel, sans mother, stood on my porch wearing a breezy, off-white top and snug blue jeans with her hair in a ponytail, tucked to her left. Her mouth slid into half a smile on the same side when I opened the door.

"Hey, Josh," she said, Pickle barreling out the door to begin his routine. Before I could say the obligatory dog owner things, apologizing for the four-legged tornado and his antics, Laurel shot me the "It's okay, don't say it" look, so I held back.

"Afternoon. You feeling any better?" I asked.

"Eh, hanging in there. I was hoping I could come in and talk to you for a few if you're free?"

"Absolutely," I said, stepping back to let her in, Pickle underfoot. "Sit down, relax. I was just about to grab a beer or something, would you like anything?"

"Thank you, but not right now."

"Okay, just give me a sec."

I reached into the fridge and pulled out a colorful can; red, green, yellow, and blue pastels, resembling a melting mountain—some Double IPA from a local brewery that was all the rage. 8.5% ABV and aroma of melons and pine that poured like orange juice into the tulip glass. The kid working at the local market deli gushed about them, so I'd purchased a four pack.

"Thank you for spending time with Ethan today. He was chirping about that for the last couple hours, wouldn't stop. Loved seeing the cars, but honestly talked about the chess game more than anything. Probably fascinated by someone that actually knows what the hell they're doing," Laurel said from the other room.

"Well, I think he's just impressed with me because, from what he's told me, you're straight up fucking terrible."

Laurel shriek-laughed, unlike anything I'd ever heard. "Oh my God, sorry. I don't know what that was," she said, almost choking the words out. "Feels good to laugh, but, afraid it may morph into throwing up again. Speaking of that, can I please just apologize for that whole situation again."

"Don't be ridiculous," I said, sitting at the other end of the couch, facing her. "And are you sure you don't want any water or..."

"No, I'm good. Thank you though."

"K," I replied, before taking a sip of the beer and placing it on the floor near my feet, a guaranteed spill. "Ethan, by the way, was a quick study and a pleasure. He's a great kid."

Laurel grinned and slid her hand over the top of Pickle's head, his gargantuan eyes staring at my beer, tongue sticking out as he panted. "He loved it, truly, and yeah he's a wonderful little guy, thanks."

"So, we both agree your kid is cool, you stink at chess, and you like to throw up around me. Is that all you wanted to talk about?"

Laurel sighed. "All true, but that's not it. Though, yeah some of it has to do with getting sick with you last night..."

"Did your mother give you some sort of injection where you immediately throw up if I get a hard on? Cause I have to tell you, I only had half-wood last night. Definitely not full bone here, so shouldn't have worked."

She giggled, but it was forced. I shut the hell up and let her say what she needed to.

"These last couple weeks have been so much fun," she said.

Holy shit, getting dumped. Mom got to her, that knee-high, buzz-killing tyrant!

"Of course, there's no way I would have ever imagined someone like you moving in across the street. How could I?

106

Compared to Barry, I suppose almost anything would be a step up, but you were nothing I expected, in a good way."

"Hey, I know your mother hasn't been keen on me, but—"

"No, no. It's not about her. Well, yes, it's true she's not your biggest fan, but I have not, nor would I ever, make romantic decisions based on her. This is about *me*, and about me being honest about some things."

I shut up, nodding, letting her continue. Pickle flopped down onto his belly, so Laurel adjusted her position to continue scratching his head.

"Barry wasn't just a mistake or some rebound situation. I think I started screwing around with him because I was bored, maybe desperate even, and probably a little terrified. When Ethan's father died a few years ago, I was wrecked. Not in the emotional way or even financially—his company life insurance policy paid a good amount to secure a solid future for me and Ethan, and I wasn't in love with him anymore—but I was a woman in her mid to late thirties, all alone with a little boy and no career. Not just no job, but no clue what I was good at, what I wanted to do, or, cliché of all clichés, who the hell I even was. Darren, that was Ethan's father, was a serial womanizer. That cheater hadn't been good to either of us in years, so when the pickup truck slammed into his Mercedes, killing him when he was probably out screwing some woman he met at another 'corporate event,' I was distraught but not sad. I don't know if that makes me an evil person, not mourning the death of my child's father, but I barely shed a tear the first couple days. Ethan was so young, he didn't really understand, and his father wasn't around a lot anyway. My mother liked Darren, shocker of course, as she's enamored with all the idiots, but she was helpful in the transition and still an invaluable caretaker for Ethan."

"I hope you don't think I take issue with your mother's disdain for me, or lack of trust, whatever it is. She has every right—"

"Oh, please. She's earned any and every negative opinion one may have of her. Don't apologize," Laurel interrupted, scooping up Pickle and placing him in her lap as she spoke. "She's a good grandmother to Ethan and loves me in the way she knows best, but I know what a terror she can be."

We both laughed, and Pickle nuzzled against her tummy, looking at me with the "Look what *I* got, numb nuts!" face.

"Anyway," she continued. "I need to focus on a few things at home right now. Sort out this Barry debacle and get my head straight before diving into something...something I would love to do, don't get me wrong, but something I need to be reasonable about. I think everything going on has taken a deeper toll on my health, which you witnessed last night. For now, I think I need to dial it down a bit. Get my strength back and take care of me, you know?"

She finished speaking, ending with the question, but wasn't really looking for an answer. Her mind existed elsewhere, and her eyes were fixed on Pickle as she stroked his round apple head.

"What's going on with your health, if you don't mind me asking? I'd never question anyone vomiting in my company after listening to me ramble on, but it sounds like this is something more serious, no?"

Her eyes stayed fixed on Pickle. She continued stroking him, his eyes now closed.

"I won't pry anymore," I told her, "and I'm sorry. As for us—I get it. You know, part of the reason I moved out in the woods was to avoid relationships all together. If you think you've had some fucktardery in that department, I'd challenge you to get me under hypnosis sometime and just sit back with a beer or something. Would scare the skin off you."

She grinned and looked over at me. Pickle let one eye creep open when he felt the hand stop moving across his head.

"I need to take care of myself is all, though I appreciate the concern. I also hope you know that this doesn't mean I want anything to change, really, if that doesn't sound too selfish? I know you guys are always worried about being in the 'friend zone' or whatever, but I promise you that my desire for a platonic relationship has nothing to do with desires elsewhere. I would totally hump you right now, right in front of this little pup, and much to my mother's and Barry's chagrin, if I didn't feel nauseous and have nine hundred things racing around my brain that would distract me from what I'm certain would be wonderful."

Our eyes connected for a few seconds before I smiled and stood up, heading to the kitchen. "Welp, if I'm not getting laid, then I'm at least going to get drunk," I said. "Are you sure I can't get you anything at all? Soda, water, wine, animal crackers, the Kama Sutra?"

"They all sound great, but I'm good, thanks. Plus, I want to hear more about what we were talking about the other day before the Barry situation erupted. The accident you started telling me about. I did a little more reading on you—amazing what Google found, seriously—and I listened to, I think, all your music. It's good, Josh. Like, really good," Laurel yelled to me from the living room.

"Well, if you want to be certain sex stays off the menu, then yeah, sure, let's talk about my music," I shouted back, pouring one of the dense, fruity IPAs into a glass.

"I saw a story about an accident you had in California, but there wasn't a wealth of information. Just a crash off the side of a road, but you weren't the driver. You weren't hurt badly either, but the woman giving you a ride home from the bar died? I saw a couple other references about the circumstances being questioned, an investigation. Was that the right one?"

I plopped onto the other end of the couch next to her and lifted Pickle up, placing him at my feet, which he gave me the stink eye for. "Yeah, if it was California, then it's the right one. Have only been in two my entire life. The other was in Canada. I got knocked off a bicycle by an asshole on a scooter."

Laurel roared, which fired up Pickle. He zipped to the other end of the room, scarfed up a stuffed turtle and shook it in his jaws, showing off.

"Please tell me you're kidding. You were on a bicycle, and you got hit by a *scooter*?" she asked, working her words out between the giggles. "Is that even possible?"

"Have you ever been to Montreal in the summer? Drunken college kids everywhere. You think they have any respect for a rock star on a Schwinn? Hell no," I said.

"Jeez. See this is why I can never fully dump you because there's no way I want to miss out on all the stories. I'd be heartbroken."

"Of course, right. If I'm going to be in misery not being able to mount you, then might as well just add the torment by revealing the details of my ridiculous past."

Laurel furrowed her brow and grimaced. "Don't give me that. I don't believe for a second that you don't relish much of your past and being famous, being on TV, all of it."

I gasped cartoonishly. "Holy smokes, am I that obvious? I mean, I do believe that I'm better and more interesting than you commoners, but I attempt to be stealthy with that opinion. Guess I need to ratchet it down even more. You want some cashews?" I asked, digging into my pocket, pulling out an unopened plastic package.

"You really like those nuts, huh?" she asked, amused.

"I have a fondness for them, indeed. You have a problem with my nuts?"

She avoided the tee up. "I *should* hypnotize you. What a world I'd find in there I bet," Laurel suggested, shaking her head. "What a sloppy, antibiotic-filled, woman-soaked mess of debauchery that must all be."

I snort-laughed. "Hey, you're the one that wants to fuck me but can't because you've got *problems*, princess," I shot back, using exaggerated air quotes as I said the word problems, regretting it immediately. "I'm sure if I cracked into that noggin with a swinging pendulum, I'd find a lot more than drinking cosmos with the girls and pushing Ethan on a swing."

"That you would. But we're supposed to be talking about you and that accident. So, what happened? Is that why the show ended? Was after the last season was on, right?"

I exhaled with intention before reaching down for the IPA, taking a long pull prior to setting it back down on the floor with an eyeball warning to Pickle. Otherwise, he would come over and start lapping at it like some fruity pug-fection he thought I'd offered him.

"Crazy thing is the five-year anniversary of that crash is the day after tomorrow. Sort of crept up on me here," I told her.

"Wow. So, you didn't know this woman at all who was driving? What I read made it seem like you were drunk, and she offered to give you a ride home, but toxicology reports showed she was completely obliterated. Did you know that at the time?"

Remember that moment—a few months ago, a year, ten years, maybe twenty or thirty, maybe when you were a child—that you arrived at the hour where you had to tell someone close to you that you'd lied to them? Maybe for years you let them believe something that wasn't accurate, a sin of omission, keeping yourself in the clear in fear of embarrassment or retribution. Maybe you fabricated an alternate version of the truth completely, sparing yourself from further scrutiny or implication. Maybe you ran from the situation entirely and avoided talking about it for years in hopes it would evaporate from your consciousness and all others. Well, when you're famous, there's always someone waiting around a corner to ask you about it. You can try to let it die an unceremonious death if your constitution is formidable enough to survive the guilt and shame, but there inevitably comes the time when the debt must be paid for denial or obfuscation. It's the gut check we have so we know we're not all sociopaths, I guess.

"Well," I answered. "Uh...fuck."

"Are you alright?" she asked, leaning in toward me.

"Might be my turn to puke soon."

"You want me to get you—"

I sighed and took two deep breaths. "No, no. It's fine. Don't get up. I'm OK," I assured her as I reached for the beer, then slugged half of the glass. "That ought to buy me some time."

Laurel's eyes expanded, surely questioning how pounding half a beer would improve nausea, which was a fair assessment.

"The woman I left with that night; her name was Sasha...I *did* know her. Knew her well. I was in love with her."

Laurel gasped, then leaned back against the arm of the couch, before sliding closer to me. "Oh my God, Josh. I'm so sorry. I...nothing I read though, none of it suggested that—"

"That's on me. The whole damn thing is on me. Been having trouble carrying it," I said, in bumbled, stuttered sentences filtered through anguished breath.

CHAPTER 15

S he was motionless when the car stopped. Her head, neck, and shoulders were wedged between my knees, while her torso rested below the steering wheel. I was disoriented, so I sat there for a few seconds before yelling her name, cradling my hands under her neck, trying to move her up. There was blood trickling from the bottom of her mouth and glass in her hair, and her shoulders and neck were contorted oddly in respect to her back. I slid myself from underneath her, laying her chest and head on the driver's seat as I moved to the other side of the cabin. I felt around her neck until, in one spot, I noticed what felt like a pulse, so I shot up out of the car digging into my pockets for my cell phone. It wasn't on me. I frantically began scouring the car, first the passenger side floor and between the door sills. Then I went around to the driver's side, leaning over the door frame and Sasha's body, scanning near the brake and gas pedal. It wasn't there. I opened the door, reaching down into the crack between the seat and door. Nothing. The smell of gas was overwhelming, though the car had stopped running, and nothing appeared to be leaking underneath. I started hyperventilating, panicking that the car may catch fire. Then I saw Sasha's head and all that glass in her hair, and just lost it. Started crying and freaking out, brushing the glass from the dark strands, cutting my fingers with each stroke.

I stood up once my hand was good and red, wiping the blood across the front of my jeans, noticing my cell phone peeking out from the cramped rear seat area of the convertible. Before I could lean in and reach for it, a pickup truck stopped about fifty feet from where we'd ended up. A woman was yelling from the window, "My husband just called 911. Is everyone okay? Are you hurt? Oh my God, what happened?" All the typical things you'd expect someone to ask at an accident, though I kept thinking, *Why aren't they helping me pull her out of the car?* because I felt like that's what I was trying to do when they got there.

I don't know.

I'd passed out. The next thing I recalled was the woman and her husband crouching next to me and the sound of a fire truck siren dying out. The husband left to speak to the EMTs as the woman adjusted the rolled sweater she'd placed under my head.

"There's...someone else in the car, a woman," I told her, and she smiled at me, that kind of smile that's really sadness pretending it doesn't know what it knows.

"They're here now. They're going to take care of her. You too," she said.

"Is she alive? Is she alright?" I asked, trying to stand, though I was still woozy. I must have passed out again because the next thing I remember was sitting against a tree. An EMT was dabbing a cool towel on my head as a police officer approached.

After I got sorted out with the EMT, I stood near the tree and talked with the officer, avoiding the obvious question. He asked me where we'd come from, how long we were there, where we'd been before, if I recalled anything from before the car went off the road. Then he asked how much Sasha had to drink and if she'd done anything other than use alcohol that day. I lied and told him I wasn't sure about drugs and answered the rest honestly, I think. He kept asking about her demeanor, her behavior—if she was angry, sad, happy, whatever. He started to ask me something else when I just blurted, "Is she dead?" His expression gave me my answer.

I started choking up and he stopped asking questions, but then I remembered he'd asked me something that didn't make any sense before I learned that she'd died. It got lost in the barrage of questions:

"Was she behaving erratically behind the wheel?"

"Is she still in the car?" I asked. He said no, that they'd taken her away. She was in the driver's seat, positioned that way when they arrived because I'd moved her there, and in that vicinity originally because she'd been climbing on me before I'd lost control.

"Do you recall why she may have veered off the road, Mr. Traxon? Was there an animal or another car headed for you two? Anything that would help explain the crash?"

I searched my mind, the recollections of the last minute before the wreck. I was absolutely in the driver's seat, controlling and then not controlling the car while she tugged at the wheel in her amorous advances. The car surged right, jumped and skipped violently before stopping. The officer waited while I assembled the pieces but offered no answers.

"You want to take a minute? Meet me up by the road when you're ready?" he asked.

I nodded.

Many minutes later I made my way toward the street. Without malice, reason, or ulterior motive I told the officer, "She was loaded, no question, and I shouldn't have let her drive."

I told the cop that she was driving.

I told him that, and then lied when he asked specific questions about speed, behavior, and other relevant details. He asked if I'd also been drinking. I said yes, though far less than her, which was true. He jotted everything down in his little pad. I watched him write my lies on that paper, and instead of feeling guilt or remorse, I felt empowerment and relief. I wasn't drunk, and if they'd chosen to field test me or run blood tests, I'd come out okay, so it wasn't to save myself, it was to...

I'm not sure, is the only answer I have. In all these years, I've never figured out why I did it. Why I told them it was her driving and not me. I told an outright lie as the woman I supposedly loved was carted off in an ambulance. Not to save myself embarrassment or persecution or legal trouble, but *just because*. What kind of person does something like that?

Sasha was never behind the wheel; *I* was. That's the truth.

One of the problems with that truth was a guy who worked in the kitchen was outside the restaurant. He saw me get into the driver's side of the car, looked right at me, think I nodded to him. I had to go back the next day and talk with him, to find out what he remembered and coax him into *not* remembering it. He was from Columbia, and that restaurant often employed undocumented workers off the books, so I knew it wouldn't take much to influence his memory. The fact I did it is fucking vile...hearing myself in my head, saying I did this, it's just—it's sickening.

Of course, if you're thinking it, you're right. She was climbing all over me, messing with the car, making the whole situation dangerous—it was a nightmare. When I've thought back to that day over the years, it's unfathomable we didn't wreck earlier, that I didn't stop the car instead of trying to race to get her home...but it's still a lie.

I knew one of the cops that ended up on the scene. He'd done freelance security for the band on and off. Several days after the crash he was asking additional questions about her driving, why her purse was on the floor of the driver's side, etc. I bullshitted him with *Maybe it was the force of the crash, stuff moving all around, whatever.* I don't think he bought it, though he never questioned me further. Sasha was in the system for a previous DUI, had no local family, no kids, and nobody pushing to make sure they get all the case facts right. The only one who had the ability to do that was me, and I flat lied about it.

She has a father who lives in Connecticut, not far from where I grew up. So many times I thought about reaching out to him, but never had the balls to pick up the phone. He deserved to know the truth about what really happened to his daughter, even if he was, according to Sasha, a "rotten fuck."

I remember hearing someone tell me once that "peace comes when we accept the closure that won't come," or something to that effect. I'd love to think this may be that scenario for me, where I'll find a way to let it go because there's just no other way. She's not here to make amends. There's no piper to pay except my own guilt and shame.

I did have a couple that afternoon, but barely had a buzz. Honestly, I wasn't impaired. I had to watch myself around her because she went from zero to sixty in a blink. I was no model of responsibility in those days, but if I didn't keep things in check when we were together, all hell would break loose. Plus, she was a full-blown addict, needed twelve steps, the whole enchilada. I'm not oblivious to the fact that booze is also my coping mechanism, just FYI, but whatever was happening with Sasha was miles beyond my own struggles.

Or so I've told myself.

CHAPTER 16

Laurel engaged me eye to eye as she listened to me recount accident. When I was done, she exuded a profound melancholy, wiping her left eye and pulling Pickle tight against her tummy.

"I wasn't hammered, I swear to you, and she was making every ounce of that drive dangerous by pulling at the wheel and climbing on me...but I was driving. It wasn't her."

Laurel stroked Pickle's tiny round head, moving her fingers methodically through his tan fur, which he adored and got him moaning. Then she slid him off her lap, looked at me misty eyed, and said, "I'm sorry," before scooching over, leaning her head into my chest and holding my hand.

She laid with me, wrapped tight against my body, for twenty minutes or more, saying nothing else. Then she got up, kissed my forehead, placed Pickle in my lap, and went out the door.

"Yup, we just got dumped, buddy. Well, I did, not you. Nobody dumps the Pickster. What do you think, Dude? Time for some chess, or should I knock one out of the park?"

Pickle stared at me, watching, waiting for the next move, his curled wannabe tail wiggling. I crept toward him, splaying my hands out like I was going to grab his head,

sending his ears up and tail into manic mode. After I moved five feet toward him, he yelped once. I then pursued him full chase, roaring and gurgling. His tiny paws scurried

underneath as he raced away with delight. I chased him around the house for

ten minutes before we both bailed, he for his water dish and me for a seven-hundred-dollar bottle

of pretentious tequila and a monster binge that would've killed a wooly mammoth.

****

I told her so many times that I was getting sick of hearing it myself.

I could see it in her face every time I looked at her, that

she was done with me telling her what to do, but how could

I stop? The pills and the coke and the motherfucking booze,

just incessantly poisoning herself. From where does such self-hatred

come, or is it just woven into the DNA? But

who the hell was I to tell her what to do with her body and mind? The

way I was always partying and screwing around, goddamn hypocrite.

I'm telling her how to live as I show up to fuck her and extract the only

value she had to me out of her, without offering salvation or healing.

I killed her. Me and a dozen guys before me, feeding the disease,

taking what we wanted. The difference was /

The sentence ended there, with the cursor still blinking. And I was reading it completely smashed, clutching the back of the chair before I fell over. I don't even recall sitting down at the damn computer, but there's no way Pickle wrote it. Where was that little shit anyway? I tried calling him, but nothing happened, so I slid down onto the carpet, smacking my head on the oak floor.

****

"Go pishh, buddy," I told him. He was upset. Hated when I was loaded but dealt with it. He got it done quick, shot back into the house, and headed for his bed on the living room floor. I looked in his bowl. There was something in it. I should eat, but it was goddamn 4:18 a.m. in the morning. What the hell was gonna be open in this town? There was no food in the house, and I couldn't drive. Nowhere to go anyway. Was going to throw up again, too.

"Go away, Pick," I told him. Dry heaving made him nervous. Better make this happen soon, or he'd be all strung out.

****

He didn't like when I cried, which was all the damn time lately, so he was spazzing out, licking me and nuzzling in. What a beautiful creature, this little thing, which only made me cry harder. The more fucked up I was, the more he wanted to love me, like some cliché love interest in an airport paperback. Pickle wanted to be as close as I'd let him, always, judging nothing, ever. I could talk to him for hours about her, or anything, and he'd listen, ears pricking when my intonation changed.

"Did you know your daddy's famous, buddy?" I asked him, his head rolling to the left. "If I'm famous, then you're famous too. Two famous, handsome dudes lying on this floor, and nobody knows but us. If the whole world knew we were here, they'd wanna hang with us, right? Josh and Pickle, the fun parade."

I started laughing, but that spun into a coughing fit, so the pup stood up and backed away. "It's alright. Not going to die tonight, promise."

I reached for my phone that was face down on the green throw rug a foot away but then decided not to pick it up. I didn't need the pictures to see her face. I didn't need pixels on a high-resolution screen to remind me of the pout in her lips and the scar to the right of her left eye. I didn't need to see what was always there, behind the eyes of all those who followed, looking back at me through a vessel of the living.

****

I must have been dreaming about the dog barking, because its tone was deeper and more menacing, like a bloodhound or boxer. As consciousness returned, so did the familiar quick jabs of an almost twenty-pound, fawn-colored dingbat. Ah, someone was knocking.

"One second," I yelled, but it came out more like 'Wuh Secun.'

I was on the floor, which by itself wasn't shocking, but being without pants was new. Often the shirt, many times underwear, but balls out pants-less with just a T-shirt was uncharted territory.

I pulled myself up and peeked around the floor for my trousers, as my old man called 'em. They were nowhere to be found so I hobbled into the bathroom and grabbed a navy-blue robe that hung behind the door.

"I'm coming," I told the knocker, which could only be maybe three people from my calculations.

"Well, you were at the top of the list of potentials. Glad it's you and not Barry or momma, as either one could kick my ass right now," I told Laurel, who was wearing a baseball hat and a Shaky

Bones T-shirt. "Holy shit, are you serious with that thing? Where the hell did you get that?"

"It came yesterday—can I come in? —and it's wicked comfortable. I love it," she said.

"Yeah of course, come on," I said while Pickle did the requisite sniffing her ankles routine, coupled with tail circles and panting. "I can't believe you bought that shirt. You know I have like a whole freaking box of them somewhere in the garage. I could have given you one, or ten. They're great for dish rags and changing oil."

"Stop it. Have you checked your phone at all?"

"Uh, not in the last couple hours, why?"

She wrinkled her face, which was more radiant and beautiful than ever, even sporting the tomboy look. "Couple hours? Come on, Josh. It's almost eleven in the morning, and I was texting you from eight o'clock last night. At least ten or twelve texts you never responded to."

"Ohhh, so I see how it is. You come over and dump me yesterday, but now you think you still own me, and I need to respond to all your check-ins? We are on a break, just like Ross and Rachel!" I shouted.

She wasn't amused. I was unsure if it was due to the lame *Friends* reference or simply because it was moronic.

"Josh, what's going on? You look like hell, you're wearing a bathrobe at almost noon, there's bottles and cans strewn all over this place, and it smells like a dive bar. If you're having trouble dealing with what we talk—"

"No, it's okay. I didn't mean to make you worry. Just wasn't paying attention to my phone. The damn agent has been nagging me about writing and I've been avoiding his calls. I was also playing chess late and—"

"Is this what you've been writing," she asked, heading toward the open laptop on my dining room table, which was fifteen percent exposed hardwood and eighty-five percent fraternity party pack, save for the computer.

"Yeah, you don't need to see that. It's straight garbage. Just the ramblings of an inebriated moron," I said, shuffling over in front of her and smacking the laptop case down with a *thwank*.

"I've read some of your lyrics. It can't be any worse than that," she replied.

With furrowed brow, I said, "You vacillate nicely between the concerned ex-girlfriend and ball busting neighbor."

Her moon-pie-sized eyes locked on to mine in full business mode. "Josh, come on. I'm not exactly sitting across the road there with an empty plate either. Don't add to it by making me worry needlessly. What the hell is going on? Do you need to talk to someone or go to a meeting or—"

I shot a stream of air out of my closed lips, startling her as they reverberated.

"A meeting? Are we there already?"

"Where?" she asked.

"That place where we're comfortable telling the other what a flaming mound of burning shit the other's life is and that maybe we need outside help? Usually, I've at least felt someone up before I do that."

"Don't be crude, Josh. Come on, I'm serious. You've got me concerned here."

"And I appreciate your concern, but who do you think moved in across the street here, a Mormon? You know the life I've come from. None of this should be a surprise to you, and it's not like I'm tearing up the neighborhood with loud parties and inebriated debauchery."

"I didn't say you were. Don't turn this into something it's not, and don't pretend it's wrong of me to care about you, regardless of our situation. You don't look healthy, and there's empty beer and liquor bottles all over this place. This isn't backstage somewhere out on the road. It's your living room. I'm sure you'd feel the same—"

I walked away, grabbing a half-empty bottle of bourbon from next to the laptop, heading into the kitchen.

"Josh, come on. What the hell are you doing here? Last night we're talking about how destructive this kind of abuse has been in your life. Days prior we're talking about Barry's childish behavior. Now you're right here, doing the same thing. Should I call him up, see if he wants to shotgun some beers and talk about all the chicks you've bedded?"

I stopped in the doorway to the kitchen, took a long slow pull from the bourbon, and began to shake my finger as I formulated a scathing, witty comeback, but the motion caused the robe to come open, and my pecker said hello to Laurel in one third of all its glory.

"Wonderful," she said, as she snuck a peek and then turned her head to the left.

"I'm a grower not a show-er, as they say, and it's freezing in here. Regardless, that wasn't intentional," I told her, pulling the fabric back together with the hand that held the bourbon bottle.

Laurel held back laughter, though her lips were wiggling more than Pickle's tail when anything human visited. "Have you got yourself together over there?"

"All tucked away."

She looked back at me, her eyes dropping at my beltline for an instant before returning to my face. "I'm just—"

"I saw that," I interrupted.

"Will you stop it? Let me finish. I know you're—"

"It's one of those things that is impossible not to do, right? I mean, if I see a tit come flying out somewhere, and the owner of said tit tells me they've squared it all away, it's scientifically impossible not to look in that direction again, regardless. It's more difficult than trying not to blink for an hour," I explained. "Don't be embarrassed, except for the fact that, had you not dumped me, you might have to be having relations with that sad state of affairs down there."

She half-smirked and then walked over to me. I balanced myself in the doorway, careful to keep an eye on my front door. "You make me laugh. I've needed that desperately. I'm sure you could make me laugh even under the most tenuous of circumstances, but that's not going to send me off course in my concern for you."

"The 'ol, 'You're using humor as a defense mechanism thing,' eh? Well, I promise you that if I wanted to keep you away, keep you from digging around in my head, it wouldn't be by showing you my dick and cracking jokes, though I'm certain that *would* keep you away."

She rolled her eyes and turned, heading for the door. "If you want to talk, you know where to find me. There's also a little kid over there who thinks you're pretty freaking awesome. I'd love for him to come see you again, but I won't let that happen if you're going to keep blazing down this road," she said, bolting toward the door, confusing Pickle, who bobbed his head back and forth between her and me.

"It's all good, buddy. She's not mad at you. They're never mad at you."

Laurel stopped after she pulled the door open. "Last night I was wishing I'd met you sooner. Like, four or five years ago at least. Maybe it wouldn't have mattered because of where your life was at that point. Maybe I'm being foolish for even thinking it, but it would have been nice to have more time. I feel like there's more to know, more to hear. I wish we'd had that time. Bye, Josh."

She pulled the door closed and was gone. Pickle sauntered over to the right window next to the door, hopped up with his front paws on the sill, and watched her walk home.

"I live right across the street. We have all the time in the world," I said.

Pickle looked over at me but then went right back to watching Laurel. His sadness was quelled by a rawhide sticking out from underneath the couch. Mine was dulled with a two-hundred-dollar bottle of Tequila Blanco. Viva la fuck you.

CHAPTER 17

"**I** appreciate that, and it's no bother. If you haven't noticed, I'm the kind of guy where the only way stuff like this will ever get done is *if* you bother and nag me. Okay, take care, and I'll make sure to be there."

In the mix of messages missed from Laurel the other day, I'd also missed a call from Lyle. The guy really wanted me to sit down with this other egghead and discuss a financial plan. I finally told him I'd do it in a couple weeks. Half to shut him up, half because he wasn't wrong. I'm barely a generation removed from stuffing wads of cash under my mattress. It was time for some evolution.

Pickle was fed, walked, played with, and visibly enamored with his stuffed crab toy in a manner unfit for publication. I had held down my first solid food in a couple days. Three pieces of nuked bacon and two graham crackers. Not ideal, but it tasted divine and felt like there was a real chance it wouldn't come back up.

I'm not sure if I mentioned this or not yet, but I grew up less than two hours from here in North Central Connecticut. Wasn't until my early twenties that I trucked out west looking for a change of scenery and better drugs. That's not entirely true. The drugs in New England were great, but the rock and roll scene was nonexistent, unless you wanted to play "Sweet Home Alabama" and "Mustang Sally" in two shows a night at the local VFWs and sports bars. Those gigs were magical. You attempting to resonate with the drunken Sox fans and miserable Pats fans in the days preceding the empires they've established since. The first band I played with had a standing bet that the dude who *didn't* get clipped by a beer bottle had to do the breakdown and load out. It was rarely me. My problem was I didn't give a crap that we were playing in a sports bar and patrons were often heavily invested in the game. We showed up to play them some great tunes, and they should be grateful to be there and hear them.

In between songs I'd call out certain patrons directly: *"Hey, Giants hat with the turkey neck, this next one is for you, if you feel like slow dancing."* That's a bad example of the beer bottle stories, though, because he whacked me in the shin with a pool cue. I think I tackled him on the edge of the bar and cracked one of his ribs. He got in a few good shots before the bouncers dragged us out because I was busted up for days after. The rest of the guys in the band were rip shit pissed, even though they were degenerate lunatic assholes, too. They just didn't start fights the way I did, which was purely a function of the booze because as I mentioned earlier, I was no tough guy in those days. Anyway, where the hell was I going with all this? Oh, right, that I'd been raised down in Connecticut. My screwed-up adolescence wasn't what got me thinking about that, though. It was Sasha.

In what had to be one of the most incredible coincidences I'd ever been involved in, Sasha—whom I "met" much later in life—lived behind my house in Stafford Springs when I was growing up. She was a few years younger than me. Her house was on a farm separated by a long stone wall bordering the rear of our property. I'd seen her riding horses and messing around in the field from time to time. For one whole year, she was on my school bus. According to her, I smiled at her far too long one morning and she went home and rubbed one out in whatever way a kid that young can manage such a thing. I don't recall that moment, and knowing her propensity for bullshit, it wouldn't surprise me if she made the whole thing up. She did, however, live in that house behind me for years. That much is true.

None of this came to light the first few times Sasha and I hung out together. Our first encounters were primal, sweaty, and brief, like most of those I was engaged in, but I remember the day it revealed itself.

"You drink like everyone back home," she'd said.

"There's a special way people drink where you're from?" I asked.

"They do that swig thing you do. Where they tip the bottle up like they're dumping some only into their bottom lip, swirl it around a moment before swallowing, and then hold it with just a couple fingers right against their leg."

"That's a very specific methodology for drinking beer. I'd argue most of the numb nuts where I grew up were more the pop-a-hole-in-the-can-and-shotgun kinda dudes, though on special occasions you may see a bottle or two. My buddy Pete may have done it exactly as you say, come to think of it. Where did you grow up?"

"The rock star, party-all-night capital of the known world, Stafford Springs, Connecticut."

I can't remember the details all that vividly, but I know I was wide-eyed and mouth agape for a while before she finally said, *"What?"* and snapped me out of it.

"There is absolutely no way you are from Stafford Springs, Connecticut. Get the fuck out of here with that. You read a bio about me or something, had to be."

"What would your bio have to do with me being from a hokey pokey town in Connecticut?"

"Sasha, are you yanking me right now? Did Marty tell you to say this or—"

"Your singer, that creep? Hell no. I don't want that cretin dribbling all over me while he speaks. Why are you so concerned about where I grew up and what does it have to do with you?"

Right there. That was the millisecond that I discovered it was *her*. The little girl that lived behind my house and rode horses and sometimes got close enough to the stone wall that I could see her smile at me. There was no discernable reason *why* I should have known it was her—no unique look or gesture or inflection in her voice—but I knew it was her, and then she knew that I knew.

"It was you, riding that caramel brown and white horse around all the time and getting chased by a dog in the field behind my house. It had to be."

"Holy shit, Josh. You are THAT Josh, THE Josh...from the bus!"

"I don't think you were ever on my bus, but I remember you in that field, riding and playing and sometimes waving, but I never went to say hello."

"Oh, I was on the bus, just one year while you were too. That was a gamechanger year for me," she'd said, before laughing and going into the story about her little crush and eventual self-gratification. We talked about the town, the landscapes of our intersecting properties, and the absolute absurdity that we'd only met so many years later after having spent months upon months just a hundred yards apart. I was too old, she was too

young, I was broke, her family had money—it wasn't that odd that we'd never connected when we hashed it all out.

Sasha was different those first few months. She was tough and sassy. Well-guarded but enough childish vulnerability that peeked out making it impossible not to fall for her. She was self-deprecating, silly, playful—whimsical almost. Nothing like the woman she was at the end. There were signs that she was being taken by the disease, but I think I ignored them when I became consumed by the rest of her. Sasha was a groupie, by anyone's classical definition, but in my eyes, she was a goddess. A sensual, intelligent, witty creature that, if she was going to shack up with a rock star, was fully deserving of the royalty in that mix. Not some backwoods bass player dope who was more interested in playing chess than having threesomes and doing coke off strippers.

I was more interested, but I'm not saying I didn't do it.

Sasha was a mint condition '62 Fender Jazz Bass in rooms full of knockoffs. She had the eyes of every dude in every freakin' band around on her, especially the ones we'd played with because, for a time, she was with me every night. I'd like to think she was faithful to me in the beginning, but how the hell would I ever know? I was loyal to her, right away and for the months that followed, until the wheels came off. With a woman like her, the desire and appetite for others receded, as she was an all-consuming mate. That's a lousy excuse—"I didn't bang other women because she was, like, really hot"—I know, but it's an honest statement, though it wasn't only the sexual chemistry. Sasha had a depth to her that I'm certain I'd never even scratched the surface of. She was smarter than everyone that worked in or around the band, including the engineers, and she could argue a polar bear into desert living.

One evening after a show, one of the roadies was bickering with our tour manager about our stage set up weight distribution. She got up off the beer-soaked couch we'd been pawing at one another on and drew some *Good Will Hunting*-esque math equation on the wall and looked at them like they were idiots for not understanding it. I dabbled at teaching her how to play chess, but I'm glad I never went deep on that because there's no question she'd have begun to annihilate me inside a week.

I'm not going to drag you through the sad and murky details of where and when our relationship began to unravel and what addiction did to Sasha because she's gone. It serves no purpose other than to illustrate yet another tale of a soul swept away into madness. What I will say, however, is that it happened fast, almost overnight, or at least that's how I remember it. When you've got both feet in and someone's altered your world so profoundly, there's no way to turn back and ignore what you feel and know. You simply must strap in and finish the ride. My last six months with her had devolved into a collection of almost embarrassing trysts, strung together by fading recollections of a more blissful time. She was someone with little remnants of what I'd fallen for remaining, and I was this pathetic sex buzzard, feeding off the carcass to serve myself. I was in no place to heal, guide, or support—though I like to believe I tried. In all honesty, my random increment presence in her life likely only served to worsen her condition. But I didn't stop. I kept coming back, telling myself love was the guiding force when any halfwit watching from the outside knew it was lust.

She's dead.

Pickle shot up when he saw me jump up from the couch and head for the bourbon sitting next to the laptop. I stopped, thinking he was looking to be chased, but his tail wasn't wagging.

He just stared at me. I reached for the bottle and the nutty fuck started barking with reckless abandon. Not someone-is-here-and-holy-shit-let's-see-who-the-hell-it-is barking, or what-the-hell-is-that-big-bag-you-just-plopped-down-in-the-corner-and-is-it-going-to-get-me barking, but furious, loud, deliberate, and angry barking, with a hint of snarl.

"What's the matter, Pick?" I asked, but he kept right on going. I let go of the bottle, walked over to him, and crouched down. He stopped barking and nuzzled right in against my knees.

Yeah, I was thinking the same thing, but come on? I mean, it's not unreasonable to think he was tired of dealing with my drunken, annoying ass and was smart enough to know what going for that bottle means, but really?

I'm no Carl Jung, but, maybe when the dog is telling you that you're a loser, it's time to do a gut check.

"Okay, buddy, I'm sorry. I'll leave the bottle," I said, rubbing his sides and then his ears. He started moaning and groaning the way he does. I contemplated letting him out to pee and sneaking a couple pulls off the bottle, but another idea scurried across my mind: I needed to go to Connecticut.

"You wanna go outside? Come on, bugger, let's go pee," I said, much to his overzealous delight. While he was outside I again considered sneaking some bourbon. It wouldn't be the worst sin I'd ever committed, lying to my dog. But, if I were going to get on the road and head to Connecticut, it was a piss poor idea.

Then again, one quick pop an hour or two before I hit the road wouldn't jam me up.

I took a long, slow pull from the bottle before Pickle meandered back inside. I glanced across the street wondering if Laurel would be willing to watch Pickle for forty-eight hours, even though the little freak loved car rides.

"Come inside," I said, resulting in a quick stare and multitude of ground sniffs before bounding in. I grabbed a fistful of Pug Nugs from the kitchen, his favorite between-meal snack. One lucky day we met a woman in Pennsylvania who baked her own treats because her pugs refused those commercially available. Chicken proteins, vegetables, rice, and a mixture of random goodies that made Pickle bonkers for the shit. They must have sold well because now I could buy them at the local high-end pet store instead of her personal website. The bag had a massive cartoon pug face, and even the sound of that material rustling sent my little guy into hysterics. I wish anything got me half excited as Pickle over those damn biscuits.

He devoured three, then stared at me with the "What's next?" face. I tossed him his stuffed crab. He pounced and shook the crap out of it before lying down to commence gnawing.

"I'll be right back, buddy. Just gonna run across the street." He paused the licks to survey my body language, listening for recognizable words. I kept my decision to go see Sasha's father alone to myself.

I'd never met her father, and it was a distinct possibility he had nothing kind to say to me, or want to speak at all, but I needed to try. If he didn't still live there or turned me away, at least it would be a scenic road trip and less toxic than kickboxing my liver the way I had been of late.

"Hey, squirt. Is your mom home?" I asked Ethan.

"She's in the shower, I think."

If this were a film, I'd have looked directly into the camera and smirked.

"Gotcha. Well, can you tell her I stopped over? I just want to ask—"

"Hey there," Laurel said, drying her hair while she made her way down the stairs. "Ethan, why don't you go finish messing with those Legos so I can talk to Josh, but don't leave them all over the rug because I just stepped on one and nearly passed out."

Ethan looked up at me and smiled, then bolted back into the house before Laurel closed the door and joined me on the porch. She had on one of those dresses that clung to the sides of the upper arms below the shoulders, floral print, per her usual, and her hair was much darker wet.

"I didn't mean to pull you out of the shower, just had a quick question," I said. "I'm going to head down to Connecticut for a couple days. Go visit Sasha's father in my hometown, clear the air with that situation. Clear the head a little, too. All that cliché shit an aging former pseudo rock star would probably do in the final act of his life. Was wondering if there's any chance you guys could watch Pickle while I'm gone? You could leave him at the house, and he'd be fine, but I'd love him to have a few visits to say hello, play and whatnot, but if—"

"Absolutely. Of course, Josh, but no need to leave him in that house all alone. Ethan will be thrilled to have him here," Laurel interjected.

"Not that I don't adore her, of course, but is there any chance your mother may actually murder the little bugger?"

She chortled and tossed the wet towel onto one of the green porch wicker chairs. "She is, oddly, quite good with animals. Although yeah, she does seem to feel like Pickle doesn't qualify as a dog. To be fair, I don't always think she qualifies as a human being, but we're working on that."

"Good luck," I told her, stretching my eyes open. "I really appreciate it, and I can—"

"What if I went with you?" she interrupted, doe eyed.

"With me?" I replied, brow furrowed. "You mean down to Connecticut?"

"Is there another destination we've been discussing that I missed?" she shot back. In that moment Laurel looked little like her mother. Underneath the bucketloads of empathy, compassion, and warmth, she absolutely had picked up the older woman's ball busting gene.

"Well, as much as I'd love the company, I wouldn't want to put you out, have you leave Ethan, you know? Then there's the dog situation, and—"

"Pickle will be fine here, honestly. Ethan is great with dogs, and my mother, for all her shortcomings and coldness, is a wonderful caretaker. If you don't want me to go, it's fine. Just don't let it be about caring for the dog or bothering my mother."

"How are you feeling? Are you sure you're up for a road trip? Also, I'm going to stay the night. I don't want our post-breakup-but-were-we-really-ever-even-together situation to get any weirder for you."

She rolled her eyes. "When are you planning on leaving, now?"

"What time is it? Almost eleven?" I asked, looking at my imaginary watch. "I don't know, maybe leave by noon or something.

"Well, why don't you go square yourself away. I'll get ready and pack a couple things. When you're all set, bring the pup over and we can be on our way. Sound good?"

I stared at her, cautiously and curiously.

"What?" she asked.

"It's just that...I don't know. I'll shut up and go get ready."

"Excellent idea. See you soon," she said, grabbing the towel and smiling at me before stepping back into the house. "Oh, and not to poke at recent wounds, but I'm assuming this will be a dry road trip?"

Fair question.

I looked away for a moment before meeting her eyes with a response. "You have my word."

She nodded. The sides of her mouth stretched upward, and then she ran the towel vigorously through her damp locks. "See you in a bit."

With every page turned, a new story begins.

Not sure where I'd heard that or why it popped into my head, but it did. She looked so beautiful with that messy, wet hair and acting all tough, interrupting me, asking to come along, making demands. I'd never been more excited to go on a road trip with an ex since the last time that had never happened.

I opened my front door to find Pickle, as expected, standing right behind it. I slowly crouched down and splayed my hands, preparing to give chase. "Let's get your tiny ass all nice and tired so you don't drive the demon across the street crazy and get evicted while I'm gone." The second I lunged forward, he sprinted off, howling and yelping like a beast possessed, his tail flattened and the sound of his nails *skiff skiff skiffing* furiously across the wood floors.

CHAPTER 18

The most desirable traits in a boyfriend, girlfriend, spouse, partner—whatever label applies—are undoubtedly the standards like honesty, loyalty, kindness, intelligence, sense of humor, compassion, and sex appeal. All valid, of course. However, one trait that can never be overlooked or undervalued, nor should it be, is the person's ability to groove with your road trip playlist.

Traversing miles of road through changing landscapes, elevations, and weather, is, by itself, an almost sensual experience. Couple that with a ferocious car and a killer playlist moves into full-body orgasm territory. If you have a co-pilot, their ability to assimilate to the playlist, enjoy it even, is crucial. Heading over ascending terrain while the sun is swallowed by the horizon, "Night Moves" by Bob Segar playing through twelve speakers, the white noise rush of tepid air swooshing by your ears outside the window—these are the moments where passion is born and euphoria lives. Now, cresting that hill, with Bob crooning away, the acoustic guitar strings a-strummin', the sun dissolving into a hazy, orange-red puddle in the sky and your passenger asking, "Can we put on something good?" Well, that's how forty percent of pre-meditated murders begin.

Laurel, conversely, sat in her bucket seat, grinning when I depressed the Porsche throttle, burying it deep into turns, tapping her hand against her thigh to the beat of every song. Barely audibly, she sang the chorus of songs she knew and hummed the melody of the ones she didn't. In the first forty-five minutes, she never said a word, except for, "Wow, I loved that song, who was it?" I nearly pulled over and proposed on the side of Interstate 91. Before we left, I'd mentioned I was somewhat anal about music in the car, but if there was anything she'd like to hear, to let me know and I'd put it on. She replied, "Nope, I trust you. Play whatever you like." If I hadn't been crying so goddamn much lately, I would have lost my shit again right there.

"I'm going to zip off this next exit and grab some gas, maybe a couple waters, a snack, take a pee break," I told her, decelerating and downshifting the coupe.

"I don't know which is a bigger aphrodisiac, this music you're playing or the engine noise behind my head. I can see why you love this car," she replied.

I'm not making this up. That's what she said.

"If you're saying that just to get me to buy lunch, I was going to anyway," I assured her.

"I'm not hungry right now, but I'm sure I'll find something you can buy me on this trip. You may have the cool car and tunes, but I'll bet this ride hasn't had legs like these in it for a while, if ever," she said with a playful wink, sliding the bottom of her lavender and blue floral print dress up from around her ankles to the top of her calf. She wasn't wrong, and now, whatever lunch appetite I had shifted to another origin, though I was determined to keep this trip respectable, friendly, and sans douchebaggery.

"You're already my favorite road trip co-pilot ever. Just catapulted to the top with that move," I said.

"Well, thanks. Can't say I've been a *co-pilot* that often, though. Most of the time I'd have to drive with the likes of Barry. I did date this guy before him who had this colossal pickup truck, with a bench type seat. You know? Anyway, first time we go out in it, he pats the seat in the middle, looks at me, like he's beckoning me the way you might Pickle.

Slide on over, girl, I guess he was thinking."

"Well, did you?"

"I did," she answered, and I blew a stream of lip flapping air from my mouth, "and you hush up. But I felt so ridiculous sitting there in the middle of the cab. I'd seen women do that before, driving down the road behind them, and I'd laugh to myself at how absurd it was. That one or both were so insecure that even the foot or two that separated them was too much space to allow. But there I was, doing the same thing with Gordon."

"Gordon? Oh, my word, Laurel."

She nodded her head, cracking up. "There were dozens of red flags. I missed them all. He wasn't that bad, but we only went out a few times. It was hard to recover from the mandatory slide over."

"Hey, you were destined for bigger things. And if you hadn't nixed 'ol Gordo, you'd have missed out on all those blissful days with Barry."

You can probably envision the eye roll that one induced.

I slowed the car to a crawl and pulled into the convenience store. "The Honey House" it was called, with a big stack of pancakes and what appeared to be bees buzzing around them on the sign. I'm no marketing whiz, but I'm not sure thinking of bees while eating my breakfast is the best campaign. And honey on pancakes? Why not *The Maple House*? I didn't ask Laurel these questions because they were dull, and so far, there still existed strong evidence she found me interesting.

"Are we still in Vermont?" she asked.

"Nope, just crossed into Massachusetts. A few exits in, I think. Less than an hour before we get there," I told her as I slid the car up next to the gas pump.

"Okay, I'm in no hurry. Enjoying the ride and the company," she said before offering a crippling smile. All doubt vanished when she smiled that way—she was happy. Sometimes, we offer or receive these half-assed smiles that are more of an acknowledgement that we heard what the other person was saying, while disengaged from the conversation. Laurel rarely did that. If she liked what you said or was offering praise, she made sure you knew with those twelve-ish muscles it took to bring the lips into position. There was never a question.

"I'm going to run inside to pee, so I'll grab a couple bottles of water. You want a snack, anything?" she asked.

"After I fill up, I'll pop in to pee too. I'll just meet you inside."

"Sounds good," she said before walking into the place that may serve pancakes and bees.

****

I hadn't been to Stafford in almost thirty years. Thirty years. That's three decades, which I realize is no revelation, but think back over the last ten years and how your life may have changed, evolved, grown, worsened, imploded, or become focused. Then multiply that by three. In thirty years, you'd see at minimum four presidents. If you had children at the start, they'd be graduated from college, maybe have kids of their own, and it's how long the band Tool takes between releasing albums. We are talking a long freakin' time here.

The town center looked the way I remembered, with brick buildings lining the narrow Main Street. Trinket shops, an insurance agency, a couple casual restaurants were all crammed together, and now a cidery to accompany the craft breweries that had popped up on every corner of New England. The road sloped downhill to a rotary, and as I made my way through it and to the left, I noticed a small black dog licking a purple ice cream cone from a crouched young child's hand to my right. The little bugger looked a lot like my first dog, Timber. He lived with me here for a while until he was struck by a car. I used to give him some of my ice cream cone from the same sidewalk vendor we'd just passed, though not sure if it was black raspberry because that was too delicious to share.

I accelerated the Porsche up the hill just beyond the rotary, sparking the interest and hollers of a few pre-teens playing by the roadside. "You do that on purpose, don't you?" Laurel asked.

"I wouldn't expect you to understand, but yes, it's a requirement of emotionally stunted, juvenile men to race their cars by groups of children to show how awesome we are. That's the only demographic willing to lavish praise on our overpriced 'look at me' mobiles," I explained.

"I told you I loved the car. Don't be dramatic," she said, patting me on the knee.

"Patronization will get you...somewhere."

I turned left at the blinking light and dropped the hammer on the gas again, heading for the lake a few miles out. The flat six boxer engine behind me whirred and screeched, and Laurel adjusted herself in the seat next to me, half aroused, and half embarrassed that she was with such a doofus, I imagined.

"So, up here on the right is a milestone marker in my universe. A site where something remarkable happened, and one whose memory may invoke some jealousy and anger in you, but I'm just going to go with it," I told her, slowing the car, and turning right onto the access road. "This is a place where magic unfolded, and dreams were crushed."

"It looks like a school, so I'm going to guess it's here that you learned how to play chess, but soon after, even though you thought you were really good, some little girl beat your ass, and you cried in front of the entire school?"

I shut the car off and locked eyes with her. "I feel like there's a little bit of schadenfreude in you, especially when it involves me. Maybe I should have taken your mother, the empath of the family, on this trip."

Laurel gasped and covered her mouth dramatically. "I find a smidge of joy in your misery, sure, but only in teeny-weeny things, like when you tripped over that sprinkler at my house. Is there any way you could do that again when we get back?"

I pursed my lips and nodded before unclipping my seatbelt. "I went ahead and got double beds, like a gentleman, but you just adjoining room-ed yourself, Mayes."

"That'll make it easier for me to sneak in the bellhop. Thanks."

"We'll be lucky if this place has running water. Only the best for my ex-girlfriend, you know that."

"And you wonder why we broke up," she said, shaking her head and stepping out of the car. "So, tell me the story here, and don't skimp on the crushed dreams part."

She followed me to the stone wall lining the parking lot rear. It had doubled as a kickball court when I was in fifth grade. I was usually picked last because I was fucking terrible, often missing the ball completely. On my very first attempt, I flung one of my shoes all the way to the wall in an overzealous kick. The crowd of kids went bananas. I ran back into the school and cried before sitting down at a chess board to practice moves. It was the only thing that kept me from diving off the roof. I decided to skip the kickball story, in fear of revisiting the howling laughter from years earlier, only Laurel's would be more uncontrollable.

"Right over here, not five feet away from you, is where I had my first kiss. Fifth grade, Kirsten Grammano," I told her, pointing to a spot along the wall.

"Aww, really?" she asked, her head tilted in that cute way that made every dude nuts.

"Indeed. Her and I, with another 'couple' standing nearby watching. Was kind of creepy, in retrospect."

"Why were they watching?"

"Well, the whole thing came together because—and yes here's where chess does come in to play somewhat—"

"I knew it!" Laurel shouted.

"Okay, settle down, Wingnut, you're scaring the squirrels."

In response, she saluted me, which I thought was the cutest damn thing I'd ever seen, forcing me to hesitate before continuing.

"Yeah, so the girl, Kirsten, wanted to play checkers with her buddy— the other one at the wall watching with her boytoy—one afternoon when it was raining, and we had recess inside. Problem was, all we had was a chess board. She had no idea how to play, so I offered to show her. I never got more than five minutes into the lesson before her attention was drawn elsewhere, but I guess that was enough to light a fire for her. The next morning, that same girl who later creep-stared us at the wall when we made out tells me, 'Kirsten has a crush on you,' and I needed to meet her out at the stone wall at recess. Most terrifying three-and-a-half hours of my life waiting for that walk out there. In this school, we had two homerooms adjacent to one another, but if you were in one, you couldn't see any of the kids in the other. We were in opposite rooms, and that entire morning after her friend told me, all I did was watch the oversized clock on the wall while the massive second hand swept around the white face. Didn't hear or learn a thing all day, just fixated on the clock, my hands and forehead sweating. We had lunch in the rooms, and following that, recess began, so I scarfed down my shitty bologna sandwich and apple or whatever the hell it was and ran outside to the yard."

Laurel was transfixed, hanging on every word, her eyes reminiscent of those cartoons where the character has been hypnotized and there's wavy lines pulsating over their corneas.

"So, I'm standing there in the schoolyard, and I see Kirsten and the two others about seventy-five yards away from me, near the stone wall. They don't motion for me to come over, but I know they've seen me, so I just stand there kicking the ground and walking in a small circle, like a moron."

Laurel giggled, or something, then covered her mouth. "I'm sorry, keep going."

"Yeah, so they're looking over, I'm stumbling around, so finally I decide that I'm not going to wait any longer or there's a real chance I'll have a GI issue in my briefs that will become the story of legends on this playground. So, I walk over to them with what surely must have looked like the most clunky, awkward gait ever used by a human, and when I get there, I just stop and stare at Kirsten with a half-smile straight out of Creeperville. Incredibly, this doesn't dissuade her in the least—she must have got off on my insane confidence, who knows—and she grabs my hand and drags me over to the stone wall, pulls herself into my chest and starts to kiss me straight on the mouth. This goes on for maybe thirty seconds, and I'm sort of opening my mouth a little, pushing back with my lips, wiggling them around, maybe a jab of the tongue, who the hell knows, and she's just going with it."

Laurel started to fall apart, but I kept going.

"By this time, the other couple has nudged their way up close to us and started watching, from like five feet away mind you, messing up my mojo, and then a few other kids wander over that way, and they're watching too. I think we went at it for about four minutes before a teacher shot over to us, but we pulled apart before they got there."

"Holy crap, Josh. That was the most pathetic, yet adorable, story I've ever heard for a first kiss. What did I miss that made it negative?" Laurel asked.

"Be patient, Miss Mayes. This story is far from over," I assured her before motioning to join me and sit on the wall.

"Oh yeah, better sit down then," she said, before pulling one of those round hair ties that every woman on earth has at the ready for any occasion from nowhere and fixing her locks into a ponytail. "Keep going."

"Cashew?" I asked her, pulling a pack from the front of my khaki shorts.

"No, thank you," she said, wrinkling her face.

"Anyway," I continued, after popping a couple nuts in my mouth and chomping them down to small bits, "for days these make out sessions went on at the wall. Kirsten and I, most of the time the other couple as well, who had by then also started slobbering all over each other, and the occasional onlooker. If memory serves, we made it about eight or nine days before it all imploded. So, I'm inside one afternoon in my homeroom, and it's game day where we have thirty-five minutes every two weeks on a Thursday to play whatever board games we want. I wasn't even planning on playing a game, as I was too obsessed and enamored with Kirsten and was drawing her name in massive letters on a piece of paper or some shit. You know when you're at the age where you first realize how to make block letters look 3D on the page so everything you put down on paper is drawn that way?"

The reference was lost on Laurel, so I moved on after tossing a couple more cashews down the hatch.

"I'm doodling on my page, and a tall girl named Heather, wearing glasses and with long pigtails, stops at my desk and says, 'Do you want to play chess? Nobody here knows how to play, but I saw you playing before.' Well, I nearly crumpled that Kirsten-covered paper up and tossed it in the trash. Heather had these pouty lips, rosy cheeks, and she wanted to play chess for Pete's sake—what chance did I have?"

Laurel was shaking her head as she grinned.

"So, I play, like, one game with her, and some freakin' narc kid goes flying over to the next room and rats me out to Kirsten. I don't see her the rest of the day, though, because school is almost over and we're on staggered bus schedules, so the next time we run into one another is recess outside the next day. I head out to the wall, loosening my jaw, puckering my lips, getting all ready to put this girl into orbit as usual, and as I stroll up, she is there with the two other loons, and a small crowd begins to filter in as well. I slow down as I get about ten feet away from her, and she storms right up to me, inches from my face. 'You're with Heather now?' she yells at me, the onlookers dead silent, transfixed. No teachers around, as though they'd been paid to stay away. I ask her 'What?' And before I even take another breath, she socks me square in the gut with enough force to blast me out of my shoes. I hit the ground, doubled over, clutching at my midsection, and the crowd roars, laughing for about thirty seconds until finally a teacher saunters over, breaks things up, and asks what happened before taking me in to the nurse's office. So, I'm at the nurse, the whole damn school is talking about me getting my ass kicked by a girl—this is the eighties remember—and the only comfort I have is the knowledge that at least I have my angelic, four-foot-and-a-half Heather waiting for when I get out of there. We will play chess and make our own memories at the wall for days on end, maybe get married someday. I think I even grabbed a piece of paper and began doodling *her* name in 3D block letters, when all of a sudden, this awful kid, total instigator and known rat, Darren Mollick, peeks his head in the nurse's office and says 'Heather likes Stanley Sherber now' before disappearing back into the hallway. There I am, sitting on the edge of a shitty, freezing cold cot, belly aching from a sucker punch by my girlfriend, and now my chick on the side dumps me through a consigliere."

Laurel stared at me blankly for a moment before reaching over and taking my hand. "Hey, I want to thank you for bringing me up here because I don't think there's a Netflix series or Lifetime movie that I could have stayed and watched that would have come close to this," she said, leaning into me before erupting in laughter.

"As long as my childhood traumas serve to entertain and delight you, then I'm a happy man," I said, gingerly pushing her away.

"Awww, you poor wittle guy. Was it tough for Joshy Woshy to get knocked out and then humiliated because he cheated on his ten-year-old lover? Poor thing. What a tragedy."

"First of all, I never got *knocked out*. I was conscious the entire time. Second, I wasn't cheating on her. I only played one game of chess, and sure, okay, there were some mild fireworks that went off, but nothing happened. Oh, and don't ever say Joshy Woshy again. That hurt worse than the sock to the gut."

"So, even at ten years old, you freaking men are making excuses for your bullshit," she said, shaking her head for what seemed like the fortieth time since we left. "How would you have felt if Kirsten were playing Boggle with some tall, intimidating boy from her class in your absence? Next thing you know she's got 'Drake' written in those huge letters you mentioned on her notebook."

"That's stupid because there was nobody named Drake at our school and we didn't even have Boggle," I shot back.

"Wow, solid comeback. I can see why you're so good at chess," she countered.

"Yeah, well, I think I've exposed enough of my pre-pubescent soul for today. How about we head out to that one-and-a-half-star motel and get settled in? I hear they have a Hot Pockets vending machine. My treat!" I shouted.

"Wow. When you take an ex on a trip to win her back, you really pull out the big guns. Throw in a juice box, and I could be naked on the ride there," Laurel said.

We started walking back to the car, and I slid my fingers into hers. She said nothing, just offered the potent smile she always had at the ready. While we walked, I let my eyes swirl around the green and brown landscape that bordered the three-story white schoolhouse where I'd spent that eventful year. The paint was chipped and fading, and the roof was covered in splotchy patches of green moss, born of the abundant shade from the massive oaks and maples billowing over the top of the structure. In the faint whoosh of the leaves blowing behind us, I could hear the long-ago voices of a few dozen kids screaming and hollering as the kickballs took flight and the swings raced toward the sky.

CHAPTER 19

"Hopefully by now you know me well enough that you *think* I might be willing to do something like this, but that I wouldn't *actually* do it," I said, both sets of eyes locked on the queen bed in the back of the modest, pastel-vomit room.

"It's fine, Josh, I told you. I asked to come on this trip and being close to you was one of the reasons. I'm a world class snuggler, so this is perfect," Laurel replied. I debated making another "but I thought we broke up" joke but skipped it. Her reply was perfect, and I didn't want to sully it with grating sarcasm.

"I just have to pee, and then we can go get some food to bring back here, if you want, before I have to take off on my business," I told her, tossing my overnight bag onto the floor at the end of the bed.

"Sounds good. I'm not starving, but I'll probably be later. I want to just call home quick, too."

The bathroom was about the size of the back seat in my Porsche, which itself had about enough room to carry two cantaloupes. There was an off-white drop sink, at least twenty years old, a similarly colored toilet with a cracked plastic seat cover, and a gray shower/bathtub combo with a murky see-through shower curtain, guaranteed to be the home of a variety of molds at the bottom. When I was out on the road with the band, we stayed at some epic shitholes in the beginning, but that was just the way the rock and roll lifestyle was. Nobody cared. When you're traveling with a companion, however, and you're now driving a hundred-thousand-dollar sports car, you don't drop anchor at Casa Craphole. There weren't a lot of options this far out in the sticks, but I could have booked something fifteen minutes away and upgraded to two stars. Laurel was the least affected person I'd met in a long time, though, so spending one night here wasn't likely to make her dump me. Again.

"Tell your mom to let Pickle kiss her right on the mouth, like all up in there, lick her gums and everything. He loves that," I whispered to Laurel who sat on the edge of the bed, the phone against her ear. She shooed me away.

"I miss you too, baby, but I'll be back tomorrow night," Laurel told Ethan I presumed. Unless it was Barry. Would be weird telling him she missed him and calling him baby right in front of me in a motel room, but it wouldn't be the first time someone did as such. I had her on a bed in a cute dress in one of the finer establishments available in North Central Connecticut though, so checkmate, dude.

"Is that Barry? Tell him I'll bring him home some taffy and a T-shirt," I said louder this time. Laurel squinted her eyes and then flipped me off, which kind of got me going, honestly.

"I'll call you before bed. Have fun playing with the puppy, and make sure you're careful. He's a little thing and can get hurt easily, so not too rough. Okay, bye, honey," she said, then tossed her phone down onto the bed.

"How's the homestead?"

"Sounds like all's well. Ethan is enjoying having Pickle around, so thanks for that."

"No, thank *you* guys for taking him. I haven't been away from him much since he's been out this way, but I'm sure he's been break ready for a while now. Has to be pretty boring sitting around a house all day with me."

"From what I've seen in that place lately, boring isn't the word I'd choose. Chaotic. Turbulent. Wild. I'm sure puppy never lacks excitement. The question is, though, does Pickle want that much—"

Laurel stopped, jumped up from the bed, and ran into the bathroom, slamming the door behind her. I could hear her vomiting, then flushing the toilet. I was tempted to knock lightly and ask the requisite, "Is everything okay?" but does anyone in her situation really want to have a conversation?

"I'm sorry," she said, wiping her hands, leaving the bathroom. "Had a feeling that was coming on."

There's a moment at the end of the excellent film *Searching for Bobby Fischer* when young Josh Waitzkin is playing another young opponent, thought to be stronger than him, and that opponent realizes he's lost. It's a classic "aha" moment where the boy acknowledges defeat and concedes. I was having one of those moments. There was no battle I'd lost, in my case, but instead a glowing, obvious truth revealing itself in all of Laurel's recent sickness.

She was pregnant. Barry was the father.

"I'm going to have to start taking it personally, the number of times you throw up in my presence," I told her, running my hand across the back of her shoulders when she sat down next to me on the bed.

She leaned her head and neck into me, saying nothing.

"I'm no Copernicus, but I've got an inkling that you're not telling me everything that's going on. Is this something we should be talking about?" I asked.

"You know what I'd prefer instead? That you lie back against the wall, and I rest in between your legs and you rub my head and hair, like you did that night I was over your place on the couch," she suggested.

I complied without resistance, sliding my shoes off, and wiggling up to the back of the bed. "Here, come on up."

Laurel pulled her slip-on shoes off and fidgeted her butt back and forth on the bed until she was in position, then let her back and head fall between my thighs, looking up at the yellowed popcorn ceiling.

"Tell me a story, if you don't mind, as you rub my head," she asked. "Maybe more about this place, your childhood. Other girls you've made out with as a pre-teen, whatever."

I could delve into the Sasha history and the insane coincidence of us being neighbors, but the vibe felt like it called for levity and silliness, not a lead up to sadness.

"Sure, though Kirsten was the only one involving soft-core, pre-teen porn. I wasn't the svelte, dashing creature you've come to know and love today. I was, quite simply, a massive dork."

"I think you give yourself too much credit for your evolution. I still see plenty of dork," she said, squeezing her right hand twice on my lower leg. "Why don't you tell me more about chess. You tried explaining the game that night at your place, but how about why you became so enamored, why you love it so much."

"Wow, so you want me to go *full-on* dork. Hey, sure. It's your money in the meter here, honey. Um, I guess—"

"Just make sure we're rubbing as we're talking," Laurel interrupted, guiding my hand to her temple when she spoke.

I hesitated for a second, then leaned down and kissed her forehead. She smiled while keeping her eyes closed.

"I think I told you my father taught me the game and that I'd progressed quickly. It was maybe around nine or ten when—wait a sec, are you sure you wouldn't rather hear about the beginnings of Shaky Bones or how the TV show started, something more exciting?"

"This is my story time, and I've made my selection. Go on, please," she countered.

"Hmm, okay. It might be you that's the dork, but whatever. Anyway, I was getting proficient at the game so my mother enrolled me in this chess club at school. I'm sure you can imagine that didn't exactly shield me from bullies, nor did it ingratiate me with the girls I had eyes on, which were all of them, just so you know. She insisted, though, and I grew to be thankful for that choice because I did meet some friends. The best connection, however, was the head instructor, Mr. Mallet. Yes, like that kind of mallet."

Laurel inched her head closer while I moved my thumbs around her temples and ran my fingers through her tangled hair.

"According to most students, Mr. Mallet was 'a mean bastard,' which pairs well with a guy named after something you might be clubbed with, but I found him to be only occasionally grumpy. He also taught science, and in that class he was ornery at times, but in chess club he was always fair, as well as complimentary, when you made solid moves or helped someone, demanding only that we pay attention and be respectful. He made it clear early into my enrollment that I was gifted and had an impressive understanding of the game, but he never made the other students feel inferior or that their time was less important, you know?"

"Did he teach you to be better at the game, or where you already better than he was?"

"Now see, that's an interesting question. Bonus kiss for you," I said, leaning down and kissing her forehead again, another smile spreading across her lips. "Mr. Mallet and I never matched up until the end of our time together, but he taught me a ton about the game's heart. How the human element and emotion can be relevant in game play, strategy, making mistakes, all that. He was less concerned about openings and more about end game—preparing your pieces and the board for the eventual finish. He always stressed that you were playing another person, a fallible, mortal soul that could appear invincible one moment, yet be taken down swiftly by capitalizing on revealed weaknesses the next. I think prior to the time I spent in that club, I'd looked at chess as some sort of mathematical puzzle that I was able to interpret and solve better than most, but Mr. Mallet helped me deconstruct and rebuild the puzzle from the ground up."

"By this point—and excuse me for not remembering this—but your dad was no longer in the picture, right?"

"He was gone about a year prior, yeah. I mean, sure, I'd agree that Mr. Mallet was a father figure type, if that's what you're getting at, but at the time I wasn't seeking that, though maybe I wasn't even aware. I think..."

I stopped speaking, though I continued rubbing Laurel's head.

"Think what?" she asked.

I had two complex memories, simultaneously vying for attention in my headspace. The first was about my dog Timber again, who'd died around the time I was in the chess club. The second was a conversation with Mr. Mallet a couple years later before entering high school. I went with the puppy story first.

"I was just remembering that my dog, Timber, died right around this time. He was hit by a car in front of our house, somehow had slipped his collar and off the run he was tied to. I wasn't home at the time but was told about it later. It's the first vivid memory I have of crying. I mean, one where I can clearly recall the intensity of the sobbing, the pitch, the volume, where I was sitting when it happened, the smell around me—a vanilla and urine mix, as Timber sometimes had accidents in the front corner of the house by the door and my mother had candles everywhere. I remember being distraught for days, and when I next went into chess club, Mr. Mallet asked why I'd missed the last meeting, and I told him about the dog. He suggested finding a memento of him, a toy, his collar—whatever—and placing it somewhere that we'd play or walk, and anytime I missed him to visit that spot. Even at ten years old, I recognized this wasn't creative or profound advice, but it helped, and he seemed to genuinely care."

"So, did you do it? Build a memorial?"

"I did, or we did—my mother and me. It's hazy, but I remember. I was also thinking of another moment with Mr. Mallet years later, and now they're both...blurry. Drinking as I've been of late, and getting old, well...it's not been as conducive to recollections as I'd like."

Laurel sat up, turned, and faced me on the bed.

"I think it's beautiful how much dogs have been a part of your life. I wish I'd had that more as a child, but, shocker, mom's never been the type to warm up to them," she said, pulling the hair that I'd mussed back, away from her face.

Before I could open my mouth about my dog being in her care, she pressed her index and middle finger to my lips. "Pickle is going to be fine. She's not evil. She's had her own tough go of things, not all her fault. She tries the best that she can."

"What I got from her, in that delightful unannounced visit at my place that morning, was that she worries about you a lot. You seem pretty tough, Mayes—no doubt—but she's just being a momma, I guess. She may not be warm and fuzzy delivering her message, but it isn't hard to see she cares deeply for you. And come on, what mother on earth wouldn't have reservations about letting her daughter hang out with a guy with all *my* shit?"

Laurel snorted and then smacked me on the leg. "You have your shit, but I think you also use that as a crutch to allow self-destructive behaviors."

"Oh, here we go, Laurel Freud. Can I go back to rubbing your head and you shutting up?" I said, my head drooping to my chest.

"What was the other memory?" she asked, bulldozing right over me.

I let it go and played along. "Right. Well, it was years later, as I said, and Mr. Mallet was in town at the grocery store. I hadn't seen him in quite a while. It was maybe two weeks before my freshman year in high school, and I was so apprehensive about that transition that I remember like it was an hour ago, oddly. He recognized me and asked how I was, if I was still playing chess, which I said I was, and we exchanged simple pleasantries. But then he asked me pointedly, 'Are you nervous about going into the high school?' And I told him, I think with my expression and not words, that I was. He put his little basket of items down and said, 'We are always afraid of the unknown and what we can't control. That's why I love chess, Josh. We can retreat into those squares when life overwhelms us and at least have a chance to regain control, and we don't have to be afraid.'"

Laurel smiled and then scooted closer to me on the bed before rubbing my knee with her hand. "Makes sense, but it feels like there's a larger component to the game here as well, no? I mean, this game has been such an integral part of your life for so long now, right? You've had a more diverse, rich, storied life than so many others, yet this game has always been in the background, arguably in the foreground even. Why do you think that is?"

"Well, I don't have an answer this second, but my guess is you're going to tell me, doc?"

She smacked my leg with the stroking hand. "Chess wasn't just a *retreat* for you. It was the world you existed in where *you* had all the power and control, whereas your life was full of things you didn't. The loss of your dad early on, followed by this beloved pet years later, and that was the time you said you started playing the game more seriously and began improving, right? So, you grow older, and even though the average guy may argue that the rock star life, getting famous and all that, is wonderful, yet again you're in an environment where you have little control. It's manic, turbulent, and unsteady, and yet chess is stable, solid, and always a place you can orchestrate the desired outcome."

"That's the thing, though. I can't *always* do that. I don't control every game. I don't win every game."

"Do you *feel* like you're in control most of the time?"

I stared at her, a half smirk on her face with those dopey, massive eyes glaring at me.

"Well?" she asked.

"I suppose I generally always feel like I'm in control, sure."

She widened her eyes and nodded, shouting, *"Seeeeeeeee!"* without saying a word.

"All right, enough head shrinking for today, and I have plenty of crap I could grill you on."

"I don't think it would be the worst thing for humanity if that head of yours were to shrink a little."

That made me giggle, and though I hate the word 'giggle,' it's the only way to describe what I did.

"I imagined you came on this trip to escape Momzilla and enjoy my always captivating company, though I'm starting to think you have more nefarious goals here."

She stuck out her tongue, then, "I wanted to be here with and for you because I imagine this is going to be an emotional experience," she said. Just like that, a playful jousting turned poignant.

"I'm glad you came with me," I told her, running my hand across her ear and through her hair.

Laurel pushed up and over me, pinning me down to the bed, kissing me, her hands wrapped into mine and flat against the bedspread. Our lips and tongues ebbed and flowed against one another for a minute before I rolled her off me and was on top of her, the kissing intensifying. I slid my hands across her chest and then moved my mouth to the front of her neck and between her breasts. She wrapped her legs around my back, pulling me into her, thrusting her hips tight against me. She pulled away from my lips and began kissing the side of my face, then licking my neck, which was unexpected though welcomed. She thrashed herself beneath me, kissing and licking and squeezing her hands tight on my ass, before abruptly sitting up.

"What's the matter?" I asked, wiping a bead of sweat from my forehead and onto my shirt. "Shit, you're going to throw up again, aren't you?"

Laurel leapt off the bed and ran for the bathroom, and when she got there, it sounded like the Lido deck bathroom on a cruise ship three days post Norovirus outbreak.

CHAPTER 20

I'm not ideal in these situations. I mean, I'm a compassionate person, I like to believe. I have empathy and understanding for others and genuinely feel bad when people suffer. However, if my on-again, off-again girlfriend was in the bathroom of our love shack hacking her guts out because Barry put a bullet in her one night while guzzling PBRs with Skynyrd blasting in the background, it was going to be challenging for me to be all hugs and "awwws."

"Are you okay?" I asked, like a dipshit, knowing she was anything but.

The toilet flushed, and she ran the water. A minute later she emerged, an off-white hand towel in her fingers, blotting her mouth and chin. "I'm fine now, thanks."

"I'm not sure what your history is, but I've had actual elephants in my room, and none of them were as big as the chubby pachyderm I feel like is here now," I said.

Laurel tossed the hand towel back into the bathroom and flopped down on the bed.

"Don't know what the protocol is for former-sort-of-used-to-be-something-maybe-but-now-we-just-make-out relationships, but I feel like this is something we need to discuss, no?" I asked.

Laurel sat up and exhaled dramatically before standing and pacing in front of the bed.

I stood up and blocked her path. "Hey, whatever it is, you can tell me. Although, I'm pretty certain I know what's going on."

Laurel stopped pacing and stared at me. "You do? Were you going through my purse?"

"Why? Is there a pacifier in there? Nanny cam? One of those Bjorn things?" I asked.

Her face wrinkled up, befuddled. "What on earth..."

"It's okay, I get it. You had a history with Barry before I knew you, and I'm sure when you're a box of wine or two deep he can seem sort of charming, even if he smells like beef jerky and motor oil. I'm not upset, but where I draw the line is that I won't let you give this kid a mohawk. I know it will seem kind of cute in the moment, and Barry will be pushing for it incessantly, but I'm going to have to see the kid from across the road and—"

Laurel began laughing wildly before turning herself around and falling onto the bed with a *thhlump!*

"I'm giving serious thought to not taking you back after we're broken up a little while longer," I threatened.

Laurel reeled in her laughter and sat up, tapping the open spot on the bed next to her, beckoning me. That move was in her top five cutest gestures, no question. Tough to fight it, so I slouched down and fell onto the bed beside her.

"You honestly think I'm pregnant?" she asked.

"Oh, what, and that's supposed to be totally out of the realm of possibility?"

"Josh, hon...no. Just, no. I may have made some idiotic choices in my life but having unprotected sex with Barry was not one on them. Not to mention it's been quite some time—"

"Yeah, I don't need to hear the details, especially minutes after you were writhing all up and over me," I interrupted. "Not that I don't find him attractive, of course. He's a dashing fella with wonderful sideburns."

"What is it with you men and this stuff? You've probably had more sexual partners than I have had long baths, and I've had a lot, and you're in a tizzy about my last boyfriend who's not even a threat. You realize how pathetic it all is, right?"

I did my best sad puppy eyes, but I was never good at that. Pickle though, wow, you should see him do it. Freaking world champion of sap.

"Josh, listen," she continued. "There are some things happening with me that I need to tell you about. It's part of the reason I wanted to come, besides be here for you, which was genuinely a part of it. I'm not pregnant, nothing like that."

I stared at her, saying nothing.

She rubbed her right hand across her other forearm for a while, and then: "I'm...sick. The serious kind. Have been for a while."

The words hung there like the cheap sailboat painting behind us on the wall. *I'm... sick.* She slid her hand over into mine, and I looked at her, but those last words held us both silent for a minute, maybe two. I moved off the bed and got on my knees and faced her, rubbing my hands across the tops of her arms.

"What's going on?" I asked her.

She took a long breath in through her nose and exhaled heavy before scooting closer to me, her butt half on the bed. "It's the C word. It's always the damn C word, isn't it? But listen, Josh, I need you to know something, okay? I didn't mean for you to get dragged into this. Right before you moved in, I was doing much better, and it was only recently that I learned...well, that

I learned that my condition had worsened. If I'd known that I was—"

"Laurel, no. I don't want to hear any apology for this, or our relationship, or whatever the hell it is we have here. All I want to hear about is what's going on with you and if there's anything I can do to help," I interjected, squeezing her arms.

Her eyes began to pool up, and then she pulled one of her arms away and scoured the bed for her phone. "Shit! Josh, what time is it? Aren't you supposed to meet Sasha's father soon? You're going to be late."

I looked at my watch, and she was right. Sasha's father lived about fifteen minutes from here and I was supposed to meet him in ten. "Fuck. Yes, but no, I can't go now. Are you kidding? I'm not going to leave a minute after you tell me—"

"It's alright. I'm not going anywhere. I'll be right here when you get back and would feel a hell of a lot worse if I make you late or miss it altogether. Go do what you need to do. We can talk more later," Laurel said before I could finish.

I made the gesture with my mouth that I had more to say, but Laurel pushed her palm gently onto my lips and mouthed, "Go." I stood up, leaned down, kissed her on the head, and scurried around the room for my phone and keys before looking at her one more time, asking without asking if she wanted me to stay once more.

"I'll be waiting for you right here. Please drive safely, K?" she said and then blew me a kiss from the edge of the bed. I returned the same and then ran out to my car.

****

As much as I'm an idiot at times, I'm not the worst guy you could have for a neighbor, a pal, or even an on-again, off-again boyfriend. I've learned over the years when callousness and indifference are necessary—usually for

163

simple self-protection—but also when I should shelve those in exchange for feelings and introspection. The latter is often terrifying but also cleansing, like any emotional purge, so it's important not to put up roadblocks just to avoid it. I don't think, in this case, a pile of freakin' Jersey barriers would have stopped the onslaught that came my way.

Driving to see Sasha's father, absorbing the news of Laurel's cancer, was the musical equivalent of finding out The Beatles broke up shortly after hearing that Hendrix and Jim Morrison died—it was too much. Driving a Porsche 911 on twisted roads with soggy eyes is no easy feat, so I pulled over and grabbed a couple Dunkin napkins from the glove box and dabbed at my peepers. The tears were exacerbated knowing Laurel was alone, back in that shitty motel, after having revealed the news to me, but she was right that I'd come here for a reason. A reason that was sure to extract its own set of emotions.

"God damn it," I said to myself, jamming the coarse sandpapery rectangles into my eyes like one of those trash TV guests that just found out their lover has fathered kids with five other women.

Sasha's dad's house was up on the right about another mile, so I balled up the napkins, tossed them into the passenger footwell, and pulled the car back onto the road. My hands were buzzing, trembling. I needed a drink. I had a bottle of bourbon wrapped in a shirt in the front luggage compartment, but if I cracked the seal now, I'd be stuck where I was, and I needed to get back to Laurel. I pulled into the half circle driveway that was 147 Lilac Road, turned off the engine, and sat in the car for a minute, staring up the house.

The home was a weather-worn, dilapidated green Colonial with an old, rusted pickup truck on blocks off to the right. The grass was overgrown, and there were vines creeping up around the open front porch that stretched to the roof. On first inspection it appeared abandoned. For a moment even thought I was in the wrong spot, until I saw the dingy white curtain pull away and someone peeking from the porch window bay. I waved. The curtain fell back against the frame.

The earth outside my car was a sludgy, wet mud mixed with gravel. The roads had been soaked earlier while we'd made our way down to Connecticut but dried when the rising sun cooked the blacktop. Spots like these, hidden in shade and long neglected, held the moisture and transferred muck all over your shoes. Most women I'd had relationships with would unquestionably claim that dirty shoes on the floor was an incessant problem between us, and now I was about to bring two sized thirteen gun boats up into this guy's place covered in sloppy, wet filth. I'd wipe them off, but you know as well as I do that shit never comes *all* the way off. I could offer to remove my shoes, but that's no bargain either, especially if he had high functioning olfactory senses.

I stepped onto the hazardous porch of rotted wood and rusty nails, though I didn't imagine many visitors stopped by from the look of things. The smell was a pungent odor of stagnant water and animal decay, which saturated my nose and mouth as I tiptoed my way to the front door.

"Hello, Mr. Darrow. It's Josh Traxon," I announced, knowing he had to be the curtain-peeker from a minute ago. I heard movement and creaking from behind the door, but it stayed closed. "Mr. Darrow, you home?" I asked, knocking harder.

The lace curtains in the door window fluttered, and I heard the knob turn.

"The flies will get in. Come on," the silver-haired man said, walking away from the door, leaving it open a crack for me, instantly unworried about those flies.

"Thanks for letting me come by," I said, following him into the house.

Sasha's father was five-nine at best, hunched over about fifteen degrees, old age pulling him from the neck down. He walked like he used a cane, but his hand was empty.

"I don't have anything to offer you other than some tap water or a can of cola. We can sit here in the living room," he said, motioning for me to head that way.

"I'm fine," I replied, navigating my way through the clutter piled on the explosive, fiery red carpet. Empty boxes, piles of newspaper, several jars with coins and nuts and bolts were strewn along the path to the couch, which rested against a water stain-soaked wall adored with two pictures. One was an image of an old house at dusk, almost impressionist, murky, and sinister. The other was a smaller framed picture of what looked like the Mother Mary. The indoor odor was unfamiliar to me, worse than outside, and pervasive enough that it had me comfortable in my decision to pass on the water.

In the dining room corner, next to a weathered brick fireplace, hung a blue sport coat with a patch on it. It was fitted around one of those mannequin busts as though it were for sale, pressed and perfect, ready for a state dinner. The patch said, "Club Champion," and there were some dates underneath it. The whole damn house was a festering wound of trash piles, stains, offensive odors and not a thing that was clean or cared for, and yet this golf jacket was pristine. A local club champion jacket, crisp as the day it was new, like it was a Green Jacket from the Masters.

He sat across from me in a recliner covered in worn gray fabric. On the wooden table next to him were fly fishing supplies and a TV remote, though I saw no TV. A tabby cat peeked around the corner from the kitchen, ran its back and tail up against the threshold the way they all do, and then walked away, giving zero fucks.

"I almost hung up on you when you called," he said, looking at the ceiling.

"You *did*, actually. The first time," I reminded him.

"I mean for good. Can't see any reason to dig into old sores like this," he said, pulling some of the fly-tying gear into his lap and fidgeting with them.

"I appreciate you seeing me, Mr. Darrow. I won't stay long, but there are some things I need to say...after all this time."

"I don't know you. I spoke to you once for a couple minutes years ago and then for less than that the other day. There's nothing I can imagine needs to be said, but I've agreed to let you speak your peace, so have at it."

I shifted on the couch and rubbed my hands together before leaning back and looking up at the popcorn ceiling. "You know, years ago, I mean a *looong* time ago, I was your neighbor on the other side of town. By the farm you owned. Not sure if Sasha ever told you that."

"I'm aware," he said, looking down at the flies on his lap while he messed with them.

"Ah, okay, wasn't sure," I said, shimmying on the couch.

"That couch isn't going to get any more comfortable the more you fidget. Be better off on the floor."

I contemplated the idea but instead let my back fall against the rear cushion and exhaled. I sat there silent for a minute. The only sound in the room was his huge hands bumping together as he worked with his fishing gear.

"I don't expect you'll find it satisfying to watch me do this all afternoon and evening, so how about you speak your business?" he said. The cat peeked out from the other room again, cautiously.

"Did Sasha talk to you much, about me or anything? Her love life?" I asked.

He stopped his handiwork and made eye contact.

"I know of my daughter's affairs, Mr. Traxon, including the one she had with you. I couldn't stop her from telling me if I'd wanted her to."

"You weren't interested? I mean, it seems like a topic fathers and daughters might discuss, no?"

This time he stopped and placed the supplies back on the table next to him before speaking, now in a more amplified tone. "Fathers and daughters may discuss those things, and in some cases, maybe enjoy it. In the situation with my daughter, however, that was certainly not the case. How much did *you* talk to my daughter? How much did you know her?"

I leaned forward on the couch, the wood frame creaking as I moved. "I like to think I knew her quite well. She was a tough nut to crack at first, I'll admit, but I was able to get inside before long."

"Of course, you and five dozen others before you. Please don't tell me you thought she *loved* you? That you meant something to her more than just a warm bed and a glimpse at celebrity?"

Not exactly Mike Brady here. Almost made me miss Laurel's mom.

"I lived under no impression that I was the only lover Sasha had, Mr. Darrow, but—"

"Only one? What the hell is wrong with you? All those years of booze, drugs, and rock and roll make you stupid? Sasha was sleeping with any man that would look at her cross-eyed from the time she was fifteen years old. Frankly, I'm shocked, based on the proximity to our house, that you never had a go at her back then," he interrupted.

I looked him in the eye, but he pulled away from my gaze. "I didn't come here to rehash her troubled past. I know she was messed up and suffering with demons I didn't understand, though I tried. What I came here for was to—"

"You think because you bed a lot of women that makes you a man? More of a man than me?" he interrupted, wagging his finger. "I know you rock and roll types. I was the head golf pro for thirty years at Cedar Springs in the next town over. I saw some of you come and go as you'd pass through our little state before and after Boston or New York. Couldn't play golf for shit but threw your money around at the waitresses and bartenders so they'd spend ten minutes in the locker room with you or a couple hours at one of the seedy motels. Thing was, those same broads were giving it to guys like me on the regular because I knew how to dress, how to carry myself, and I wasn't a damn cartoon. You were merely the distraction, the opening act."

My eyes tightened as he spoke, leaning towards me. When he stopped, he sighed and slammed himself back into the chair before picking up the flies again.

"I'm not sure what your angle is with all that, Mr. Darrow, but I didn't come here to measure dicks. I would, however, question how Mrs. Darrow may have come into this whole equation, with you apparently banging most of the Country Club behind her back while—"

"You leave her out of this, and don't try to claim some moral high ground either because if I know anything about you assholes, it's that morality isn't your strong suit," he interrupted, this time without the leaning and finger wagging.

"I'm not understanding why we're getting off track here. I came here to talk about Sasha and my role in her death. Is that something that interests you, or should I just get the hell out and let you play with your little macramé toys there?" I

169

said, with intentional condescension and ignorance, knowing it would bother him.

He looked up, dropping the project in his lap. "Did you kill her?"

There was a perverse near grin on his face, and a whimsy in his tone that was unsettling. "Did *I* kill her? No, I...I didn't kill her, but she was with me when it happened and—"

"I know the story, and I remember the phone call. If what you told me was true, that she was hammered and crashed your car and died at the scene. What role did you play other than being an unfortunate party to her irresponsibility, just as others before you had been?" he asked, steamrolling over my words again.

In that moment, I recalled the way my father used to respond to my mother when she was upset or fearful. An indifference to the tone, emotion, and language. An almost total disconnect from the reality at hand, and zero empathy. This crusty fuck was listening to someone discuss the last moments of his daughter's life and was crowbarring in suggestions that other people had suffered at her hands while she was alive.

I looked over and saw the bottle of whiskey resting sideways, half empty, on the ground near his feet. I was clenching my fingers against my palms.

"Huh. So, you've got the bug, too," he said, smirking like a child that just caught his little brother stealing cookies before dinner. "Go ahead, take a hit off the bottle. Nobody here is going to give you any shit."

"Easy there, Kreskin. Just because I look at a bottle of booze on the floor doesn't mean I'm an alki," I said pointedly.

"So, the fact that your hands are trembling and you're trying to squeeze them so damn hard to stop it that they'll be bleeding soon is, what, because there's a draft in here?" he questioned, still with the stupid smirk.

"Do you want to hear about Sasha or not?" I shouted as I stood up.

"Oh, come on. Settle down, kid. Sit, and say whatever is so bloody important. That's the other thing with all of you musicians—everything is so damn dramatic. Not everything in life needs to be a story. Sometimes things just are what they are, and nobody needs to know any different."

Fucking Aristotle over there had my blood boiling, but I wasn't about to give this guy the satisfaction of seeing me come unglued.

I sighed and indulged in a minute-long pause, before leaning forward to speak. "That day in the car, with Sasha, she was out of her mind from drinking and drugs. Which, based on what I'm hearing from you, wouldn't be a big surprise. I was trying to get her home, but she was agitated, moving around the car, climbing over to my side and distracting me. It was a nightmare from the moment we drove off."

"If this big revelation is that she crashed the car and you feel bad you let her drive, you can stop now. I know what a conniving, ornery bitch she could—"

"Shut the fuck up," I screamed, much louder than I'd planned, startling him. He rolled his eyes and leaned back deeper into his chair. "Let me finish what I came here to say."

I stood up and began pacing over the flame red carpet, its long strands tramped down from age, traffic, and a wealth of unknown stains. "I was driving. I left with her as the passenger from the restaurant. Sasha was out of control in the car, but I'd almost had her home. I thought she'd passed out when we were on the last stretch before she began flailing around and trying to climb over to my side, and at one point it was simply too much, and I lost control of the car. We careened off the road and down an embankment, and somehow, in the violent turbulence of the accident, she broke her neck, and she'd come to rest nearly all the way on my side. I don't know why or how I was able to let it be assumed she was the driver, but I did. Fear, shock, embarrassment, probably all of it, but that's what I did. I let her take the blame for what was absolutely my responsibility. A dead woman who had no voice. A woman that I loved. I lied to protect myself, as there was no other reason to fabricate what I did. I was only able to make it work because I visited the single witness to us leaving the place and—"

"Hold on, hold on a sec here," he interjected. "Are you telling me you're having some moral dilemma, crises of conscience, because for all these years you've let others believe it was her—an almost lifelong drunk and addict—driving that car and not you? You, who if you're being honest, was sober and just trying to get her home safely while she attempted to run the two of you off the road? Is that really what I'm hearing?"

His tone of veiled laughter stopped my surprised feet from pacing. I dropped back down on the couch.

"Kid, I'm not sure if it *is* an 'artist' thing or something I'm just unable to understand, but if you're feeling guilty because you told a little white lie to save your ass, then I'm not sure how the hell you've made it this far in life. My daughter was a goddamn mess. It surprises me not one iota that she made you wreck your car, and frankly, I was dumbfounded that you'd let her drive in that condition. It makes sense now. Instead of feeling like you need to clear your conscience to find some catharsis, how about you just stop shacking up with drunken whores and avoid this in the future?"

"Seeing red" is an expression used by people who snap. That very moment, as the sweat trickled out of my clenched hands, felt like a viable reason for the phrase to exist. All those mad bastards must have been staring at this horrendous, glowing red

172

carpet, listening to Mr. Darrow trash his dead daughter as he tied flies in a room that felt like two hundred degrees, because the red was everywhere for me.

I watched his hairy fingers work around the material. His indifferent expression fixed on his hands as they pulled, wound, and tied. I slid off my right shoe and pulled it into my lap, the leather sliding against my sweaty digits, my heart slamming into the walls of my chest.

I shot up off the couch and lunged at Sasha's father, pulling him off the chair and tossing him to the ground before pinning him with my knees. He was stunned, but thrashing beneath me, trying to free himself, shouting muddled obscenities.

"You motherfucker," I screamed in his face as I drew back the shoe and smacked the ball side across his head. "I know what you did to her, you monstrous fuck!"

He struggled to free himself after the blow, trying to roll to his left, but I leaned into his chest, drew back the shoe and hit him again before tossing it aside.

"I'll kill you," he shouted up at me, his cheek bleeding from the second blow. "That little bitch was—"

I punched him with my right hand, square in the jaw, before gripping his throat and squeezing, eliciting gurgles and chokes. His thrashing lessened. I clamped down harder for a few seconds, watching his eyes bulge before releasing my grip and stepping off him. He hacked and spit a half dozen times before rolling and pulling himself toward the couch I'd been sitting on. He slid his arm underneath, running his hands across the carpet back and forth until he grabbed hold of something. I knelt on him again, grabbing his forearm as the weapon revealed. It was a hunting knife with an eight-inch blade and flesh-colored scales. As I leaned my knee into his neck and applied pressure to his forearm and wrist, he attempted to roll his torso to gain leverage, but I held him by constricting my lower legs around him. When his movement stopped, I pulled his arm up six inches from the carpet, smashing it down to the floor, over and over, until the knife broke free from his grip and smacked into a ceramic jug, cracking it.

"What else have you got hiding around this shithole? Maybe I need to cut your hands off with that knife, so you don't go scurrying around looking for your twenty-two or baseball bat," I said, still on top of him and latched onto his arm.

"Let me up," he said, barely audible.

"What's that?"

"Let me up. I think you broke my rib."

"I didn't break your goddam rib," I said, letting go of his arm before standing up.

He rolled away from the couch and propped himself against the chair he'd been sitting in, wincing as he moved. "Cracked it or something, I can feel it. You're twice my size."

I watched him in agony, and then imagined him having his way with Sasha as a young girl. Creeping down the hallway, Sasha hearing the footsteps and the floorboards creaking, and then the turning of the knob, bile rising in her stomach. "There's still a good chance I pick up that knife and cut you open, old man. You think you're in pain now."

"You didn't have to live with her mother. That woman was a cold hearted, asexual bitch," he forced out through labored breath. "I gave her a beautiful farm, horses, a lavish home for her child, and she repaid me with indifference. Sasha was the only one who—"

I picked up the shoe I had thrashed across his face minutes earlier. "Sasha was your daughter. A little girl you were supposed to love and protect from monsters like you. Say another word, just one more word, and I'm going to beat you so fucking hard with this thing that the lights are going out. They're going to go out, and you won't be coming back."

He wanted to say something but instead leaned deeper against the chair, coughing several times.

I looked around the house while he sat there in pain, blood leaking from the laceration on his face. The home was a dumpster fire compared to the thriving farm they'd had when I lived next door as a child, though I'd never been inside. Messy, cold, filthy, and no signs of life other than the evil old pig sitting on the floor. On a rack of metal shelving, cluttered with miscellaneous papers and trinkets, I noticed a picture of a man and a teenage girl. It was Sasha and her lecherous father. She wasn't smiling, but kind of grimacing. He had his chin up in an arrogant pose, wearing the same damn golf club coat that hung on that mannequin. I grabbed the picture and walked back into the room where he was still sitting against the chair.

"How's the pain in the chest? Still aching?" I asked.

"Screw you. What were you messing with over—"

"Shut up," I said, kneeling and picking up the hunting knife. "How well have you taken care of this knife? Sharpen it regularly? When's the last time you used it to cut something?"

He dead stared me but didn't answer. His breath was wheezy, and he flinched with each inhalation.

"Well, as much as this entire place should be burned down, with you in it—something I'm still contemplating, by the way—I imagine you probably keep things like this knife in decent shape," I said, lifting it skyward in front of him.

"Hey. Hey! Don't, please," he shouted, covering his face and neck with his arms and hands.

I slammed the knife down into the picture of the two of them, the blade plunging into the carpet and down to the subfloor. I pried it loose and pulled the blade down through the picture lengthwise, separating her from her father in the shot. I took the half with him in it and jabbed the knife into it repeatedly and then tossed the torn up remains at him before sliding the picture of her into my front pants pocket.

"Still bleeding pretty bad there, huh? Let me get you something for that," I told him after standing up. I walked over to the golf jacket hanging on the mannequin bust and pulled it from its perch, tossing it down onto the floor and then kneeled on it. I dug the knife into the fibers, tearing at the sleeve until it broke free from the rest of the jacket. I took the piece in my free hand and then wiped my feet on what was left.

"Here you go. Why don't you clean yourself up," I said, tossing the torn jacket sleeve at his bloody face.

He pulled it from the side of his head and placed it next to him on the floor. He started to say something but stopped as his eyes met mine.

"Only out of my desire to not be as deplorable a human as you, I'll call the EMTs if you want. Have them come take a look," I offered. "Otherwise, you can just die right here on the fucking floor for all I care."

"Call the cops. I'll tell them what you did, and you'll be locked up. I know the sheriff here," he responded, his breathing heavy and sputtering.

"You tell them whatever the hell you want. Please. I hope they come find me. I will tell them what you are, what you've done, and let them do with me that what they will. And no matter what that is, I'll come for you again. And at that time, we will say our goodbyes," I replied.

He winced, and then, "I saw you on that stupid goddam TV show. Drunk as a skunk, making an ass out of yourself, and here you're judging me. You looked like a clown, copulating with a kitchen utensil."

176

I contemplated picking up the shoe again and just bringing the full force of God, gravity, and fury down on his head, but if there was a place beyond this life, where he was headed was worse than anything I could do to him here. And if there wasn't, well, he'd rot away alone in a box without his beloved fucking golf jacket and a set of scars put there by me.

"I have my regrets, asshole. I'm not proud of everything I did. But I never touched a kid. *My* kid. I never did something so vile and evil that it made a man walk into my house and beat me with his shoes. Plus, I'm famous, which doesn't mean a whole hell of a lot except that there are people out there who feel like I entertained them, made them laugh, bob their head, enriched their lives in some way, however small and trivial. You're just an ugly, old monster, bleeding on his floor that will be dead before too many years click off and nobody fucking cares. Except me, but only with hopes that I sped up your journey to hell."

I slid the hunting knife into the back of my pants, navigated my way around the garbage and left without a single look back.

CHAPTER 21

As each mile passed on the road back from Sasha's father's, I considered calling 911. I left the old bastard pretty banged up, but he deserved every violent blow. Each time I reached for the phone I thought of Sasha's picture in my pocket. He could tend to his own wounds. They were far from fatal. That motherfucker was lucky I left when I did.

Laurel. The motel. That's where my focus needed to be, but just as that thought crossed my mind, another mental image flash interrupted. It was Timber again. The intensity of the situation with Sasha's father, the proximity to where I'd lived with the dog …it had extracted a long suppressed, though vivid, memory.

I was so distraught by my pup's death as a child that I was inconsolable, crying incessantly. My mother was a wreck, not knowing how to help, and even missing work the day after he died to stay with me. She asked if I wanted to bury him in the backyard. We had ample land and maybe that would help me heal, knowing he was close by, if only in essence. She went outside that afternoon, in the pouring rain, and walked along the stone wall bordering Sasha's farm. I watched from the kitchen window. She walked and then crouched, over and over, until far off in the distance and barely visible in the sheets of rain. Finally, she latched onto something. My eyes trailed her all the way back, carrying the heavy stone in the downpour. When she got close—even though she told me to stay inside—I ran into the backyard to see what she discovered. She dropped the rock at my feet, saying, "This is for Timber. It was meant for him. It was meant for both of you." It was a large, heart-shaped rock, appearing to be carved, the lines perfect and true. It was the size of a car tire and my mother had carried it in the rain for at least a quarter mile. She was convinced that finding it was destined. I had no reason to question that belief.

For thirty years, this piece of the Timber's memory had been dormant. I forgot about the bleeding old motherfucker of a man, pegged the accelerator, and raced backed to Laurel.

****

"Hey, I was just about to call you. Wanted to make sure you were okay," Laurel said when I walked into the motel room. "How did everything go?"

I felt sweat running down my forehead and my arms ached from the struggle, but otherwise, I imagined I didn't look like I'd just been in a violent tussle with the old man. "We hashed some things out. I said what I needed to say. He responded. I left."

"That's it?" she asked with a furrowed brow.

"I'm more concerned about how *you* are doing. I really didn't want to leave you—"

"I'm fine, but look at you, Josh. You're sweating like it's a hundred degrees out. Let me get you a towel," Laurel said, hopping off the bed and slipping into the tiny bathroom.

"It got a little heated there for a minute, but all good," I told her as she sat on the bed next to me and wiped my forehead.

"Hmm," she hummed.

"I had another Timber memory driving back," I said, hoping to divert the conservation from Sasha's father. "It popped in out of nowhere. Lotta stuff been doing that lately."

"Your pup?" she asked. "What was it?"

I ran my hand over the small of her back and nudged myself toward her. "He was the first dog I ever had. He was the first living creature I was—at least partially—responsible for. He'd sleep in my bed every night with me. I'd run around with him in the huge open field behind the house, chase him as he'd bound after sticks I'd toss for him. I'd take him for walks along the stone wall that bordered our property, down to a stream that snaked around the back. He was with us for just about a year before he was hit by the car."

Laurel stroked the side of my head with her hand, her dewy eyes fixed on me.

"My mother wanted to console me after he passed, obviously, though nothing was helping. One day, in the pouring rain, she walked the backyard along the stone wall edge and finds this stone. It was a huge, heart-shaped rock pulled from the wall bottom, way at the end. She carried it back, soaked from head to toe, and placed it near my feet. 'This is for Timber. It was meant for him. It was meant for both of you,' she said after laying it down.

Laurel's eyes leaked down onto her cheeks. She rubbed her hand over the top of mine.

"I recall being bothered by that last part, 'It was meant for him, for both of you.' How could something like that be meant for him, for us? Was he supposed to die? What the hell was she talking about? All I felt was sorrow that he was gone. I missed that dog so much, cried so many days. That anguish was the only emotion I knew for weeks."

"Pretty amazing she found something that perfect, that germane, right? A heart-shaped stone in a rainstorm right after he died. I mean...it's beautiful."

"I can see how it may seem pre-ordained, supernatural even, but at the time, all I could feel was misery. I vaguely recall, now, thinking about the stone, maybe ten years later, during a vicious bender. Think I was crying on the floor in some Midwest hotel, yelling about Timber's stone, sobbing, probably had pissed myself."

Laurel laced her fingers into mine from over the top of my hand.

"He was such a great dog. Losing him just eviscerated me."

"What about your mom? You don't talk about her much. Have you guys discussed that event at all?"

"She passed away several years back. Long illness, but she'd found a man late in life that took great care of her. I saw her shortly before the end. We reminisced a lot about childhood and my asshole father, but, oddly, the stone never came up."

Laurel squeezed my hand. "Where did you put the stone? In your backyard, you said?"

"Yeah, behind one of the sheds on the property. In front of a maple tree that was a few yards past it on the left."

Laurel's eyes as wide as frisbees. "We need to go find it."

"Find it? For what?" I questioned, dabbing the towel Laurel had handed me across my forehead.

"You said this memory appeared out of nowhere. That it was vivid, intense, unexpected. That must mean something, Josh," she assured me, hopping off the bed.

"Right. It means I'm back in the little Podunk town where I grew up and a bunch of things happened, so it makes sense I might have a flashback or two. I may have to take back the

181

'you're smarter than me' thing," I quipped, which brought a smack to my left arm, eliciting a groan.

"That hurt? Okay, you need to tell me what the hell happened when you were gone before we do anything," Laurel pressed.

"Nothing. Other than I'm an old man and shit hurts sometimes for no reason."

"Oh please. You're in good shape and have one of the most juvenile personalities I've ever known. I mean that in a sweet way, of course."

"Well, then maybe it's Lyme Disease. I don't know, but, regardless, it's fine. Now, can you help me understand why you want me to find this rock where Timber's buried?"

She whacked the arm again, this time less aggressively, and then kissed it three times quickly. "I told you. I don't know why, but we need to. So, let's get some food and head out there before it gets dark."

"A couple hours ago you started telling me you've got health problems. We haven't discussed that at all. Can we talk about that? Help me understand what's going on?"

"It's nothing that won't still be here when we get back. Besides, this is your trip, I'm only along for the ride. It's not about me. Let's go on this adventure and we can talk about unpleasant hings later."

Looking into her doe eyes when she wanted something was like staring down at Pickle when he knows you've got grub. Right or wrong—they're going to get what they want.

"What am I supposed to do? Walk up to whoever owns my old house and say, 'Hey, I used to live here like a million years ago. Can I scout around your back yard for my dead dog's grave?' People get shot for shit like that. These country folks have guns, babe."

"Oh, stop it. You're charming, and remember, you're *famous*. People love doing things for celebrities."

I grimaced. "The chances that the old timer who answers the door knows who the hell I am is about one in a thousand at best. This part of the world is more *CMA's* and *The 700 Club, not* reality TV and rock and roll."

"Well, then maybe I'll need to take off my top. Whatever. Just stop making excuses, and let's go find this thing."

That comment got the ol' pants pony wiggling, not gonna lie. I thought about revisiting the canoodling we'd been engaged in earlier, but she was on a mission. I didn't want to disappoint her, and let's face it, anything in the sexual realm was likely to. Also, I'd like to apologize for "pants pony" and "canoodling."

"All right. Let me pee. Then we can go bother strangers at their homes," I said, rustling her hair as I stood.

"Normally that move would add fifteen minutes to our departure time, but considering where we are, I'm going to just put my hair up in a ponytail and stick a hat on. Feels more home-invasiony anyway."

"Now you're catching on," I said before shutting the bathroom door. After peeing, I washed my sweat-soaked face and hands, suffering another moment of indecision about not calling help for Sasha's father. I pulled the adolescent picture of her from my pants pocket, stared at her sullen eyes and the tear in the paper where her father had stood.

"Fuck him," I said, staring at myself in the mirror, tucking the precious image back into my pocket.

CHAPTER 22

"It's coming up on the right, at the top of the hill," I told Laurel. "Looks like the entire place has been renovated. Holy crap. That barn was barely standing last time I saw it, and the house was ten years overdue for paint and trim work. Looks immaculate now."

"It's gorgeous. Wow. Did you bring your checkbook? Be a lot easier to get him to let you dig up his yard if you just bought the place," Laurel said, checking her face in the visor mirror.

"Maybe we ought to scrap this. I feel like a moron pulling in here, asking to go rooting around their property."

She looked at me, face freshly painted with only a dusting of makeup and lipstick. Running her hand across the top of my knee, smiling, she said, "This is your life, your experience, Josh. Don't make this decision because of what I think or feel, but don't be surprised if you have night terrors and a lifetime of regret if you bail out now."

I squinted my eyes and pursed my lips. She was the only woman I'd known since my mother that sometimes left me speechless, unable to formulate a witty commentary comeback.

Without another word, I pulled into the long gravel driveway that stopped a hundred feet before the house.

The updated version of my former home was a green and white Colonial with new windows and a recently installed cobblestone walkway leading to the front door. The tiny shed we'd had years back had been replaced by one three times its size and painted to look like a smaller version of the main house. From where we'd parked, I could see a swimming pool, a backyard entertainment area, and a figure walking behind the fencing.

"I think I saw someone out back, so I'm going to head out there. You coming?" I asked Laurel before tossing a few cashews into my trap.

"Do you want me to?"

"Of course," I told her. She smiled, flipped up her visor, and exited the car.

As I walked along the side of the house, I recalled a Sunday morning when I'd taken one of my mother's towels, tucked it into my back shirt collar and climbed up onto the shed from the adjacent tree. I'd watched a marathon of the old *Superman* TV show episodes, and something about the weather that morning. The eerie breeze and Indian summer sky, coupled with imagination and stupidity, had me thinking the bath towel was enough to get me airborne off the shed. It wasn't. A sprained ankle and broken thumb had followed. My mother was angry but fought back laughter the entire time she tended to my wounds Later that night, I heard her say to a girlfriend on the phone, "He really thought he could do it!" She was right. I did. Seriously.

"Hello there. Didn't mean to startle you," I said to the salty-haired man in shorts and a Harley Davidson T-shirt exiting the fenced area around his pool.

"Good afternoon. Saw you pull up the driveway in that fancy car. Figured it was my neighbor, Donald, coming to tell me one of his scratch tickets finally hit. What can I do for you?" the man asked.

"Well, first let me apologize for the intrusion. I don't often show up unannounced to people's homes I don't know, and I'm sorry for that. My name is Josh. Josh Traxon. This is my girlfriend, Laurel," I said, extending my hand to the man while noticing that Laurel didn't flinch at the girlfriend comment. Bonus.

"Grant Dawkins. How are you?" he replied, shaking my hand with a firm grip and two-second hold. I liked it.

"Ah, like Richard Dawkins, the evolutionary biologist," I added.

"Not familiar with the fella, and no relation. So, what can I do for you?"

Laurel peered over at me with an eye roll. A certain judgement for the Richard Dawkins reference, apparently knowing it was going to bomb.

"Well, believe it or not I used to live here as a child. Moved away from town many years ago."

"Why wouldn't I believe it? I've only owned the place for ten years."

I felt like Carrot Top telling jokes in front of a room full of engineers.

"Good point," I offered before putting my arm around Laurel and pulling her toward me, though she hesitated, smelling the stench of loser.

"Looking at that car, my guess is you were hoping to what, buy the place again? Make me an offer I can't refuse," Mr. Dawkins said, using an awful pseudo-gangster affect at the end. Laurel

186

stepped on the side of my foot with an *OMG did you hear that?* subtext.

"The place is beautiful. If I was in the market, I certainly would. The visit here today is purely nostalgia," I told him.

"Funny how people do that. I couldn't care less to see where I lived as a child. A tiny box outside of Hartford with no air conditioning. Families on both sides that beat the tar out of each other. No need to look back."

Laurel pulled away from me and stepped closer to the man. "I think that's what makes human beings so interesting, how we're all different like that. See, if I'd lived where you did, with those memories, I'd want to go back and see if things had changed, see if some good energy was there now. How it made me feel to revisit what I experienced as a child versus where I am now."

Mr. Dawkins furrowed his brow, looking over at Laurel like Richard Nixon at David Frost after one of the heated exchanges in those tapes.

"Why we stopped by today, Mr. Dawkins—"

"Just call me Grant," he interrupted.

"Sure, thank you, Grant. When I lived here twenty years ago, I had a dog named Timber, my first pet. He was hit by a car out on that road," I said, pointing.

"Horrible street there. Between the kids racing up and down in the summer with their crotch rockets to the damn eighteen wheelers zooming up to the highway, it's a damn nuisance. I have a run for my Shephard. Won't take the chance."

"I hear you," I said, though all I really heard was 'I don't really care about your dead dog story, so let me just tell you about one of my gripes and why you're stupid.'

"What was the dog's name again?" he asked.

"Timber, like a tree," I answered. "He was caramel and black, looked like bark. Think that's why I named him that. We buried him here on the property. There was this stone my mother placed on his gravesite. I know it may sound a little morbid and strange even, but..."

The man started walking away from us toward the shed, but not before he went two knuckles deep into his ass and pulled the wedge of his crack through his shorts. Laurel silent laughed and gave me the thumbs up as we started following him.

"When I started renovating the place, I began with the landscaping and this shed here," he said, stopping at the left front corner of it, at least thirty yards from where Timber had been buried around the other side. "I dug this out of the ground maybe five years ago. It was overgrown and only caught it because my mower blade clipped the edge on a soggy morning cut." He crouched down in the grass and pulled some wood and debris he'd stacked there aside, revealing a heart shaped stone.

"Holy shit," I said. Laurel grabbed my hand and threaded her fingers between mine.

"Oh my God, Josh. Is that it?"

I knelt next to him, causing the man to stand, giving me space.

"It's been here since I dug it up. Was going to maybe paint it and incorporate it into the garden next to the pool area but never got around to it."

The painted letters on the stone were barely visible, worn away from years of weather and earth. Most of the black 'Tim' was still noticeable, and the left half of the B, but that was it. "Do you mind if I pick it up?" I asked.

"Go ahead. It's a heavy little sonofabitch, I recall," he replied.

I wiggled the stone from the overgrown grass, adjusting my position to gain leverage and tip it upward, facing me. Laurel crouched down beside me.

"I have to say, I'm beyond shocked that it's still here, or that someone found it. I know it's a big hunk of stone but...it's been so long," I said.

"Geez, you can't imagine the amount of stuff I've found here since I bought the place. Got myself one of those metal detectors and covered most of the landscape with it. Found a ton of coins, some copper wiring, at least five or six Matchbox cars—I'm guessing those were also yours—and a metal box with several old pictures inside, before either of our times."

Laurel ran her hand up my back and onto my neck, caressing it.

"I hate to be douchey here, Mr. Dawkins, and I don't want this to be weird, but is there any way you'd consider letting me take this? It, well, it has a lot of sentimental value. I used to come out and sit by this thing when I was depressed about losing Timber or getting my ass beat at school or whatever dilemma I was suffering from at the time. Would mean a lot to have this back in my life, I think," I said.

"I can't see any reason why I'd need to keep it. I don't have the same affinity for rocks and such as you do, but I wouldn't deny a man his," he answered.

Laurel smiled up at me, squeezing my hand.

"Much appreciated, Grant, and again I'm so sorry for the intrusion. Can I offer you something for this? Buy you and your wife dinner, something?" I offered.

"Oh, heavens no. It's just a rock, son. Plus, the wife is at her sisters until next week, which I'd be a liar if I didn't say I was thrilled about. Gives me a chance to get some things done around here. Have almost finished the grotto, as I call it. Just a few more flowers and some stonework, and it will all be done. Come take a look," he said, heading towards the pool area.

As we walked into the backyard, I noticed a marble chess set resting on a rock table he'd made inside the pool area. Laurel noticed at the same time and mouthed, "No" as we approached.

"I started with just the pool at first and then began building up everything around it. Has taken a few years, but it's coming along," he explained.

"It's stunning, truly," Laurel said. "Must have been a lot of work, but what a magnificent result."

"Agreed," I added. "I also see you have a chess board there. Did you make that?"

Laurel squeezed my hand firmly enough to comprehend her message wasn't amorous.

"Do you play? Can't get the wife to play with me anymore. Don't understand why she quit. She improved quite a bit over the years."

"I do play. I'd be a liar if I said the game doesn't consume me most days, but I'm learning to let other things do that," I responded, smiling at Laurel. I didn't mean it sexually, and somehow, she knew that as her eyes softened when she acknowledged me.

"If you have a few more minutes then, let me grab us some beers or iced tea or whatever you prefer and play a game?"

"That sounds great, and...iced tea would be fine. Laurel?"

"If you're getting some for yourself, then sure, iced tea sounds wonderful," Laurel told him.

"Back in a second," he said, stepping inside the back of the house.

"What are you doing?" Laurel asked while smacking me on the shoulder. "This nice man lets you on his property, is giving you the stone, and now you're going to humiliate him at chess in his own back yard? Come on, Josh."

"Who says I'm going to humiliate him? He has a chess board. He knows how to play. And who am I, Magnus Carlsen?"

"Is that a chess guy? Yeah, no idea who he is, so that reference did nothing for me."

"Are you feisty because you want to get out of here or because you know my car has no storage space and I'm going to make you keep that stone on your lap on the way home?"

"I'm happy to sit and have drinks with this nice man. I just don't want to see you embarrass him."

"You're such an empath," I told her, rubbing my hand over the back of her neck, inducing a half smile. "I promise I won't, okay? I'll make a couple mistakes, let him win some pieces, and then I'll just finish him off easy."

Mr. Dawkins returned before Laurel could argue further.

"Here you are," he said, handing us the drinks. "Just grab any of the chairs near the board there, whatever's comfortable."

We followed him into what he referred to as The Grotto, which appeared to be lounge chairs surrounding a pool, along with a monstrous stainless-steel grill and smoker. No playmates, no splashing, and no Hef.

"What a spot to spend a summer day. If we had this when I lived here, I'd probably never have left," I told him, munching on some more cashews.

He didn't respond and just slid the folding chair up to the chess board. I pulled a zero-gravity type reclining chair over for Laurel and then parked myself in one identical to what he had chosen, nudging myself up to the other side of the board.

"White's move," he said, eyes fixated on the pieces.

"That is customary," I replied, drawing no response. Laurel went from concerned I was going to humiliate the poor fuck to clutching my upper thigh in panic.

I opened E4, shocker. He countered Knight to F6. I went D4. He looked up from the board, and that's when I knew I was toast. Not that I'd lost already—that would be absurd—but that I was outmatched.

I could illustrate the whole game for you, which lasted less than forty-four total moves, but chances are you wouldn't understand, nor would you care, and I get that. Chess is something for me that it will likely never be for you. I honestly prefer it that way. Which is why this loss—this rare and devastating loss—was so beautiful in its doom. Few people who walk the earth would be able to fully grasp the dichotomy of a brutal defeat on the chess board. The savagery of watching another tear down your defenses, outthink you, outplay you, anticipate your every move, mercilessly striking you down in the end, entwined with the awe of witnessing such wizardry. It had been many years since I'd watched another human being—less so on the virtual boards—eviscerate me. I wanted to both pummel and hug the man equally.

"Well, I have to say that was something to behold. I don't lose much, which I'm sure you may have gathered, but that was as sound a defeat as there is," I said, extending my hand.

"You're a strong player, much like I was years back, but you have to be willing to die to live, as they say," he replied.

"Take more risks, not play so conservative, yes, you're probably—"

"No, not the shit the chess coaches tell you. You play like you're on that board with them, or you don't play at all. Your only purpose is to win, be in control, and yet you're bleeding the entire time. Only then will you get at the heart of this damn thing. That's how you find the game."

"Every time I think I have it mastered I'm reminded I don't have a clue. You were that reminder today. Holy smokes. I think

I'm shaking," I said, standing up, fishing for my cashews in my front pocket.

"When I was learning the game as an adolescent, someone said to me, 'When you think you've mastered chess, you've finally become a beginner.' I can't imagine putting it any better than that," Mr. Dawkins said, looking through my soul.

"Profound, indeed. Though at this point, I think I'm just going back to playing tiddlywinks for beer money."

He smiled, his first of the day. Laurel was still in shock, I think, so I grabbed her hand and led her from the chair.

"I can't thank you enough for letting me take this stone, Mr. Dawk—Grant, excuse me. It's very kind of you, as were the drinks and the chess lesson, brutal as it was."

"I don't imagine you'll forget where I live, and I'm sure that car is anything but loathsome to drive. Come down and play a game or two, anytime."

"I just may do that. Give me at least a year or so, though. That game is going to take a while to get over, not to mention I'd like to show up and feel like I have at least a *chance* to win."

"You had a chance, twelfth move in—not much of a chance, but it was there—you squandered it on castling."

I looked at Laurel and she gave me the "Even I could see that," stare.

"Thanks again, Grant, and I'll see you around," I told him.

"Enjoy your day, folks. Oh, and Josh, seems that I recall you being on television for a bit. Maybe a rock and roller at one point. That right?"

Laurel clenched my hand again, cracking a knuckle.

"You'd be correct, yes. Was in a band called Shaky Bones for a few years and then a reality TV show for a stretch. Wouldn't have guessed either of those endeavors would have drawn your attention, though."

His eyes squinted and his head tilted to his right. "Making the same assumptions you made on the chessboard, I see."

I felt blood rush to my face, which was intriguing for a guy who didn't get embarrassed the time someone in the bank line told them he was wearing underwear and not shorts.

"You're right. Sometimes I forget that I have fans across a wide spectrum. Thank you."

"I didn't say I was a fan, just that I know who you are. The music had its moments, a couple solid tunes, but that TV show...then again, you're the one driving that German rocket ship, and I have the beat-to-piss pickup truck."

"And this beautiful woman on my arm. Check-fucking-mate, Dawkins."

That got Grant laughing a bit. The only victory I'd take from him today, besides the stone of course. I took them both and headed for the car. Laurel looked up and smiled, leaning her head into my shoulder.

"Don't castle so early, Josh. Play like your life is on that board," Mr. Dawkins yelled from fifty feet back.

It used to be. Might be headed somewhere else now.

****

"Do you want to bring it inside?" Laurel asked, the late day sun illuminating lemony hair strands dancing in the breeze.

"I think I'll just leave it here," I said, looking down at it resting in the small space under the hood of the Porsche. "I wasn't sure it would fit, but it's almost like it was designed for it."

"Did it make driving your car feel any different, with more weight over the front wheels?"

Talk about foreplay.

"That may be my favorite question you've ever asked, but no, I don't think I noticed anything. The stone can't be more than

194

thirty pounds, so not enough to have any discernable difference, at least to a ham-fisted moron like me."

I slammed the hood shut and walked back to the motel room, Laurel in tow. She'd called home on the way back, reminding them she would be home tomorrow. From what I overheard, Ethan was thrilled Pickle was staying for a sleepover, while Mom's long pause indicated she wasn't quite as thrilled about Laurel's sleepover plans.

"You hungry?" I asked Laurel as we got into the room.

"I have those extra sandwiches and that bag of chips I bought earlier. Not feeling like anything fancy. How about you?" she asked back.

"Simple sounds good. In fact, it's not that late. If you did want to head back to—"

Laurel sat on the edge of the bed, her eyes welling up. I knelt in front of her, resting my hands on her knees "What is it?"

Her lips quivered, and a tear leaked from each eye. One raced down the left cheek, but the other stuck midway, clinging, not ready to drop to the floor. I rubbed my hands over the tops of her legs, waiting until she was ready.

"That was such a beautiful moment for you today, Josh. Thank you for bringing me along. It meant a lot to me," she said, working through it.

"It wouldn't have been half as meaningful had you not been here, Laurel. I mean that."

"I wish I could be more than...more than what I can be, or what I am, for you. I...I just..."

"What?" I asked her, before biting my bottom lip.

Laurel wept heavily, wiping her eyes with her sleeves, so I went to the nightstand and grabbed the tissue box and placed it next to her. She pulled one out and dabbed her eyes.

"I want to be strong enough for myself and for you, but with what's going on, and Ethan and everything, it's just so difficult."

I took a tissue and wiped it across both cheeks, then slid up onto the bed next to her.

"Spending time with you has reminded me what it feels like to live and be in love, to feel beautiful and excited and hopeful...but I can't let that overtake me. I can't live in a fantasy world with you, Josh."

"Well," I began, dabbing at my own leaky eye with the back of my hand. "First of all, let me say that I'm glad you finally admitted you're in love with me. I mean shit, it's been pretty obvious from day one."

She laughed through the waterworks and pushed herself against me, nudging me sideways.

"I'm serious, though. *This* is serious, my life...my fragile, damaged life is something more serious than anything between us, and it's killing me."

I slid off the bed again and faced her, kneeling. "Laurel, whatever it is that's going on, you can tell me. Whatever your health, your history, your fears. I can handle it. You have cancer. I know. I haven't forgotten. It scares me too. But you're not alone in this, not if you don't want to be. I'm not a destiny guy, but I feel pretty confident saying I didn't show up across the street from you just to drink myself to death and watch your mother saunter around in her evening wear, as hot as that would be."

She chuckled again before grabbing ahold of my wrists and looking down at me, square in the eyes. "Josh," she started, her lips vibrating again, her eyes filling up. "This cancer that I have...it's aggressive. It's, well, it's eating me up inside, and I don't have a lot of time. The options I've had in the past are...they're gone. I wish this weren't the truth, but it is."

I took a deep breath before speaking, though my words were bumpy, stuttered.

"How much...how much time? What did they...how do you know it's—"

"My time has already passed, Josh," she said, squeezing the words out through labored breath. "Every day I've had with you has been borrowed. My oncologist called me a miracle when I last saw him...they'd missed the spread, the rapid growth and...I'm out of time."

I stood up and went to the bathroom, taking a baby blue hand towel from the O ring near the sink and rubbing it into both eyes. Laurel softly wept, still sitting on the edge of the bed.

"There are always options, Laurel. I've known people that—"

"Josh, please," she interrupted. "Please don't do this right now. I love that you want to be that person who wants to talk about fighting and surviving, but there's nothing about this disease I don't already know. There's nothing left to fight, no treatments that remain viable, no roads I haven't already been down. Just sit with me, okay?"

I shut up and went to her side on the bed, trying to quell my shaking before I sat.

She let her back and head hit the bed, pulling my arm, drawing me close to her. I lay on my side, facing her, brushing my hand across her forehead and into her hair. We stayed that way, silent, for maybe five minutes.

"Just what you always wanted after moving from your rock star life in L.A. To get mixed up with some chick who has cancer, a child, and a mountain of baggage. If they ever do a *Where Are They Now* segment about your TV show, you're going to look like a sap."

I wanted to laugh, play along, say something witty, as was my nature, but I didn't have it.

"If they *do* end up airing a show like that, can you at least tell them that I looked great in a pair of jeans up until the end? I really worked hard on myself in the last few years. Nobody tells you that when you have a kid your body is going to wage a civil war on itself," she said.

"The only thing I'm going to say today, tomorrow, or when-the-fuck-ever about you is that you're the only human being I can possibly imagine spending every day with without interruption," I told her.

"You haven't spent enough days to make that determination, and my guess is that had you, you too would be singing the praises of my ass versus my companionship."

"Whatever, Mayes, but I'm not going to be doom and gloom right now. I'm here with you right now. I'm happy *now*."

She recognized my discomfort and gave me a look of empathetic resignation.

"Want me to get one of those sandwiches for you? Anything else?" I asked her.

She didn't answer but instead rolled her body toward and on top of mine, kissing my mouth. Her hands ran up over my shoulders and onto the sides of my head as I felt her hips push down into mine. She cradled my head with her forearms, sliding her mouth across my neck, kissing it tenderly as her breathing intensified. I almost rolled her over and positioned myself on top, but I let her have her way, exploring my neck and face with her lips. A minute or two later, she pushed her hands up underneath my shirt, massaging and stroking my chest and stomach before letting her hands slide down to my jeans and unbuttoning them. My heart surged, and my arousal peaked as Laurel pulled off her top before reaching down for my jeans again, this time pulling them down and tossing them to the floor. She paused, her doe-like eyes finding mine in the dimly lit room that dusk had just crept out of. In that look we said all that needed to be said before making love the rest of the night.

I don't need, nor would I want, to describe every detail of what transpired in our room. Most of my life, sex in motel rooms, or any room, has been a torrid, haphazard, furious, sloppy, meaningless collision of two (or more) bodies, but not this night. This night was a harmonious union more perfect than any chess game, more beautiful than any song. Feel free to paint whatever picture you like, and as a kindness to Laurel, imagine her backside even better than you think it is. She deserves that, and it's true.

Other than that, mind your business. But imagine it was really hot.

CHAPTER 23

- -

"**D**id you sleep well?"

"More soundly than I recall in a long time, thank you," she replied, kissing me on the cheek.

"Good, and I hope I wasn't snoring too much? This damn deviated septum sometimes makes fireworks."

"I was out like a light. Didn't hear a thing."

"Well, I did take you through a set of acrobatics that would have tuckered out a cheerleading team."

"I won't argue that."

I smiled, kissed her back on the cheek, hopped out of bed and headed for the bathroom.

"Josh," she said, turning me around. "Last night was beautiful. I wish I had a more descriptive or original word for it, but that's all I've got." Her eyes were misty, wide, and alluring as ever. My knees wobbled.

"*You* are beautiful, last night was...nirvana."

"Can it be Pearl Jam instead? Always liked them better."

"I'm going to pretend you didn't say that, and in no way will I let it detract from the hypnotic afterglow I find myself in right now."

"How are you going to pee with that thing?" she asked, tilting her head towards my morning stiffy standing inside my boxers.

You wouldn't have to be Nostradamus to figure out what happened next, and once again, I'm not going to Harlequin Romance this up for you here. Just picture two incredibly sexy people doing things you wish you were nimble and adventurous enough to do, and you'll probably get it half right.

****

The ride back to Vermont was to be expected, I suppose. The emotional intensity of the previous night and morning had vanquished all our reserves. Neither of us had the energy, nor the desire, to chat. At least, that's what I'd like to pretend. In truth, it was more likely a result of two people facing something they had no idea how to handle, being terrified of what was next, and still not knowing one another well enough to find the right words, if there were any.

I wanted to pull the car over at least a dozen times, let my head fall in Laurel's lap, sob like a child, and let the comfort of her hands stroke my skin until I felt calm again. I wanted to tell her I loved her and that whether I had an hour, a day, or a lifetime left with her, that I didn't want to be away from her for a moment. I wanted to ask her to be my wife, to tell her the cancer didn't matter, that we could beat anything together, and that her fears were unfounded. I wanted to make love to her in one of the rolling fields we passed on the way back. Lay a blanket out there, let the chirpers play and the breezes trickle by as we kissed and writhed and touched for hours, oblivious to broken bodies and responsibilities. I wanted to scream out the window at the universe for the giant fuck you it was giving me with this love affair with another dying woman that was better than me.

Mostly, I wanted a drink.

"Did you want to stop for a snack or anything?" I asked her.

She smiled and just shook her head before reaching her hand over, placing it on mine as it rested on the Porsche's shift lever.

That little gesture almost had me crying again, but I wanted to remain as strong as I could for her because, well, honestly, I don't even know why. They always say, "You have to be strong for them," in these situations, but why, exactly? And who the hell said I was strong anyway? This woman that wiggled her way into my heart almost overnight was dying, and the idea of not seeing her for ten minutes, never mind a lifetime, was terrifying, and I was supposed to stay strong? Get the hell out of here.

The miles clicked over in chunks of ten, with the Porsche gobbling up the asphalt happily. When we approached central Vermont, my streaming playlist that was at whisper level for the last couple hours played "Goodbye, Dear Friend" by the band Deer Tick. Laurel wasn't familiar with the song, at least as far as I was aware—and her mind appeared to be elsewhere—so I let it play, which was a mistake. One of those sneaky tears that always finds a way to leak out when you're trying to choke back emotion, jumped from my eye and rolled down my right cheek. Laurel saw it, I'm sure, halfway through the song, but said nothing. I'm glad she let it go because, at that moment, I wasn't prepared to open the floodgates and deal with the onslaught. Too fragile. Too sober.

"I was wondering if I could drop you at your place, help you in with your stuff, and then you could keep an eye on Pickle for another couple hours while I run into town?" I asked Laurel, approaching our road.

"Oh, sure, that's fine, but I think the text I got a little while ago said my mother and Ethan took him to the park, so he may not be there anyway. Do you want me to go with you? We can just stop now if you want?"

"No, no, it's alright. Just a couple quick things I need to pick up. You must be tired after all this, so probably wouldn't hurt to rest for a bit. Is there anything I can get for you while I'm out, or did you want me to stay with you until they get back?"

Laurel stretched her arms up over her head, hitting the roof of the car, and then squeaking the way some do when they stretch. From many others, that would have been annoying, but when she did it, I wanted to cry. "I think you're right about the nap, and yeah, I'll be fine until they come back. When am I going to see you again?"

"Should be in a couple hours, when I grab Pick, and then, you know, whenever you want, and always."

She turned in her seat and faced me when I pulled into her driveway and put the car in park.

"I know this has been a lot, Josh. This was supposed to be about dealing with things from your past, and about you, and then it became about me and I'm sorry for that. I don't know—"

"Laurel," I interrupted. "Come on. You don't need to apologize for letting me into your life, ever. And I'm so happy I took you with me to Connecticut. Truly. I don't want to let sadness be what resonates here, though I know what lies ahead, and I'm not avoiding it."

"I almost believe you," she said.

I stuck my tongue out. She snickered.

"I'll check in when I make my way back home. Call me if you need anything. Anything at all," I said.

"Thanks for bringing me along, Josh. I still want to hear what happened at Sasha's dad's place, so don't think I'm going to forget," she replied, wiggling her finger at me. Not in the horrifying manner her mother did, but disturbing still.

"There's lots to talk about, I know. Let me grab your bag and bring it in for—"

"It's one tiny bag, Babe. I got it," she interjected, pulling it from the pseudo back seat of the 911. "I have cancer, but so far, all my muscles still work." She flexed her arm as she stood next to the car, holding the bag with the other, smiling. That wrecked me.

"I'll call you in a little bit," I told her before mouthing a kiss.

"See you soon, and drive safely," she yelled over the engine as I pulled out of the driveway.

I straightened the car out onto the road, clicked it into first gear, and drove off, watching Laurel wave in the side mirror. I stuck my hand up through the open sunroof and gave her the peace sign, holding it for the duration of the street and until I took a left onto the main road.

****

One of the benefits of living in Podunkville, USA, is that there's only a few bars in the area and it's unlikely anyone will know you if you show up. I'd passed this place—Woody's—several times when I took the longer route back to my place, choosing to carve up more enticing roads instead of the straight shot home. It was as okey doke as a place got, with a crappy green, weather-worn, hand-carved wooden sign drooping off the front of the building and a couple neon signs that were barely lit, advertising beer that hadn't been popular since the Vietnam War.

I parked my car against the side of the building, behind a dumpster, because even though the place wasn't on the main road and I didn't know many people in town, a car like mine stuck out like a tuba in a bathtub. I didn't need any of the ten or twelve people I did know stopping by to chat about the fucking weather or what it was like to be on TV. I scanned the landscape and didn't see anyone coming except a kid on a bicycle a few hundred yards away, so I locked the car and popped inside.

The décor didn't deviate from what I'd expected, though it was cleaner than I imagined. The walls were adorned with more

204

of the classic beer and liquor brands, a few *Life Magazine* covers, and newspaper clippings. Behind the bar hung a pump action shotgun and a massive machete, biggest I'd ever seen, which was either for killing Brontosauruses or chopping down redwoods. The fella behind the bar watched me come in, dropped his rag at his end of the bar, and left his conversation companion to head my way. Like most of the dudes working in bars like this that I'd been in, he was a goddamn giant. He was wearing one of the denim button-up, long sleeve shirts that had somehow survived the nineties, the ends rolled up so that his tattoos were visible. His face was alcohol and smoke worn, rugged, and I'd venture a guess he was missing a tooth or two. The hair was almost military-cut short, the dirty blond strands receding at a good clip.

"What brings you in?" he asked, letting his monstrous hands and forearms hit the bar in front of me with a thud.

"It's not for the clam chowder, my friend," I answered, which inspired no smirk or chuckle, but instead a dead-eyed stare that would terrify a Komodo dragon.

"Sorry. I'm just here for some whiskey. Dealer's choice. I'll trust you," I told him.

He turned around and grabbed a bottle of Johnny Walker Red, probably my last choice if I had a say, but I wasn't about to tell Ivan Drago I didn't approve of his selection. I was fond of my head being attached to my neck.

"Thank you. Can I start a tab, or do you want me to pay as I go?" I asked.

"I'll leave the bottle. Pay when you go," he answered before marching back down to the other end of the bar to his conversation companion, who looked like Burgess Meredith in the *Grumpy Old Men* movies. He wore too big and warm a coat for summer and oversized, black-rimmed glasses. I raised my glass and nodded toward them but got no response. I suppose if your goal is to get shitty, it's preferable to be ignored and anonymous.

Before you start judging, which wouldn't be unfair—no, I wasn't planning on driving home. I've stumbled out of a lot of bars, some far more horrible than this place, and staggered home on foot for three or four miles. This was probably seven or eight, so it would end up a personal record, but it was a gorgeous day outside.

I missed Laurel and my ridiculous dog. Checking in on them before the afterburners kicked in probably made sense, but—

The bell above the door, one I hadn't noticed when I walked in, chimed, and like every other human on earth, I had the Pavlovian reaction to move my eyes to the sound and see who'd walked in, right when I'd pulled the glass to my lips.

"Hi, Mister Josh," the voice said, and although I couldn't make out his face with the sun blazing in behind him, I knew it was Timmy from the hardware store.

"Hey there, kid. What, uh...?" I mumbled, genuinely shocked.

"I was riding my bike to the store, and when I rode past, I saw your car and knew it was you. Nobody else has a car like that around here. But you parked it near the garbage, which probably will make it smell bad. You should move it I think," he answered.

"I hadn't thought of that, buddy. Thank you," I told him. He hopped up on the seat next to me, prompting the hulking proprietor to come down to us as I placed my drink back on the bar.

"What are you doing in here, Tim? You know your uncle wouldn't want you in here," the bartender said.

"I was just visiting Mister Josh. I like his car," he told him.

"Why don't you get on down to the store. I'll call Dan and tell him you're on your way," Drago said.

See, this is where a smarter man might ignore what was going on and leave the situation alone. Acknowledge that he may not have all the information needed to make the most reasonable decision or take responsible actions. I'm not that man.

"You're headed to work, you say, Tim?" I asked him.

"Yeah. I left my bike out front," he replied.

"Anyone ever try to steal your bike?"

"I don't think so."

"Why the hell are you asking him that?" the hulking bartender asked.

"Tim, what say we pull that bike behind the building here, and I'll come back and get it for you later, drop it off at the store. This way I can give you a ride in my car. Sound good?" I asked him.

"In your car, the one out back?" he asked, visibly excited.

"The Porsche, yes. I'll take you to work, and we can get your bike later," I told him.

Timmy jumped up and hollered before running out the front door, the bell ringing and dinging wildly when the door shoved open.

"Hey, how do you know him, and why the fuck are you taking him in your car? He rides the bike to work and if—"

"Here's what's going to happen, okay?" I interjected. "I'm going to leave this twenty-dollar bill on the bar to pay for the one shot of whiskey I never drank, meaning I'm not impaired, and then I'm going to take Tim to work in my car because he's told me several times he likes it. It's as simple as that, and if you want to call out the National Guard or summon your buddy from his stupor at the end of the bar or come around and try to pound me into the floor, so be it, but Tim is going for that ride. I'll be back to get his bike for him later."

His eyes tightened up, and I could hear his teeth grinding, but instead of reaching across the bar and grabbing me by the throat, he picked up the bottle of whiskey and my twenty dollars and walked back over to his elderly pal.

I stood up, said thank you, and went out after Timmy.

CHAPTER 24

I rolled down the passenger side window as soon as Timmy got in the car and cracked my own as well to avoid the inevitable ear destruction caused from single-open-window Helmholtz resonance. He was leaning out, letting the breeze gush across his face, intermittently yelling and cheering, as I zoomed down the backroads of Vermont. There was no pleasure, no sensation or experience I'd ever had that brought the visceral joy that Timmy was experiencing.

He was buckled in, but the stretch coming up was all switchbacks and elevation changes, so I told him to hang tight onto the top of the door. I think he heard me, but he was in acceleration-palooza and not listening to my bullshit. I downshifted entering the first decelerating radius turn, and then hammered the gas on the way out before backing down again for the next. Timmy was glued to the door, yelling to go faster, so I stabbed the throttle for the small stretch before the next bend. We weaved in and out of the turns at a healthy clip until coming out to the final straight, which lasted about a mile and half before I'd have to turn left and head back toward the hardware store on Main Street. As the road straightened, I jabbed the accelerator and let the revs build, eventually upshifting into fourth gear and letting it ride out to redline down the stretch. Timmy was roaring out the window, fearless and free, forgetting any other mode of transportation existed. It was Porsche or nothing for this guy in that moment.

At the end of the straight, I tipped back on the gas and nudged the brakes. Tim was fixed in his position, though the gleeful, exuberant howls had stopped, likely sensing the end was near. I stopped at the cross street, looked both ways, and then turned left for Main Street.

"I wish I didn't go to work today, Mister Josh," he yelled to me from outside the window still.

"I know, buddy. I could do this all day," I told him.

As I turned on Main, I could see Tim's uncle standing outside the store, which wasn't unexpected. I assumed the bartender would call him. *"Some fucking D-bag with a Porsche just kidnapped your nephew!"*

Tim unbuckled his seat belt when we pulled up to the curb. When he saw his uncle, he exited the car and yelled, "Mister Josh took me for a ride in his race car, and we went fast up and down the hills!"

"That's great, Tim. Now why don't you get on inside. You can tell me more about it when I come in," his uncle said. Timmy's enthusiasm wasn't swayed by Dan Toggins's indifference, pumping his fist into the air on the way into the store.

"I don't know who you think you are, asshole, but if I find out you take my nephew for a ride in this thing, or what the hell ever again, you and I are going to have business. And it won't be pretty, understand? This particular business here ain't over either," he said, leaning down into the passenger's side window.

"We've already met, so you know who I am." I quipped back. "But today, all I am is a guy that gave a sweet kid a ride in a car so he could smile from ear to ear for ten minutes. His smile and joy kept me from drinking, so that's pretty cool. Anything more than that is just something you're inventing, though I mean no disrespect. I will go grab his bike and get it back here—"

"There's no need," he interrupted, slamming his hand down onto the top of my car door windowsill. "Jack from the bar is bringing it by. And if I find out you were driving my nephew around hammered, our business will continue today because I'll come find you."

Here's where I do something stupid, yet again.

I shut the car off, leaving the key in the ignition, and walked around to where he stood, stopping about two and a half feet from him.

"Look, I know this is a small town, and everybody knows everybody. I'm the asshole interloper with expensive cars, apparently here only to shake up the serenity of this normally tranquil place, but that's a bunch of shit. Everyone I've met here so far is just as fucked up as me, no offense—well, maybe not quite as much, but close—anyway, I'm not here to cause problems. I wasn't drunk when I took your nephew for a ride. You have my word. If you feel like you need to kick my ass, so be it. I'll even let you have a free go at me because I took Tim on a ride without clearing it with you first. But—and I say this with absolutely certainty and conviction—I'll probably take him on another ride sometime. Because the dude was happy as hell, and that's something beautiful to watch. I wish I could be half as happy, about anything, as he was on that damn ride."

He stared at me, his left eye twitching, teeth clenched. I'm sure if I broke eye contact and looked down at his fists, they'd be balled up like boney sacks of flour ready to pound on me the moment I leaned closer, but I didn't flinch. Neither did he. Both he and that bartender had to be suffering from hemorrhoids. So much rage.

"Move that car so someone can park there. It's for customers," he said before breaking our standoff and heading into the store. I'd call it a stalemate, but in that situation, both sides have put themselves in an unwinnable position. In this case, he broke away and effectively resigned. I can't call it a checkmate, but I wouldn't concede it was a draw either. Yes, I know I sound like a petulant child, but at this point, that should come as no shocker.

I clicked the car into first gear and drove home, eager to see Laurel and Pickle, surprised and relieved to be sober.

****

When I pulled into Laurel's driveway, Ethan was rolling on the front lawn with my dog going bananas trying to lick his face as he tumbled to and fro. Laurel was sitting on the front steps, her flowery summer dress fluttering around her calves in the breeze, per usual, and her arms between her legs, hair in a ponytail.

Pickle shot up when he saw the car and started barking in explosive, gurgling bursts before blasting off toward me. Laurel smiled and waved. Ethan stood and put himself back together, the Pickle lawn romp leaving his shirt untucked and hair sticking out in every direction.

"There's my little buddy," I said, cupping Pickle's tiny head in my hands when he jumped up on my thigh, sitting in the car with the door open. He frantically licked my hands before hoisting himself up and into my lap, then placed his front feet on my chest and slobbered my face with ten trillion kisses, his curly tail wiggling in frantic, non-concentric circles. "I wasn't gone *that* long, buddy. Holy smokes."

"Probably seemed like a year to the poor little guy," Laurel said, approaching the car. She looked tired, though more beautiful than ever, with the summer sun fortifying the vibrant life in her eyes.

"Kinda feels like it's been a year since I've seen you," I told her, trying to be in the ballpark of romantic, but it just sounded dumb when it came out. She tilted her head and smiled though, acknowledging my feeble attempt.

"I didn't expect to see you back here so soon. Thought you had things you needed to do?" she asked, Ethan sliding up next to her.

"Well, you know, what I thought I needed to do turned out to not be so important and—hey squirt, how are you?" I answered, addressing Ethan. "I hear you and Pickle had a blast. You know he talks to me in this weird pug language that only I can decipher. He told me he had such a great time with you and can't wait to come back."

Ethan looked up at his mother, and she widened her eyes and let her mouth fall open.

"I hear you went to a park. That's always fun right? Plus, I saw you wrestling out here, which looked like a blast. You do anything else?" I asked him.

"Won't Pickle tell you?" he questioned.

Laurel and I locked eyes, exchanging a telepathic *awwww* while smirking. "You know, he probably will, but how about you first." I said.

"He likes to eat," Ethan shouted, before petting Pickle's back while he sat in my lap. "We played outside, and he chased me around and went after the frisbee I was throwing a lot, but he mostly wanted treats."

"Yeah, this little fatty does like to eat. Such a tiny thing, I don't know where he stuffs it all," I said, looking under Pickle, which made Ethan chuckle. "Was your grandmother okay with him being here?"

He looked at the ground. "She doesn't really like doggies, but I think Pickle made her like them maybe a little bit. She was laughing at him a couple times, and she didn't spank him when he chewed her slipper."

I could see Laurel's face scrunch up as she heard Ethan casually mention Slippergate.

"He did whaaat?" I asked, adding a cartoonish exuberance to the last word.

"He didn't chew them up, honey, he...well, he sorta did I suppose, but it was just one, and they're still wearable," Laurel explained, fighting laughter while rubbing the top of Ethan's shoulder.

"Pickle, you little slipper gobbler," I said to the oblivious dog who was enjoying my cranium massage.. "I won't be able to leave you with these nice people again if you're going to be a bad guest."

"Those were Grammy's old slippers. She has lots of pairs," Ethan said.

"Pickle is always welcome here, Josh. He's a sweetie," Laurel declared, stroking the back of his neck, which prompted a quick lick of her hand.

"Alright, before this furry nut turns into a pile of mush from all the affection, I better get him home and settled in. Any idea the last time—"

"He went pee pee a lot today, and, in the morning, he pooped near the trees in our yard," Ethan announced.

"Precisely the answer I was looking for, my friend," I replied, mussing Ethan's hair, because what else do you do to a little kid when they say something cute?

"Am I going to see you later?" Laurel asked.

"Absolutely," I told her, followed by what had to be the most genuine smile that's ever crossed my lips.

Her reaction was tepid, and I ascertained that was because in the distance a rumbling, snorting American automobile was approaching the house.

Fucking Barry.

"Ethan, go inside," she told him.

"Why?" he questioned.

"Just go inside," she shouted, and he complied.

I rolled the window up halfway for Pickle and then got out of the car before shutting the door with him still inside.

"Please let me deal with this and don't get into anything, Josh. I can't handle a big dustup right now," Laurel pleaded.

"Yeah, it'll be fine. Any idea why he's here?"

"Not a clue."

Barry pulled into the end of the driveway, a Vermont State Trooper car right behind him, parking against the curb.

"What is this shit?" I asked no one specific.

Laurel grabbed my arm, holding me back when I tried to walk down the driveway towards Barry, who'd just exited the car.

"Maybe in Los Angeles you can assault people and get away with it, but up here we don't tolerate that, assh-ole," Barry yelled, leaning against his car. The trooper got out and walked over toward him without any urgency.

"Barry, what the hell are you doing?" Laurel snapped. "And you, Jason?"

"Hey, Laurel. I'm sorry to put you out," the officer answered, removing his hat, "but I'm going to have to take your friend here in. Barry says he attacked him, showed me some bruises."

"Oh, give me a break, Jay. Even you must know that's bullshit. Barry, what are you trying to do?" Laurel yelled. Her mother stepped out on to the porch with Ethan tucked behind her leg. "Mom, is this you're doing?"

Her mother said nothing, just stood there, watching things unfold.

"If you want to have this asshole in your life, I can't stop you, but I'm not going to let him get away with attacking me unprovoked," Barry said, the smell of distilled spirits barreling out of his mouth and washing over my face.

"Unprovoked? Are you kidding me? Why you little shit," Laurel said before charging at Barry. The trooper and I reeled her in, but that turned me on if I'm being honest. Not the cop with his hands on her, I'm not a freak, but her passionate defense of me and the truth wrapped in retaliatory rage.

"Officer, no disrespect here, but you do know that Barry is hammered, right?" I asked.

"He's alright," he replied, releasing Laurel and standing directly in front of me. "You are Joshua Traxon, correct? Reside across the street there?"

"Yup."

"Okay, well then I'm going to have to bring you in. Mr. Blevins informed me that you attacked him and showed evidence to support that claim, so I'll need to take you in after Mirandiz—."

"Jay, this is ridiculous, come on. Josh was defending me after your blockhead cousin here put his hands on me, and I know you're not dumb enough to think otherwise," Laurel yelled while I kept her tight against me. "And you're going to let him drive up here drunk, where my little boy plays in the street? What the hell's wrong with you?"

"He may have taken a poke at something before he pulled in, but he was fine when we left. I'm sorry to roll in here like this, mess up your day and all, but I'm going to need to take Mr. Traxon with me."

"This is bull—"

"It's okay, Laurel. Let him do his job. This will all get sorted out. I'll leave my keys here, and my phone is on the seat in the car. If you could toss Pickle in my place and then call my lawyer—name is in the contacts under Lawyer Dave—see if he may have a referral for a criminal attorney up this way. If not, try my accountant, as he seems to know everyone around here. I'm sure I'll be out soon enough," I said, interrupting Laurel before she got too excited. She had enough garbage to deal with, never mind this convoluted, pathetic Barry revenge. I thought in the beginning he might be the Boris Spassky to my Bobby Fischer but turns out he's just a pre-teen nerd using a chess cheat program.

"Jason, come on, seriously with this? What if I want to press charges, right now, for Barry attacking me? In fact, I do. Put him in cuffs because he absolutely assaulted me," Laurel said, pointing at Barry vigorously.

"I'm sorry Laurel, I can't. Plus, it wasn't just Barry that witnessed this," he said, his tone falling to a whisper. Laurel's face reddened, and her head shot around toward the porch. Her mother slipped into the house when Laurel made eye contact.

"Unfuckingbelievable. I have too much going on right now for this!" Laurel exclaimed.

"I'll go with you, no argument. Just give me a second?" I asked the officer, and he nodded.

"Hey, this is nothing. Call my lawyer if you would, and I'll be back soon. Don't let it get you all worked up. He's not worth it. Think about...you know what to think about," I said, kissing her forehead and then turning around and offering my wrists to the officer.

"I don't think that will be necessary," he said, instead putting his hand on my back and guiding me down to the car. "Barry, get in the car, and drive on out of here. Go back home, and I swear if I see you swerving even a few inches, I'll haul your ass in too, and the two of you can share a cell and have a cage match for all I care."

"You should put the cuffs on him, he's likely to—"

"Get in the car, Barry, and don't drive like an a moron," his cousin interrupted. Barry complied.

"I'll see you soon, Laurel. Don't rip into your mom, either. You don't need the stress, and we always knew she was in Camp Barry anyway. I'll win her over by sending nudes, not with my personality."

That got the corner of her lip raised, but she was still fired up, understandably.

"Sorry, Pick. I'll be back soon, buddy," I told him as he stared at me with his tongue flapping out of his mouth, paws on the half rolled up car window.

"I'll take care of him, and I'll call that lawyer. I...I love you, Josh."

I mouthed it back to her, not out of embarrassment, but to avoid confusion for Ethan if he was listening, though I'm sure he was plenty confused already. I got into the back of the police car, right as the obligatory hand on the top of the head eased me downward to avoid wailing into the door frame. Barry rolled his car out and drove away slowly with his cop cousin watching for thirty seconds before getting in and taking me *downtown*.

CHAPTER 25

I 'd been in a jail cell before. More than once, less than five. In each previous incidence, the cell itself was rather large and packed other unsavory characters in there with me. In this case, however, the cell was no bigger than a large bathroom and the only other guests were a few ground beetles scurrying across the floor. They looked like tiny, armored black station wagons zooming across the cement, following unseen roads on a journey only they were certain about, but determined to get there. Ants tend to move in jagged, zig zag patterns, affected by any nuance, like air currents, scent, or vibration. Where beetles, once mobile, just put it into top gear and motor on undistracted.

The cell was nicer than I'd have imagined. The mattress on the steel slab was about five inches thick. There was an actual pillow, not just some strip of foam padding covered in fabric. The sink was stainless steel, looked borderline immaculate, and the toilet had a sulfur stench to it speckled with only a spattering of yellow and brown stains, probably all from Barry.

Obviously, speaking of that dum-dum, the dude was pissed that some Hollywood asswipe came in and stole his woman. I got that. However, there's a code out on the street, and on the chess board: when you know you're beat, you lay down your crown. You don't scramble around like a buffoon pulling useless moves out of your ass just to stay connected to a game you've already lost. Align your pieces, put up a fight, execute your plan—absolutely. But when your queen is gone and that knight has you pinned, you lay down your sword, man. It's bad juju otherwise, and I don't even believe in juju.

Part of me wanted to find Barry the moment I got out of the oddly charming prison and throttle him for robbing me of even five minutes with Laurel, while the other felt sorry for him that he had to go down this pathetic road at all. He wasn't the monster that Sasha's father was, that I could tell. He was, from all indications, a drunk like me, yet without as much common sense and not an iota of charisma. Laurel's mom got warm in the shorts for him, though, so maybe I'd missed something. Probably had a tool belt. It's always the damn tool belt.

In the distance, I heard chatter on a telephone before the receiver smacked down into the cradle. Then footsteps approached. I figured there was at least a ten percent chance I would die there. Barry and all his hillbilly relatives could be let in by his cop cousin who'd turn his back and chew on some deer jerky while they took turns beating the piss out of me with soap wrapped in old socks. You may be smirking, but you know it's not that far-fetched.

"I'm waiting for a call back from Judge Patterson, but looks like I'll be able to let you go inside an hour," Officer Jason told me. His badge, which I'd missed before, said "Sanborn," so I assumed that was his last name. He was a couple inches shorter than me, in solid shape but no hard ass. A square, tight jawline and dark brown hair that I saw only now, being the first time he'd had his hat off.

"Am I being charged with anything? Have to go to court?" I asked, walking up to the bars that separated us.

"I think Barry has decided to drop this. Judge Patterson is annoyed I called him in the first place, but he's annoyed by most things."

"So, the judge got him to drop the charges then?"

"No, it wasn't him, but he may have given Barry a rash of shit if he hadn't decided to anyway."

"I can't imagine he just up and had a change of heart, though. The guy has been gunning for me from the day I rolled into town."

Officer Sanborn pulled a plastic and metal chair, like the kind you have in grade school, up underneath himself and sat down, facing me in the cell. "Well, he's sobered up, so that's part of it, I suspect."

"I guess, but something tells me that I'm going to see him back at Laurel's place before long, and now is really not a great time to be dealing—"

"I'll make sure Barry doesn't trouble you folks anymore. Now that I've met you, had a chance to size you up and all, I can see that his concerns were misguided," Officer Sanborn interrupted.

"Concerns?" I prodded.

Sanborn pulled a stick of gum from his front shirt pocket and pulled the silver wrapper down before biting half of it off and chewing it. He folded the wrapper down around the remaining piece and tucked it back into the pocket. That was a new one. Had me fidgeting for my cashews, but my pockets were emptied, I recalled.

"Barry had an old man that, in addition to kicking the crap out of him daily, had a habit of muscling in on his girlfriends from as early as I can remember, grade school even. Didn't matter if they were young, old, skinny, fat or whatever—if Barry had his eye on them, his old man was going to creep up all over 'em. My uncle, his father, was an absolute behemoth too, so if you're wondering why he didn't do something, well, would have needed three Barrys."

I nodded before wrapping my forearms through the bars and leaning into them. "Fair enough—and I'm familiar with shithead fathers—but aren't we all grown-ups now? At some point, don't we have to leave the past and the wreckage of our messed up, tumultuous childhoods and move on? Stop being victimized by it and using as an excuse to commit our own ugly behavior?"

Officer Sanborn stood up, which startled me somewhat, though he hadn't made an aggressive move. He approached the cell, and then pulled that other half of the gum out of his pocket and slid it into his mouth before speaking. "A guy like you—wealthy, not trying to hide it—and a celebrity of sorts, rolls up into town out of nowhere and moves in across the street from the woman you're seeing. Right away you catch her looking too long, talking too often, and noticeably mesmerized by this fella. He's good looking, he's got money, the cars, the charm, oh, and by the way, her kid likes him more than you just to crank the clamp down tighter on your pecker. How's that going to sit with you?"

I loved that he said, "celebrity of sorts." Perfect. I also wanted to thank him for telling me I was good looking, but it seemed outside the spirt of what he was trying to say. Was fond of his use of "pecker" as well. It's an all-time classic.

"I hear you. It's a perspective I lose sometimes, the fame thing, and how it makes others feel, but honestly, it's all bullshit. I'm not *that* famous. I mean, seriously, had you ever heard of me before Barry or whoever told you?" I asked.

He turned around laughing, sliding the little chair back against the wall and then leaning against the concrete doorway threshold. "Whatever you were doing with that potholder, that screwy dance, and the tune you were mumbling...that whole situation made you a goddamn legend with just about everyone I know. Certainly, up in this area, where reality TV is almost as revered as Sunday Pot-Lucks."

"The fucking potholder. It's never the music, never the band anymore. It's always the goofy show and my drunken stupidity."

"You were in a band?"

My eyes shot over at his, but I caught him grinning. What an insufferable douche cannon to be that surprised and bothered that he might not know I was *also* a rock star in addition to my television legacy.

"Funny. Why should I expect that you'd know though, right? I wasn't in Zeppelin or Aerosmith or even The Killers for God's sake. Maybe you should leave me in here another day or so, humble me out a bit."

"Somehow I don't think that would do it."

I laughed out loud. Like, for reals.

"I think I follow you on Twitter, though I don't log on there much. Started an account a few years back 'cause everyone was, but not much more than political garbage and porn from what I can see."

"Ugh, yeah, don't get me started on social media. It's a necessary evil when you're in that world, but it's a dumpster fire."

"How many followers you got?"

I'm not going to lie; I did get a few tummy butterflies before I answered him. That makes me sort of horrible, I know, especially with everything that's going on.

"Last time I checked it was about eight hundred thousand. Most of those are from the stupid TV show though, and not the rock and roll, sadly. What are you into for music?"

"More of a punk rock fan, but don't take it personally. I've heard of your band though," Office Sanborn assured me.

"We had a few solid tunes, some that cranked and shrieked a bit, but The Ramones we were not. Nor Husker Du or Black Flag. Ever see any of them live?"

"Never had the chance, no," Officer Sanborn answered as a phone started ringing down the hall. "Probably the judge. Be right back."

I nodded before untangling myself from the cold steel bars and sitting on the even frostier metal bed. I thought of Laurel at home with Ethan and her mother, dealing with this unnecessary garbage on top of her health. I didn't feel much like drinking in case you're wondering. I knew I may later, but not right that second. The only thing I wanted to do was see that ridiculous little dog and have Laurel's hand in my own while we listened to the summer critters in my back yard. I'd trade my fame, the cars, and that big check the nerd accountant gave me for another thirty years or more of that scenario. I would have traded half of it for a Moon Pie or a Ho Ho right then too, as I'd suddenly realized I was either hypoglycemic or had forgotten to eat for a few days. Before I went into insulin shock, Jason the cop made his way back into the room where I was jailed, carrying a comically huge key ring.

"Are you shitting me with that thing? I thought they only had those sorts of keys in the Old West?" I observed.

"This?" he asked, jingling the massive O-Ring in front of me. "This has been here longer than any of us. Might have been made by the same folks who built this place in 1912. Only four keys on here open any of the doors inside this whole building, though. The rest have just always been attached."

The tumbler fell over, and the door clicked open. He slid the bars to his left and motioned for me to come out.

"Well, that giant metal donut with six hundred keys is the best-looking thing I've seen all year, besides Laurel of course." I declared.

He tossed the key ring onto the little chair, which clanked in rebellion, and its screams reverberated off the cement walls of the tiny room.

"Knew that was going to happen. Sorry," Office Sanborn said.

"You let me out. I think deafness is a fair trade. So, am I *out* out, or what's happening?"

"That should be it. Barry, in his own meat-headed way, isn't handling Miss Mayes's illness very well, so he makes bad choices. I know he probably doesn't deserve it, but, if you could be a little easy on him after all this, I'm reasonably sure you won't have trouble with him again."

Fuck.

"I wasn't sure he knew she was sick. Feel like sort of a dick if that's the case."

"No need to. We all handle grief in our own way, but that's no excuse for bad behavior. I just need you to sign a couple forms, and then I can get your stuff back and hustle you back home. So, what kind of a name is Traxon anyway?"

I chortled. "The kind of name an asshole gives himself so he can stick it to his old man even after he's in the grave, I guess."

Officer Sanborn smirked and nodded.

"Sorry for all the hassle and BS. Small towns, you know?"

I did know, yeah. But I still loved small towns.

CHAPTER 26

When you've lived the life I have, or even if you haven't and you're just an idiot, you make decisions that you know the moment you make them, you'll regret horribly. The beauty of a guy like me, though, is that I can liquify my bad choices after they're complete. Okay, that's a poor example of beauty, sure, but it doesn't make it any less true. Problem is, eventually the liquid dries up, and you're left a terrifying and coherent world to navigate where the only way to escape is...more liquid. It's a hell of a life management system.

I had no plans on drinking my way out this current awful decision, though I allowed for the possibility of amending that plan later as I walked up to Barry's house a half mile from the town center. While Officer Sanborn was kindly handing me the contents of my pockets before releasing me, I managed to get a peek at one of the forms on his desk and discerned an address for Barry. The only reason I knew it was close to town and how to get there was because it was on the adjacent corner to the boutique where I get Pickle's food, based on the number and street. The sign out front was hand painted and had a cartoon bulldog on it that was utterly ridiculous, and I would shop there even if they only accepted rolled coins.

I had Officer Jay drop me near the market. I walked from there, careful to avoid the hardware store and another run in with Toggins, who'd surely find out about my incarceration before sunset, along with the rest of the town. I'd called Laurel and let her know I was out, but it went to voicemail, so I told her I would stop by soon to check on her and rendezvous with my strange little dog. I desperately needed a shower to wash away the sweat and grime that had taken residence on top of the sweat and grime that had petrified days earlier, but I assumed Barry's biggest complaint wouldn't be that I smelled poorly. He was just exiting his front door and walking onto his front porch, littered with a greatest hits of beer bottles and containers, as I crossed the street and made eye contact.

"What the hell do you want? I told Jason I wasn't pressing charges, but if you think you're going to come here and stir up some shit, I'll get my licks in. You'll be back in there inside an hour," Barry said from the porch.

I kept walking, and when I reached the sidewalk, he took a step back and put his hand on the doorknob.

"I'm not here to cause trouble, Barry, I promise. I was hoping to talk is all. We can do it out here if you feel more comfortable," I told him.

"I'm not scared of you, asshole. But if you're looking for a fight, I'm gonna do it where there's witnesses," he yelled back at me, stopped on the sidewalk.

"I smell like a week-old hockey bag left in the car on the equator. You *should* be scared, but like I said, I'm not here to brawl."

Barry took his hand off the doorknob but kept a watchful eye on me as I reached into my front pocket and pulled the bag of cashews out. They'd been thoroughly seasoned by the heat, sweat, and time, so I was sure they'd be a treat.

"Cashew? I love these 'lil fuckers," I said.

"What do you want? My cousin said I need to stay away from you. I suspect that goes the other way too. So, state your business and get a move on," Barry answered.

"Can I sit here on the steps?"

"As long as you tell me why you're here."

"And you really don't want any cashews? They're a delicious snack. Very underrated."

He ignored me, so I sat down and chewed up the last of the four nuts I'd tossed in my mouth before tucking the red and blue wrapper into a *Natural Light* box to my left on the porch.

"Laurel isn't well. I understand you're aware of that fact, and I'd like to know what you want to do about it."

Barry shuffled behind me. For an instant I almost expected the heel of a steel-toed boot to slam into one of my kidneys, but he stepped down onto the street and faced me instead, folding his arms across his hunter green, oil-stained T-shirt.

"*Do* about it? What am I supposed to do? And she's with you now, so why is it my problem?" Barry asked.

"This isn't West Side Story, man, come on. Laurel isn't *mine*. She's not my property. She's a woman that I care for, that...yeah, she's a woman that I love. I'm sorry if that pisses you off, but if she means something to you too, then this macho bullshit needs to stop. I didn't plan any of this, Barry. It wasn't by design. I've had other women in the past, as I'm sure you have, but—"

"I'm aware of your other women, asshole. This whole town knows who you are. Just because you drive expensive cars and were on television doesn't mean everyone is blind to your game, that they can't see who you really are. We're not all stupid hicks."

"Who do you think I am Barry?"

Barry nodded his head but said nothing, arms still folded.

"I know who you *think* I am, and most of that's probably right, but I don't know if you, or I, know much more than that."

"What the hell are you talking about? And what does this have to do with Laurel?"

I stood up, and Barry uncrossed his arms.

"Relax. I'm just stretching my legs. Might want to get that step painted, or sand it, something. I've got ten, maybe twelve slivers in my ass already."

"I don't need to relax—"

"Barry, for fucks sake, take it down a notch, will ya? You probably have a bigger banana than I do and can bench press more than me. Sure, if I was without use of my arms and missing half a leg, you might be able to kick my ass, but can we just dial the testosterone back?"

Barry didn't laugh, but somewhere on the other side of his eyes, I saw something. A twinkle of an acknowledgement that he found my words amusing yet clouded by utter disdain.

"Listen," I said. "The only thing I know is that I'm a drunk. Is that what you know about me? It's no big secret, Barry. I'm a drunk, just like you—whoooa, don't be getting antsy there, buddy," I said as Barry abruptly started fidgeting and clenching his fists.

"Who the fuck do you think you are, telling me I'm a drunk?" Barry yelled. "You don't know me. You didn't grow up here. You don't know my family. I'm—"

"Hey, stop. Come on," I told him, moving in closer. "As easy as it was for you to peg me, it was twice as easy for me you, man. Wasn't like you did a damn thing to try and hide it. I've been around drunks and addicts my whole adult life. They're easier to spot than a week-old cold sore on a Vegas hooker in a dental chair."

Barry folded his arms again, saying nothing.

"I bet you measure your time between drinks in hours, right? No way it's days. You're fidgeting right now; I can see it. What's it been, Barry, three, four hours? Is it a beer first, or do you go to the nips right out of the gate? There's forty, maybe fifty right behind me in bags up here, you want me to count them?"

"Shut up," Barry yelled, sliding several inches toward me, his forehead beading sweat in the oppressive heat of late day summer.

"I used to always mix my nips with the beers too. Not pour them in but put down a few after I'd already loosened up with a few beers. *Beer before liquor*...yeah whatever, right? Would take a keg full of arsenic to crack this gut. What about you? Those nips going down first, or you need to feel that hop buzz before—"

Barry took a swing at me, his right hand to the left side of my face. I let him have this one, and truth be told, I was goading him. A giveback if you will, for embarrassing him in front of Laurel. He didn't deserve it. Just like I didn't deserve a People's Choice Award for one season of *Melting Pot*, and yet somehow that happened.

I crouched down after the blow, running my right hand across the left side of my face, while Barry stood over me. I didn't attempt to block it, but I tilted my head some, let the blow slide off a little easier. My hand showed a thin line of blood, from my cheek I assumed. Barry still had his hands up like he was ready to box me in the streets of Vermont while I continued wiping blood onto my shirt.

"I'm going to stand up now, and if you take another whack, I'm not going to stay dormant this time. Just letting you know," I said, straightening up. "Not a bad shot. Quicker than I'd have imagined, but you still telegraphed it."

Barry was beet red, almost hyperventilating. "You go ahead and call my cousin, you little bitch. Probably been planning this since you got out," he shouted, keeping his eyes locked on me, hands still defensive at his chest.

"I gave you that one. Not gonna lie," I admitted, wiping my face on my sleeve again. "It wasn't my plan when I came over, though. Just decided in the moment that you deserved to take a poke at me. I could be wrong. I often am."

"Get the hell out of here, and if you're going to call my cousin, at least let me know so I can be ready."

I continued rubbing my face before spitting on the sidewalk, see if any blood found its way into the 'ol cakehole. "I have another idea. Why don't you let me inside so I can clean up, and then we can talk about Laurel? This time without the fisticuffs."

"I don't think so, asshole."

"Well, let me rephrase that then. How about you let me inside, or I call your cousin and tell him you assaulted me here, right in front of your house with those couple of fat kids watching the whole thing—yeah, don't pretend you didn't see them across the street. Whaddya think?"

Barry stared at me, then glanced back at the two tweens peeking over at us from next to the pet shop I frequent, one shirtless and the other wearing a tank top and apparently videotaping us on his phone.

"I mean, you just slugged an award-winning reality TV star, dude. If that video of theirs doesn't go viral, then nothing will."

"Hey, you kids, fuck off, you hear me? I know where you live," Barry shouted at them.

"I'm still taping you, dummy," the portlier of the two yelled back, eliciting a chuckle from me, which Barry hated.

"Let's just go inside. I'll clean up, and I promise if you give me fifteen minutes, I'll be out of your hair," I told him.

Barry stared back at the kids, then down at the sidewalk before looking back at me and walking past me up onto the porch. "Come inside and clean up, and then I'll give you ten minutes. That's it."

"You got it, buddy."

"We're not fucking *buddies*, understand?" Barry snapped, and with his finger jabbing at me in the air. They really liked fingers up in Vermont.

"I'm sorry for the assertion. After you," I replied, motioning for him to go in first.

He opened the door, and immediately I heard the rattle of several beer bottles hit one another and then fall to the floor and roll. Barry scooped them up, placed them on a chair, and walked into the kitchen of his modest apartment. The walls were bare, and the only colors were the multiple brown-orange water stains on the off-white ceiling, with some creeping down across the sheetrock. There was a white-faced analog clock above a rickety kitchen table with thin metal legs and beige surface, and most of that was covered with pizza boxes and beer bottles. It was Alcoholic Starter Pad 101.

"Just use this sink here. That towel hanging on the faucet is clean," Barry told me. I was suspect that his version of clean might be worse than mine, which was somewhere just south of stained, crusty, and smelling of old pennies.

"Thanks. Can I use this soap dispenser here?" I asked, referring to the large jug with a pump handle next to the kitchen sink.

"Fine."

I lathered up with the goopy solution and vigorously rubbed my hands together before rinsing them in the running water and dragging my finger across the cut on my head. The blood was minimal, so I tore off a half a piece of paper towel that hung above the sink and ripped a small piece from it to dab on the cut. I left a sliver of the paper on the wound to soak up whatever continued to flow as it did its clotting magic. While drying my hands off with the towel Barry offered, I watched him lean up against the refrigerator and fold his arms, eyes carefully glued to me.

"Do you want to search me for weapons or hogtie me to the chair? I just let you sock me for free. You remember that, right?" I reminded him.

"Say what you need to say. I have things I need to do," he told me, chewing his lip.

"You don't have any snacks, do you? Cashews would be the best, but I'm not picky right now."

"I don't—what's your deal, man? No, I don't have any snacks. What do you want?"

I dropped the towel next to the sink and pulled one of the kitchen chairs toward me, spinning it around and sitting backwards in it, facing Barry. "I was going to ask you the same thing. I wasn't going to say 'deal,' but instead opt for 'story,' but deal works. Is this you, twenty- four seven, raging, pissed off at the world, flexing all the time? Must be exhausting."

"Oh, is this where you tell me I have too much toxic masculinity? You can take that hippy shit back to La La Land, fuckhead," Barry said.

"I wasn't going to say it, buuuut, now that it's on the table..."

Barry huffed. "See, this is why guys like me can't stand people like you. You show up in a new town and immediately you act like you're better than everyone else. You flash your fancy shit around, use big words, eyeball our women. Why the hell you think most of America can't stand you Hollywood liberal types? You don't just think you're better than the rest of us, you're upset that we don't understand why you are."

I pursed my lips and folded my hands in front of the back of the chair. Barry's eyes were locked on mine as he finished talking but then looked away after about five seconds. I could hear the second hand of the analog clock *click click clicking* behind me.

"You're not wrong, I guess. I mean, I can't say that's an unfair assessment. I appreciate you lumping me in with the Hollywood elite, but I'm not even third tier of that club, obviously. There's no question I've spent a lot of years as a bit of an elitist, sure, and it's probably an honest observation that I did it here, with you. With everyone, really."

Barry started chewing his lip again while he leaned against the fridge but remained silent.

"I don't know why I'm like this, Barry, truth be told. After a couple years of yes men and starry-eyed women, swirled in with a pile of cash and some notoriety, guess it puts lead in the pencil, and it makes you strut around with your chest puffed out. I always hated those types, though, because they reminded me of my old man. In a less douchey and violent way, I sort of became him. He stormed around bitching and moaning that he was tougher than everyone else, but the only person he ever took a swing at was my mother. Real bad ass. He'd come home and whine that everyone he worked with was stupid, but he could never finish the crossword puzzle in half the time it took my mother, and I was kicking his ass at chess before I was out of Underoos."

Barry flinched like he may say something but then turned away and took the other kitchen chair and sat in it, seven or eight feet away from me.

"Anyway, I'm sorry for how things unfolded when I moved into town. Even though I'm not going to give you a free pass for your shitty behavior, I can imagine dealing with the likes of me suddenly...well, it probably rattled your cage a bit."

"Yeah, well...what is it you wanted to say about Laurel? I have things to do," Barry said, looking up at the clock on the wall.

I fidgeted with my chin a bit. "I don't know how much time she has. I don't think anyone does, but I'd like whatever days she does have left to be peaceful. I'd like Ethan to feel like the last days with his mother weren't filled with anger and drama. I'd like to find a way that I can respect that you've had a relationship with her and her son, and that delightful mother of hers, and we can coexist in this delicate space without it being volatile. Is that something you can do?"

Barry gawked at me and then stared down at the floor before getting up to lean against the refrigerator.

"I'm not going to let you take any more swings at me, but I can dial it back a bit, try not to be so arrogant and annoying. I mean, assuming you want time with her after all this."

"I haven't always been a saint to her, but I care about her. Don't go assuming you know everything about me just from a few interactions."

I laughed. "They were pretty intense interactions, Barry, and you were cocked every time. All I'm saying is I want to respect your desire to stay connected if that's what you want. But it must be in a state of calm and definitely in a state of sobriety, you feel me?"

"See, that's what I mean. What dude over forty says 'you feel me?' Can't you just act like a normal person?"

"I sexually assaulted an oven mitt on national television. What part of normal is it you think I'm connected to?"

Barry didn't laugh, but he cracked, and that was enough to get him antsy again.

"Okay, I listened to what you had to say. I'm not going to make any trouble for you or for Laurel. Never was going to anyway," Barry said, "so this whole visit was pointless, except I got to slug you. I still don't trust that you're not going to call Jason, and this wasn't all some—what the hell are you staring at?"

My eyes were frozen on a pile of board games sitting on the living room floor next to the dingiest, puke-green upholstered couch on earth. The bottom box was Parcheesi, the middle Monopoly, and the one sitting right on top, off center and angled away from my location, was chess.

"Do you play chess, Barry?" I asked, wide eyed.

"Rarely, but I know how. Why?" he answered.

"All right, Spassky, enough of this cat and mouse mental shit. We need to make this happen for real," I said, storming into the living room, picking up the chess set, and bringing it back to the kitchen table.

"What? I don't have time for this. I need to—"

"Oh, for fucks sake. Where do you need to go that's so urgent? I gave you a free shot at my melon, a not half bad one I may add, so the least you owe me is one game here."

"Don't be calling me spazzy, either," Barry instructed as he opened the fridge and went for a beer.

"Spassky, and no way man, come on. This game is going to be sober. If I can sit here with you for five or six moves sober, you can do the same with me. Screw the beer," I told him.

"I don't like to be told what to do in my own house," Barry said, slamming the fridge door shut as I set up the pieces on the board.

"I understand," I assured him, while I rooted around for the last white rook in the box. "I don't like to be told what to do in any house. And you can do whatever you like once I'm gone, provided it's not at Laurel's, as we discussed."

"So, what, you're sober now? Put the plug in the jug? Bullshit."

"I'm not sure, but I know I'm not drinking *now*, and that's a good start. Okay, white's move. That's you."

Barry stared at the board, then back up at me from across the corner of the table where I had the game set up. "Who the hell is Spassky?"

"This game isn't going to last long enough to tell that whole story, but maybe if we play another?"

"How do you know? And so much for the ratcheting down the arrogance."

He was right, but so was I after I watched him make his first move. White Knight to b3. Holy smokes.

"I'm sorry," I said, as I countered e5. "Will probably be a bit of a learning curve on that one. Anyway, Spassky was the Russian rival to a famous American chess player named Bobby Fischer, have you heard of him?"

"Yeah, maybe," he answered, staring at the board.

"Well, these two had a couple legendary battles over the years, and—whoa, what are you doing there, buddy?" I asked him as he moved the opposite knight to the edge of the board, g3.

"What, I always start this way."

"Are you finding that you're winning a lot, or..."

"How about you just play your game, and I'll play mine," Barry suggested.

I chortled, and then that's exactly what we did.

CHAPTER 27

- -

"Hey, it's me again. I'm on my way over. I just needed to stop and take care of something. Should be there in about ten minutes. Hope you're doing well, and that Pickle isn't driving everyone nuts. See you soon," I said into Laurel's voicemail. Her not picking up knowing I was in the pokey had me concerned, but I wasn't going to let it consume me before I knew what was going on. Laurel wasn't glued to her phone the way I was, so she could be playing with Ethan, in the shower, working in the garden—anything.

"You look familiar. You in a TV commercial?" the Uber driver asked.

"Nope, just a guy with a familiar face," I told him. I wasn't lying.

"I've seen you somewhere. I knew when I took this job I'd probably run into famous people and stuff, but this is the first time since I started. Where do I know you from?" he prodded.

"Expect you'll be getting a lot of celebrity pickups here in central Vermont then?"

"Same as anywhere else, my friend."

I was perplexed how that answered my ball busting question.

"No part of my history is that exciting, so..." I thought back to the conversation with Barry and our discussion about my "elitism" and arrogance. The guy was only asking where he might know me from, and that *is* an annoying situation to be in, recognizing someone but having no idea where from.

"I was in a rock band for years. Shaky Bones was the name. It's more likely you saw me on a TV show, though, called *Melting Pot*," I told him, staring out the window at the passing greenery.

"Holy shit," he blurted out, which startled me. "That's what it is! Dude, I was just listening to *Fire in the Bone*. I love that album. Saw your picture on the back of the CD."

Impossible.

"I noodle around with bass and guitar a little bit but pretty much suck. That bass line on 'Standing' is so epic though, been trying to figure it out for a week," he explained.

"So, *you're* the one that owns the *Fire in the Bone* CD. I didn't name the band or that dreadful album, just FYI. Kind of you to offer the praise though," I told him.

"Oh, man. Come on, that album rocks. It hit when everything was getting swallowed up by R&B and pop garbage. Never had a chance to take root, but it's a great album."

Was kinda glad I hadn't opted for Lyft suddenly.

"It's a bright spot on an otherwise dimly lit album."

"Naw, 'Better Not Forget' is awesome too, and 'Steal It' I love."

"Solid straight-ahead rockers, and thank you, That album never resonated with me. Probably because it was our last and there was so much tension and infighting among the band. Happy to hear it has for you though."

"Absolutely. Man, I can't believe I'm talking about the bass line I've been trying to sort out *with* the guy who freakin' wrote it. Holy shit! Blows my mind," the driver shouted louder than was necessary.

"The line itself is really just a blues—oh man, gimme just a second," I said as I noticed Laurel's number ringing on my phone. "Laurel?" I'd just missed it. I went to hit redial before noticing we were turning onto my street. "Hey, can you drop me off up there on the left, the house with all the flowers out front?"

"Sure," he said as he slowed down, approaching Laurel's place. "What were you saying about that bass line?"

"I'll tell you what. Why don't you give me your number, and I'll call you some time? We can talk about the bass line, music—whatever. I have a few things happening right now that have me all jammed up, but I promise I'll give you a ring," I told him, sliding across the seat to open the door.

"Are you serious? Oh man, that would be epic. So, it's 860-874-5415."

I tapped it into my contacts. "Your name is Adam, according to the app here, right?"

"Yeah, that's me."

"Okay, cool. Take care, and I'll talk to you soon. Thanks for the ride."

"Yeah, anytime. Have a great day man, and thanks."

"See ya," I said, slamming the rear door shut and walking up to Laurel's front porch. There were no signs of activity, and the daylight was fading, but the outside lights hadn't been turned on. I got to the door and rapped on it five or six times.

"Hello? Laurel? Ethan? You guys home?" I didn't hear Pickle barking, and nobody responded. I rang the bell a couple times and still nothing.

As I went for my phone to call her back, I saw a text message from Laurel light up the home screen.

It's L's mom. She's in CVMC Barre.

Fuck.

CHAPTER 28

"I'm looking for Laurel Mayes. Her mother texted me, said she's here."

"Do you happen to know which area?" the silver-haired woman asked.

"I don't, but it has to be a recent admission because I just found out about this."

The woman shifted in her chair and grimaced. "Well, I can try to look her up by last name, but if she just came in, she may not be viewable yet. Can I ask why she was brought in?"

Now I was grimacing. "Because she's sick."

"I understand, but might you know if she was admitted to the ER or..."Her voice was lost in the background, and I heard the familiar timbre of a small, venomous woman begin speaking to me from my rear left.

"She's not on this floor. Best that you don't see her right now though. She's being looked after and not feeling well," Laurel's mother explained.

"Why is she here? What happened?" I questioned, out of breath.

"Well, while you were incarcerated, she was having tremendous pain and started vomiting, so I brought her in. I left your dog at your place. Laurel had the key."

Incarcerated. The ol' bird didn't tone it down on me even when her daughter was lying in a hospital bed. Consistent at least.

"Thank you for that. Pickle, I mean. And I'm fairly certain my *incarceration* had your wiggly little finger all over it."

She didn't like that. Or she just passed gas, based on the contortion of her face.

"Whatever trouble you got yourself into with Barry isn't of my doing, though it's not surprising you're looking to blame someone else," she said, dialing back her finger, embarrassed maybe.

"Is that why you texted me to come down here, so we can fight while your daughter is suffering?"

Her face changed, almost to remorse or regret, before converting to indifference.

"I'm not moving away anytime soon," I announced, "so, you and I will have plenty of time to spar if that's what you want, but for now, can I just go see Laurel? And where's Ethan?"

"Ethan's here, in the daycare. He's fine."

"Gotcha. I see how this is going to be. Ma'am, can you look up Laurel Mayes again so—"

"Come with me," Laurel's mother interrupted when I questioned the desk clerk.

"Thank you," I told her.

We walked silently down a long hallway. Typical hospital set up with the sterile, chemical solvent smell and too much light and intercom noises competing for the senses. Laurel's mother had an odd gait, where one arm sort of rolled outward from her body in an exaggerated oval and then thumped against her thigh, while the other arm remained stationary with the fingers curled into a ball. The leg adjacent to the wandering arm rotated outward in its own miniature circle and back to her midsection. The poor woman may have had a stroke at one time or an injury I wasn't aware of, but that made watching her oblique shuffle no less intriguing.

She pushed the up arrow between the row of elevators and said nothing, gazing at the creamed-corn colored wall.

"What floor is she on?" I asked.

"Seven," she answered.

"Lucky number at least."

Her eyes left the wall and denounced me with their icy beams.

"You know, Helen, I'm thinking we're going to see one another a lot from this point forward. I realize that's not a choice you'd ever make voluntarily, but it's happening, like it or not. I'm half a shithead on most days, three quarters on the rest, but I'm not without my shine. It doesn't have to be this laborious for us," I suggested. The doors opened and we stepped into the elevator.

Nothing, but her child was upstairs, sick and in pain. I shut up and waited for the doors to reopen.

"I'm going to ask the station nurse if she can have visitors, and if so, I'll go ask her if she wants to see you," she told me as we started down the seventh-floor hallway to the right.

"She's definitely going to want—"

Helen slowed her pace when I said that, but then picked back up when I cut myself off. The two of us had miles to travel in our relationship. Longer than the awful hallway even.

"Stay here," Helen said, approaching the nurse at the desk outside the double doors.

"Alright," I told her, nodding.

She walked to the horseshoe-shaped desk staffed by three nurses in pea-green scrubs and all wearing glasses. After speaking for ten seconds, the nurse she was addressing looked over at me, followed by Helen, and I thought I heard a moan but couldn't be certain. *This is her 'boyfriend,' or at least he thinks he is. Any chance we can get this dummy in for a few minutes just so he'll leave me alone?* Wouldn't be shocked if that were verbatim.

Helen motioned for me to make the twenty-five-foot walk over to the desk. I was in.

"She's conscious but in and out, and she's asked for you, I guess. You can go in, but don't stay too long if she's feeling ill. You'll only upset her," Helen told me.

"Thank you. I'll keep that in mind," I replied before offering a quick smile.

I pushed through the double doors when I heard the buzzing.

"It's room 717," Laurel's mom yelled as I crossed the threshold. I put my hand up to thank her without looking back.

The area beyond the doors was a corner of the hospital. To my right, there were five rooms, most with their doors open, and all full of patients hooked to tubes, wires, and beeping machines. To the left, it was six rooms full of the same, with the sixth corner room being larger and revealing the parking lot through its back windows on both walls. When I approached the right turn at the bend, I heard a young voice tell someone inside a room on my left that he "wished you could read that story about baby's boats to me when I go to sleep." The statement made an older woman start crying before muffled voices blended in and the young child began sobbing. A roadie in my band told me once that "Hospitals are the least happy place on earth" after he sliced his arm open while arm wrestling another roadie, hammered, of course. The dum-dum loses and topples over sideways, landing on a metal lighting rig with edges like buttered glass. Blood gushing everywhere, grown men screaming and wailing, and the drummer's girlfriend passes out cold as soon as she stumbles on the scene. Anyway, he's sitting on a gurney, leaned up against the wall with his arm in stitches and bandaged up tight, waiting to see a plastic surgeon in case he needs some magic performed on his mangled-as-fuck arm, and spills this profound nugget about hospitals and their lack of happiness. I told him I thought a cemetery would be the least happy place on earth, on account of everyone already being dead. At least in hospitals sometimes people are saved, babies are born, diseases are cured, and whatnot, but he just groans and asks if I can find him some smokes.

At that moment, however, I agreed with Jake the Roadie. That little boy and those folks in the room I'd just passed had no joy or hope left, from what I'd heard. They were saying their goodbyes without saying them.

Up on my left, I saw Room 717. There was a doctor standing outside the open door with the standard long white coat, holding a clipboard, her hair in a ponytail. A younger, much shorter blonde woman, stood to her right. They were speaking to one another, though I heard a voice from inside the room, or maybe it was the TV.

"Is this Laurel Mayes's room?" I asked the taller woman in the white coat, leaning to peek inside.

She looked down at her chart. "Yes, 717, Mrs. Mayes. Are you her husband?"

"No, no, just a...a close friend. I was told by the nurse outside I could see her. Are you her oncologist, primary or...?"

"No, they've already left. I'm her gastroenterologist, Doctor Fournier. Were you headed in to see her?"

"Was hoping to, yeah. Is she up?"

"She was several minutes ago, but that can change quickly."

"Right."

I couldn't see Laurel from my current angle, so I smiled at the women and stepped inside.

The inside of the room was more visually pleasing than expected from such a place. It was warm browns and reds and earthy tones, with pictures on two of the opposing walls, both Monet-esque watery pastels drenched in blues, greens, and whites, likely for their dull, calming effect. The odor was more sterile citrus, but less pungent than the hallways. There were two upholstered chairs in opposite corners, one seafoam green. The other a textured beige. Someone, or some group of folks, took their time creating a space that felt safe, comfortable, and unthreatening with elements of home. But this wasn't home.

Laurel lay in the metal hospital bed, which had no cozy embellishments or charm. Behind her to the left stood various machines with colored lights, blinking and pulsing in random rhythms, one beeping every few seconds almost out of ear's reach. A vast and intersecting highway of tubes and wires hung from the nearby machines and weaved their way across Laurel's body, connecting at select points. The eggshell white blanket on her bed was pulled up to her tummy, and she rested on her back, eyes closed. I stood at the foot of the bed, arms folded, listening to the gentle whooshing of one machine and the beeps of the other as my eyes fixed on her, sleeping. I'd had to visit roadies and other musicians over the years in hospitals—that crowd is always fucked up for one reason or another—but couldn't recall a scenario where someone got this sick, this fast. An older neighbor in L.A. suffered a long bout with cancer, several years. My mother's passing was peaceful, expected. Laurel was just in bed with me this morning, and now she's here in this faux Holiday Inn death cabin, pale as a ghost.

"Josh," I heard her squeak out. I unfolded my arms and slid over to the left side of the bed.

"Hey, gorgeous. I thought we had a date tonight. You get this fancy room and don't even invite me? Had to hear about it from your mother. Jeepers, thanks," I said.

Her mouth bent upward into a smile.

I crouched down next to her, grabbing the metal side rails with my hands and resting my face on top. "Sleepy? If you want to doze off, that's fine. I'm still going to stay here a while and just watch you, though. I know it's creepy, but I don't think there's much you can do about it."

She let out a sniffly nose laugh, barely audible, her eyes opening and closing. I watched her drift in and out of consciousness for a few minutes.

"This wasn't really the plan I had for us, Mayes," I said, running my index finger over the cool metal rail, back and forth. "I mean, shit, this wasn't the plan I had for myself. I wanted to come back here, decompress from that L.A. nightmare and just drink myself into a long-bearded coma and watch Pickle pee on some pretty trees. A nice Zero Gravity chair, some distilled spirits, my Grizzly Adams face, and that wingnut dog. That was the extent of my ambitions. I wasn't going to play any music, dick around with television again, or begin any project more ambitious than flossing my teeth. But then I see you across the street, and, well, you got me all turned around. Now you have the balls to go and get sick? The nerve on you."

"Your book...you write," Laurel muttered, her eyes still closed.

I stopped sliding my hand over the railing and lightly tapped at her forearm. "You know, when you close your eyes, you give the impression that you're sleeping. Had I known you'd been eavesdropping—"

"Water," Laurel interrupted, her eyelids bobbing up and down at an easy pace.

"Oh yeah, hon, right here," I told her, pouring some from a beige container with a white top into a plastic cup on the nightstand. I smelled it, knowing it had to be water, but not taking any chances.

She sipped at the liquid as I tilted the cup into her mouth, her eyes opening and closing.

"You want more?" I asked her. She gestured no with a sway of her head.

She opened her eyes fully and slid her shoulders and head further up onto the pillow. "No, that's fine, thank you."

I smiled at her because that's the only goddamn thing I wanted to do besides cry. She grinned back at me.

"My book? Best if we talk about things that don't exacerbate the nausea," I told her before inflating my cheeks.

"People want to hear what you have to say. *I* want to hear," she said, ignoring my silly fat cheeks.

I pulled myself off the metal rail and sat back. "I know you're feeling sentimental and saying things you think you're supposed to say and all, but let's not do that. Plus, now that you went and got sick on me, I've got to add this clichéd ending to my story, where I'd originally planned on us having an orgy on a blimp over Mount Vesuvius and living forever or some shit. *That* I could write about."

Laurel chortled or sneezed or something.

"We can talk about the vomitous, banal words I've been scribbling when you're back home. For now, how about you roll onto your side and let me see your caboose peek out of those dingy white backless wonders you've got on," I suggested as I lifted my eyebrows a couple times.

She chuckled, which then morphed into coughing, so I went for the water again.

"No, it's alright," she assured me after sorting herself out.

I poured the water anyway. She waved it off.

"I'm serious, Josh. I want you to keep writing, and I'd love to read anything you've got so far. In your case, your mind is a lot sexier than your caboose."

I stood up from my chair and grabbed my own ass, then smacked it twice. "Whoa, have you even looked at this thing? I was doing Pilates before anyone knew what that was," I shouted, owning my adolescence.

"I want to hear more from the inside, Josh. What it was like being the center of attention for so long and then pulling yourself out of that fishbowl. I want to know what really happened with Sasha. Why you loved her so much. I want to know about your mother and if that relationship was as challenged as the one with mine. I want to know why I was lucky enough to draw your eye after all the gorgeous chicklets I'm sure you've been with. Mostly, I just want to hear your voice in my head. It calms me."

"Chicklets?" I asked.

I sat back down in the chair, again tempted to be flippant and dismissive, but resisted, instead rubbing the back of my own neck with my hand, looking over at the wall of machines flickering and chirping next to Laurel.

"I'll tell you what, when you get out of here, and you're recuperating at home, in your bed, and possibly sometimes my bed when your mother is at least fifty miles away, I'll read to you, okay? A little passage here and there of my swamp heap of a memoir-novel, or whatever the hell it is. Deal?"

She smiled, easy and deliberate, with a glint of sensuality in those massive eyes that were locked on my own. "Deal."

"First, obviously, we need you to get the hell out of here, so when is—"

"What happened with Barry?" Laurel interrupted.

"All good. Hopefully should be the end of it. I wouldn't bet the Porsche on it, but maybe the lawnmower," I answered.

"He's a jerk, I know that, but there's a part of him that's good in there. I don't think he knows, or nobody ever showed him, how powerful that is versus the angst. He'll figure it out. You can help him."

I stared at her quizzically. "*Help* him? We came to an understanding—I think—but I wouldn't go expecting any fireside chats or cigars on the porch for Barry and me. I like where your heart is though. Still not as cute as the caboose."

"Staaahpp. I'm gross right now, and I'm sure my ass looks like Renoir dragged a dirty sponge across it."

I leaned back over and onto the metal railing, grinning at her with my face planted on top of my folded arms.

"What?" she asked.

"Nothing. Except that even your little self-deprecating pity party isn't going to dissuade me in my lust for you, even dressed like one of the Ingalls kids from *Little House* while they lay in bed with cholera," I told her.

"I'm not letting you peek in my robe, you sicko."

"Just half a cheek, come on. I'll text you a dick pic so you'll have a little something to look at when I leave," I said, before drumming out a *Ba-Dum Dum* on the railing.

"You're that pathetic that you'd ask a woman lying in a hospital bed, dying of cancer, to show her ass cheek?"

"I'm okay with a tit."

Laurel rolled over and belly laughed, pulling her legs up toward her chest, wincing in pain at the same time, though doing her best to blend it into the howling.

"Hey, hey. Come here," I told her, taking her hand in between both of mine. "Don't hurt yourself. Plus, I'm pretty sure you just farted, which we both know is not the first time, so maybe dial it back a bit."

There was no dialing it back. Laurel giggled, guffawed, chuckled, and came apart like I'd never seen her in all the short time I'd known her. Color returned to her face, weight returned to her voice, and she writhed and wiggled in that bed like the pea soup kid in *The Exorcist*.

Then she rolled onto her back and fell asleep.

I stayed at her bedside for half an hour, and twenty minutes in, a nurse came into the room to check her vitals and make a few scribbles on the chart at the end of her bed. Laurel remained asleep, and I smiled at the young woman and asked what time I needed to leave, to which she replied, "When you're ready."

Outside, Laurel's mother either sat more patiently than I'd ever imagined she might, or she'd left, but I wasn't ready to go regardless. Laurel slept like a young girl who'd just chased a new puppy through the hills and valleys of an enormous back yard field. She looked youthful, vibrant, and very much alive in her slumber. Her skin glowed with the ambient light of the room and its own natural sheen. The left bottom corner of her mouth twitched every ten seconds or so as she dreamt of unknown pleasures or foes. I traced my eyes around the curve of her face as I rested my own on top of my crossed arms on the railing. Moments later, her eyes stretched open.

"Well, hello again, hottie. Though I probably should stop complimenting you seeing that you apparently have narcolepsy now too, brought on only when I start talking," I said.

"I love to hear you talk," she whisper-spoke.

"Wow, me too!" I blurted out. "You're a sleepy girl, so I think I'm going to let you crash and come back and see you in the morning, if they'll let me," I told her.

"I think...I think mom said Ethan...that he was here?" she asked.

"Uh, you know I'm not sure if he still is, but I would imagine she's bringing him tomorrow again if not."

"I need to see his little face," she said, easing onto her side and pulling herself into the fetal position, as though she was cuddling something.

"I'll check with her when I go and see if—"

"No, you stay," she said, when I pulled myself off the railing.

"I don't know if they're going to let—"

"You staaaaay," she demanded, in the most non-threatening, kitten like voice a human could construct.

"Okay, I'm here, and I'll stay," I told her, clutching her forearm, giving it a gentle squeeze while I stood over her.

She rolled onto her side, facing opposite me, and then peeked back over her shoulder, just as her hand slid down over her lower back and lifted the flimsy hospital gown across her backside, revealing a flawless, curvy butt cheek the color of peaches and cream oatmeal. Without the lumps.

"Have I mentioned I'm in love with you, like, a way lot?"

She smiled and let the gown fall back over her skin. She was asleep again seconds later.

I made my way to the awful little chair beside her and sent a text to her mother:

Can you take care of Pickle for the night? I'm going to stay with Laurel. Thank you.

I never saw the reply because the tendrils of sleep pulled me under shortly after the last of my tears ended up on the arm of the rotten chair.

CHAPTER 29

It was just before five a.m. when a nurse tugged at my sleeve, repeating, "Hello, sir. Hello. Hello," until I disengaged from dreams of dozens of snakes wrapped around my ankles.

"Oh, I need to go?" I asked her, thankful she had a face, stood upright, and her tongue wasn't flicking in and out of her mouth.

"We don't allow overnight visitors, but I let you stay this time. You looked so peaceful," the woman in a fifteen-color, pastel top told me.

"Interesting," I said. "This chair may have caused permanent ligament damage, and the dream you just saved me from was utterly horrifying, but maybe subconsciously I enjoyed it."

She laughed before handing me my phone, which had slipped out of my pocket.

"Thanks," I whispered, peeking over at Laurel. "She sleep through the night?"

"She's been out since I got here at two a.m.," she said. "I know she's fighting. I'm going to say a prayer that she wins."

That was just about the nicest damn thing this agnostic asshole had heard in days.

"Hey, thank you, really," I told her, sliding my phone into my back pocket.

"I remember you on the TV. What a silly man. I think she's lucky to have you here, though. You've got a kind way about you is what I'm thinking.

"I'm *capable* of kindness, Tara," I replied, reading her nametag. "I think it's natural for you, and that's a gift. One I wouldn't waste on me or my silly little show."

"Oh, I didn't say I liked the show, but I remember it," she fired back, erupting in hushed cackles.

"You're not the first person who's said that to me, and I'd like to retract my previous statement," I said, as Tara placed her hand on my shoulder before walking to the door.

"I'll give you a couple minutes. Nice meeting you..."

"Josh."

"Sorry, I couldn't remember. I remember a *lot* about that show, though," she said, her eyes widening in the doorway.

Potholdergate.

"I'd say I'm a different person, but I'm not going to lie. I still find certain kitchen items attractive to this day," I said.

She let the door close and guffawed like a crazy person out in the hallway. Men have been having sex with their socks since before we had automobiles. It was one potholder, one time, I was shithoused, and we didn't even go all the way. Time to let this one go, people.

I walked over to Laurel's bed and stared down at her, fast asleep with eyeballs rocking back and forth. She looked placid, tranquil.

"I'll see you soon. I'm counting on it," I said before kissing two of my fingers and dabbing her forehead.

I felt in my back pocket for my phone, which was still there, and then left the hospital, headed for Pickle.

****

Laurel's mother wasn't thrilled about the puppy pickup just after six in the morning, but Pickle was positively balls-out ecstatic. I had to take an Uber again, and I'll say that the Uber fella—not my pal from before—wasn't too giddy himself. Can't imagine he gets many calls for 5:10 am pickups, save the occasional traveler headed to the airport, but his lack of enthusiasm and audible groans made it clear he didn't enjoy our little jaunt. I over-tipped the hell out of him and gave him five stars, so hopefully that took the piss out of his vinegar a tad.

"Pickle! Hey buddy. I missed you too," I told the frantic pup back at my place. He was sloppin' his tongue over every square inch of my face while I held him to my chest. Normally, he got squirrely when held up high too long, but in that moment, he cared not a sliver, painting my face with his slobber stick.

I popped him down onto the couch. He stared at me with curly tail swirling in furious circles, panting like he'd just had a threesome with two Bichons. The look behind his bulging globes, hidden beneath the manic elation, was, "You're not going to do this to me *again*, right?"

"I'm sorry. I hate being away from you, too. I'm sticking around for a while. Promise."

He wiggled his rump like he'd understood what I'd said, but I could have been speaking HTML and he'd still be losing his mind.

I rubbed his belly and wrestled around with him on the floor a bit before heading over to my laptop, intent on writing a few things down, keep my mind from going to melancholy places, when there was a gentle knock at the door. So gentle that Pickle didn't even hear it.

I mouthed, "Stay there," to him on the couch, but when he saw me make my way to the door, he was having none of it, so I scooped him up and held him under my right arm.

It was Laurel's mother and Ethan. She was in the same bathrobe she had on when I picked up the dog twenty minutes earlier. Ethan was wearing navy blue shorts, a black ball cap, and a T-shirt with avatars and something called "Fortnite" scrawled across the top.

"Good morning. Again," I said, leaning into the side of my front door.

"May we come in?" she asked, as Ethan's mouth curled up at the sight of Pickle under my arm, turning the pup into a vibrating blob.

"Sure, of course. Everything okay? Laurel?" I questioned.

"No changes," she told me, closing the door behind herself. "Ethan, honey, why don't you take Mr. Traxon's dog and play on the floor or something, or outside, if that's alright?"

I frowned. Not because I was upset she wanted to send Ethan off with the dog, or that she still wouldn't call me Josh, but that, apparently, we were set to have some sort of heart-to-heart I wasn't up for.

"Yeah, no problem. Hey, Ethan, buddy, how about you take Pickle out back on the deck. He has a bunch of toys out there and you can use the hose to put water in his bowl. Or spray his butt. That makes him craaaazy," I said, which got Ethan wide-eyed.

I placed Pickle on the floor, who instantly made a bee line for the little fella, no longer interested in me and my recent return. The two of them shuffled out back and onto the deck, Ethan peeking back once, apprehensive about what the grown-up pow wow was all about, I assumed.

"Do you mind if we sit down?" she asked me, motioning toward the couch.

"Absolutely. After you," I replied before sliding to the other end of the sofa, facing her.

She rubbed her hands together, her leathery, dry skin covered in a sheen of white. Her eyes stared down at them when she spoke. "I'm not going to pretend, just because Laurel isn't well, that suddenly I've developed an affinity for you—I haven't. However, my daughter is fond of you. Ethan is as well. And I spoke with Barry last night and—"

"My new bud?" I interrupted playfully. She wasn't playing.

"I spoke with Barry, and we discussed how difficult some of the days ahead are going to be, and...well, I don't feel that Laurel would want me to leave you out of the equation."

"I'm not sure I'm following you," I told her.

She sighed and realigned herself on the couch. "The equation. Going forward. You know what I mean."

"Are you talking, you mean, after Laurel passes?"

She leaned forward again, rubbing her hands together more vigorously this time.

"Yes, that's what I'm saying."

Shit.

"I don't know, or I'm not sure how you mean. Isn't it very premature to be—"

"No. It's not. It's here. It's right now," she interrupted, dead eyeing me.

"You told me she was alright when you got here."

She fidgeted again and let out another sigh. "Are you fully understanding what's going on with my daughter? This isn't influenza or pneumonia—she's terminal. This is all borrowed time. You were just with her; did she seem well?"

Her agitation radiated through her and at me. She stood up, still rubbing her hands, but now pacing.

"I'm sorry, Helen. I understand how difficult this must all be, though I know I can't fully grasp how much grief it's causing you. I just...I suppose I wasn't ready to look at her situation as...as what it is."

She moved back to the couch and then sat down again, sitting silent for a minute or more.

"I knew when this began where it was headed. I've prepared myself and Ethan as best as I can. But it's never enough," she said, looking into her folded hands.

"Can I get you some water, coffee, juice, anything at all?" I asked her.

"I'm fine, thank you. Can't say I'd have a lot of comfort drinking anything out of that fridge, either."

"Most days neither am I."

She leaned back against the side of the couch and her eyes began to swell up, so I shut up and let her words go where they needed to.

"I haven't always been the best mother to Laurel, with emotional support and all that. I was never wired that way. One might assume if you have a child you soften up, warm to the sentimentalities, but I can't say that I ever did. At least, not in any way she deserved. I loved her, cared for her, nurtured her as I was able, but I know she needed more. Something more maternal. I failed her."

I straightened my back and angled myself to face her more directly.

"It doesn't mean I don't love her, or I don't feel sympathy for her, aguish that she may be suffering, Ethan too, but I'm also angry, and that makes me sick to my stomach," she continued.

"Imagine being angry at your daughter because she has cancer. What kind of a person feels that way?"

I hesitated to answer because she looked poised to keep going, but I did anyway. "I've been with actual monsters, Helen. What you're talking about is natural human emotion. The whole stages of grief thing. It's not something you need to punish yourself for."

"I wish I could punish myself. I wish I could make myself feel the way I'm supposed to feel, as a mother, but all I feel is fear and anger."

"Well, at least you're *feeling*, right?" I told her. "'The opposite of love is indifference.' You're not indifferent to any of this, Helen. You're just feeling it in your own way, and that's okay, I think. I can't speak to the origins of all this or what it means for you and any reconciliation you need, but I know you love your daughter. I know that she loves you. Maybe just exist in that space for a while as all this is going on?"

She stopped writhing her hands and made seconds worth of eye contact before focusing her gaze out of a side window.

"Listen," I continued. "This isn't something either one of us ever figured we'd be dealing with. Had we just been neighbors and there wasn't a Laurel or an Ethan, maybe we'd be buddies, playing cribbage out on the porch and drinking lemonade. But that's not the case and no need to pretend. I'm okay with being civil, decent, and respectful and just acknowledging our vastly different perspectives on life. At the same time, I'd love to leave the door open for more than that, should the opportunity present itself. More so than it already has, I mean. Sound fair?"

"Not every woman over sixty-five plays cribbage. I'd say I was offended, but the whole damn world is offended by everything these days. I'm more of a poker player anyway," she answered, fishing her phone out of her pocket.

"Poker does seem more like your style, sure. Hey, I've had some offers from a few fine locals here to get in on a game, and before long, Barry and I will be thick as thieves, so I'd imagine we could get a game together soon."

Laurel's mother hadn't heard anything I'd said. Her eyes were fixed on the phone.

"She's coming home. They're sending her home," she said.

"Whoa, that's a good thing, right?" I asked excitedly, nodding my head, puppy faced.

Her eyes had welled up when she slid her phone back into the side pocket of her robe. She dabbed at one of them with the maroon sleeve. "They're sending her home to die."

CHAPTER 30

Laurel came home the following morning. Helen and I never resumed our conversation. There was too much commotion and activity surrounding Laurel's return. The hospice folks set her up nice in the house, with a huge, comfortable bed that adjusted like seventy-five different ways. She was in the living room. I'd helped Helen and Ethan clear that area out, so she was comfortable. Barry came by one afternoon and helped me move furniture from that room and others, to make things less cluttered. We played chess out on the front porch, and the fucker moved his knight right to the edge of the board four moves in. No amount of wincing nor head shaking deterred him before he did it with the second knight. I'd tried to play soft and easy, setting him up for opportunities to align pieces and make strong moves, but he was struggling to unlearn his old ways and preferred reckless, odd moves meant to startle me, I guess. Startle, they did. Win, they did not. I'd keep at it with him in the weeks that followed.

Twenty-two days. That's how long she'd been home. I counted while I stood on Laurel's porch, with Pickle and his stuffed crab tucked safely away at home, and Ethan and Helen

261

at Barry's place having lunch. I'd give you a play-by-play, but there's not much to tell. Laurel had been in and out of consciousness for days at a time, some lucid moments more coherent than others, and some not reminiscent of the woman I met not long ago. I visited her many times, sat beside her, helped her sip drinks, eat applesauce, peas and shredded chicken. I showed her ridiculous cat videos on my phone, laughing far too enthusiastically even after the twentieth one. Usually by then she had already slipped into unconsciousness. I laid beside her and read some of the more amusing sections of the "book" I was putting together, careful to avoid the many depressing parts. I brought Pickle to visit. He licked her face until she giggled and wiped off the slop, then nuzzled into the nook of her arm, falling asleep together. I'd stroke her forearm with my fingers while she listened to songs through headphones. She picked the topics. I picked the songs.

"Find me a song about escaping on a boat," she'd say, and I'd pop on "Southern Cross" by Stephen Stills. Taking some liberties there, as it was more of an escape from pain after a breakup.

"Play me a song named after a state in the West," and I'd put on "Idaho" from Gregory Alan Isakov.

You get the idea. She loved the little game. We'd play until she couldn't escape sleep, or until the pain took her to the hand-held clicker and she had to fade away.

On this morning, Helen called and said Laurel was more alert than usual, that she wanted to give me something. I coordinated a time to be alone with her, a couple hours before the nurse would be coming by. I stood on the front porch, about to open the door. One quick peek back at my house found Pickle staring out the front window with his paws perched on the sill, as he often did. There was less anger in that dog than a Buddhist

monk on morphine, but there was no question he was miffed
I wouldn't take him every time I went across the street to visit
the pretty lady in the bed.

"It smells like the Betty Crocker test kitchen in here again. Has
someone been burning incense this morning?" I asked, walking
through the door toward the living room.

Laurel said something, but it was hushed, and she was too far
away for me to hear it.

"You have something to say, beautiful? I hear you mumbling at
me."

She was laughing when I got into the living room, though it
was barely audible. She was paler than I'd seen her since arriving
home, with her face a faded chalk white and tighter against her
bones than days earlier. When she laughed, however, she still
did the three little head nods that I'd been so smitten with early
on, just not as pronounced.

"So, Mom tells me you have something for me? I'm really
hoping it's sexual because I can tell you that if Pickle catches me
slapping the ham one more time, he's going to call the ASPCA."

"Staaahp," she said, pushing her hand into my shoulder when
I leaned down over her.

"Oh, I see how it is. I get a little stressed, put down a few more
E.L. Fudge cookies than normal and suddenly you don't want to
shag me anymore. Real nice, Mayes."

"You look great, actually. Have you been going to meetings?"
she asked, referring to AA.

"I've been to a couple, yeah. I need to go to—"

"Every day. You should go every day," she interrupted. "Have
you shared yet?"

I rubbed my hand over the front of my head and then back
down onto my neck, pulling the folding chair beside the bed
over and sitting in it. "Not yet, and you're right. It's just that,

in this Podunk little world we live in here, there's not a lot of anonymous around so, I may need to head farther outside the circle."

"There's nothing wrong with seeking help for addiction, Josh," she whispered. "Screw anyone who has something to say about it."

"I know. It's not an embarrassment thing. I'm not going to kid myself and pretend anyone gives two shits about a has-been like me and that TMZ will be knocking on my door if they find out I'm a drunk, but..."

"You're not a has been, and it should inspire people that you're trying to get better. Anyone who says otherwise can pound sand."

"Wow look at you. You *are* fired up this morning, just like Mom said."

"If this is fired up, then I'd hate to see mellow."

That made me chuckle before reaching for her hand and squeezing it.

"So, whatcha got for me? Whittled a Porsche from driftwood in your spare time? Carved a bust of Pickle out of alabaster? Paint a nude self-portrait?" I asked, rubbing my hands together vigorously for effect.

"It's just a letter and something small I made. It's over on the kitchen table, but I don't want you to read it right now, okay? Not with me here," she said.

I reached into my front pocket and pulled out a small bag of cashews. I tore the corner open and dumped a few into my mouth.

"Is that alright, Josh?" she asked.

"Of course," I lied. Not that it wasn't okay that I not read it in front of her, but that I was fine with reading a *goodbye letter* at all.

"It's easier, sometimes, to say things that way than to..."

"I understand, hon. You don't need to explain, and I look forward to reading it," I told her, choking back the distress. "You want some cashews?"

She giggled and shook her head. "You really love those things, don't you? What is it about those nuts, versus, say peanuts, or filberts, or some other snack? I mean, they're good and all, but..."

I dropped a couple more in my mouth and chewed them before placing the bag onto the nightstand beside her. "Filberts? Really?"

She puckered her lips.

"Well, when I was around six or seven," I said, wiping my hands together, "a neighbor came over as she did from time to time, likely at my mother's request, to break up some of the fighting that went on between Mom and Dad. After she spent a few minutes diffusing the situation as best she could, she wandered into my room with this giant freaking jar of cashews. She tells me that they're mine and I don't have to share them, which I thought was so cool, but I wasn't a huge fan of them at that age. She smiles at me, leaves them on my dresser and walks back into the arena where my old man is whipping things up. Didn't love the taste or texture at first, but just for shits and giggles, I kept at them. Over time they grew on me."

Laurel laughed. "Shits and giggles. You crack me up. Who says that? And my guess is that it was more about the smile from little miss neighbor than it was about pooping and laughing. Aww, was she your first crush?"

I rested my chin on my hand, grinning over at her. "Makes a lot of noise in your head, chewing those damn things. Distracts from...other noise."

Laurel stared at me, silent and still, squeezing my hand. Her eyes were leaky. They'd been leaky a lot, right along with mine.

"Hey, none of that. This isn't going to be a sobfest, okay? Laughs, nudity, or intrigue is all I'm on board for today. So why don't you tell me something about your childhood. Something you haven't already. Maybe, and believe me it pains me to say this, but how about a memory with your mother. Something sweet, unexpected—whatever."

She cringed. "Oh jeez, Josh. I'm not saying there weren't any sentimental moments with her, but...how about you see if you can discover some of the sweetness with Helen when I'm gone."

When I'm gone.

Laurel sensed the way that gut punched me, deflating the energy in the room, so she shuffled herself up onto her pillow, sitting more upright and looked down over the edge of the bed.

"I'm sorry, I didn't mean to—"

"It's okay. Not ready to let the mind go there yet is all," I cut in.

She frowned while she clutched my hand.

"I wish my mother could have met you," I said after an extended silence. "Man, she would have loved you."

She beamed. "Why do you think so?"

"Besides the fact that 'who wouldn't,' she just would have adored you. Your wit, your wisdom, your courage and your soul—all of it."

Laurel's face took on a light burgundy hue. "I feel like there's so much more to know about her, but you don't speak of her much. The stone though, she was so connected to that memory and basically raised you by herself. Did something happen between you two before...before she passed?"

I pulled my bottom teeth in tight, anchoring my trembling chin.

"It's okay, Josh, we don't have to talk about it now. Another time," Laurel said, leaning her head into my hand. "It looks like you may have brought something for me. What is that?"

"Oh, uh, it's a second pair of headphones and a splitter thingie, so we can both plug in at the same time," I told her while dabbing at my left eye, appreciating the deflection.

"Here," I said, pushing the splitter into my phone jack and attaching each set of headphones into the adjacent connector. "Now we can both listen to the same song together."

Laurels lips stretched across her face and turned upward on the ends, and then her eyes got leaky again, so I tried to curb that by asking her a question, but now she was caught in a moment and I let her have it.

"I love you," Laurel mumbled after a minute, as both her eyes spilled tears out onto her pale cheeks. "Thank you for being everything I needed in this."

I wasn't any good at dialing back the waterworks at this point, so my levees broke, and I wiped at my cheeks while she stared at me, blurry eyed.

"I love you, too. I...I wish that," I said, before she mouthed, "I know," as she'd done several times in the last few weeks, sparing me the undoing.

"What do you want to hear?" I asked her, both of us wiping our eyes with our arms.

"Play me something about wishing, hoping. Lovers...in a warm place," she answered. I thought about a dozen choices with cheesy lyrics and overt messages, and then I thought about one not so obvious and outside the mainstream. A song from a popular band, but not one of their big hits, whose message was maybe vague to most. But not to me.

"I've got it," I said. "It's the Counting Crows. A song called 'Miami,' and when you listen to it, just imagine we're driving down the coast, the nutty dog in the back, sun toasting our skin, and that coral blue water awaits us at the end."

"Mmm, the ocean, my favorite. Sounds perfect," she said, closing her eyes. I slipped the buds into her tiny ears, followed by mine, and nudged myself up close against the bed. I closed my eyes with her while the song played, taking firm hold of her hand, her frail fingers squeezing down on mine.

****

Laurel fell asleep somewhere right at the end of the song an hour earlier. I made my way to the kitchen table and grabbed the thick, brown envelope of my letter with something larger and squishier in it, then outside to the front porch, where I'd sat since. The warmth of the late summer air crept up my ankles and shins and over my legs as I fiddled with the package. I squeezed and fondled it but didn't open it. I glanced over at my front window where Pickle had been earlier, but he'd abandoned his post, aware finally that he wasn't part of this most recent endeavor. Through Laurel's trees in the side yard, I could hear kids playing, hollering, and laughing while they jumped through sprinklers or chased one another around in the final stretch of a near perfect summer. I felt the lump in the bottom of my throat that came with wanting a drink, but I bit it back and took a long slug of some iced tea from Laurel's fridge. The glass I'd chosen at random had giant sunflowers on it, layered on top of one another, covering the entire surface of the container. It somehow made the iced tea taste better than it probably was. Cleaner, icier. You could probably put battery acid in the right container, and it would be yummy.

The humidity in the air, and darkening skies to the west, suggested storms would find their way east. They would end up making Pickle mental, but find me sitting on my back deck, hoping for electrocution. Not really. Maybe just a gentle little zap.

I folded one corner of the packaging over then back again, wiggling it in opposite directions until the crease made it weak. Then I tore off the corner. I spread the sides open with my fingers, then ripped the package down the seam. A folded letter and a soft, wrapped, square something or other fell into my lap. I put the wrapped item aside, took a breath of that humid air, and began reading.

Dear Josh,

I wanted you to have this letter, not just because it contains words I wanted to say to

you, or because soon after you read this, I'll be gone. I wanted something

tangible for you to remember me by, yes, but there was another significant reason.

This entire letter was transcribed, as I spoke it, by my mother.

Yes, Helen listened to every word of this and penned it for me, as my hands were too weak to put pen to paper at this point. In some ways, I feel badly that I let her into our little world and that you may be embarrassed by that, but I weighed all sides of the equation

here and landed on letting mom do it because I'm hopeful I've already left you

with some happiness, some joy, maybe a little lust and longing, and hopefully some

love, but to capture the true essence of our too-short time together, I feel like it

needed a large dose of awkward. So, you got it. ;) (I made her write that winky face)

I picked my head up from the page, laughing, and dragged my shirt sleeve across my left eye, which had started dripping onto the paper.

I suppose the moment I knew I had feelings for you, which was the day we met, I

should have told you that I was sick. I shouldn't have allowed emotions, sex, and

laughter to swirl itself all up and over us knowing my time was short, that any real

relationship would be impossible. I'd like to say I couldn't help myself or that I

was confused and didn't know what to do, but anything like that would be a lie. I

knew what I felt and what I was doing and why I was doing it. Yes, I pushed you away

after the Barry nonsense and made feeble attempts to keep you at bay, but they were

half-hearted, which I feel like you saw through anyway. Now, as I lie

here dictating these words to my mother (just thought I'd remind you again, lol), I

wish I had told you I was sick. Had I known the man you

are then, I never would have been concerned about it pushing you away or you

feeling burdened. I suppose it's selfish of me to think you'd be able to love

me, or that you'd want to, with all you'd been dealing with concerning Sasha and your

own struggles, adding cancer into the mix. But, knowing you as I've come to, I believe

that you would. I'm fully aware of what an immense gift that is, and I only wish I had more time to pay you back for it.

Needed to dab the other eye.

Speaking of Sasha, we never got around to talking about what really happened when

you went to see her father, and I feel like that's something you needed to explore.

I hope that, whatever transpired, it wasn't something that leaves you with scars that

won't heal, especially because I won't be there to tend to them. I know you loved her,

and part of me feels like I'd never be able to have the place in your heart that she did,

but I wish I had ten thousand more days to try. You know, when you showed up on my lawn that day, for the first time since bringing my beautiful Ethan into the world, I felt like I may need something again. That's the truth.

I'm not going to lie; Mom just sighed a little bit there, but she's going

to get past all this. You two are going to figure things out, I truly believe it. Yes Mom,

I want you to write that down (LOL).

In addition to asking that you'll keep an open mind with Mom here, and that you two work things out, I have one more request for you—and it's a big one, so I'm sorry to lay this on you without first speaking to you about it.

Ethan. Now I was fully leaking onto the pages of the letter, so I wiped both eyes hard and swiped across the page with my sleeve before going back to it.

My mother, for all her quirks and rough edges (sorry Ma), loves Ethan to pieces, and he adores her. I've entrusted her as his legal guardian and feel as comfortable as a mom could feel leaving her

271

son with someone other than herself. However, he needs more than that.

He needs other voices, other experiences, other guidance. People he can trust to bring

his fears, questions, and desires to. Mom can't do it alone. I'm asking if you'll

find it in your heart to be that beacon for my little boy. He absolutely adores you. He hasn't spoken this way about a man in his life ever before and I'd be a liar if I said it didn't have me tearing up now and then. It would mean everything to me if the two of you were in

each other's lives. I know I never had the chance to fully learn and understand everything about you, and I'd be trusting my little baby with you, but something tells me, or feels, that it's a good thing. This is a very personal, and maybe selfish, thing to ask, but please think about it. However—and I'm sure you know this—you'd need to be sober. Taking care of yourself. I can't pretend I know anything about addiction and what demons you suffer through that lead you to a bottle, but I know that you know, as well as anyone, that I can't expose my little boy to that. I just can't. I don't expect one ever "beats" this thing that grips you, Josh, but I think you can keep it at bay. I really do. I hope you do it for you first, and then for my little boy, who I know loves you already. Oh, and as much as Barry is a knucklehead and all that, I've told Mom, and I'll mention to you, that as long as he's also sober, he's welcomed to see Ethan. I have hope for him yet. I expect Mom will be around for long into Ethan's adult life, but in the unlikely event that's not the case, I've spoken to her about a more formal arrangement for you and Ethan, if you were so inclined. That's a discussion for another time, between the two of you, were it to become relevant. I expect you both will value the significance of all this and shelve whatever petty grievances *you have with one another going forward. For Ethan, for me, and mostly for yourselves.*

That's all I have, Josh. I know it's a lot, this whole thing is a lot. I never figured I'd be

staring into the abyss at such an early age and that it would be accompanied by such

strong feelings for someone I just began to know, though entwined with a tangible sense of peace. That may sound crazy, but it's true. I'll leave this place knowing my son is in good hands and that I had a chance to feel love in my final hour. I wish, like so many in my position surely wish, that there was more time to embrace and nurture this little thing we started, but I've accepted there's not, and I'm ready to let go, Josh. I'm not scared anymore. I'm not angry. I'm sad, of course, but I'm ready. I hope you find the peace that you so deserve and that your life takes you to all the places you want to be. Thanks for loving me. Thanks for making my son smile. Thanks for buying that place across the street. Thanks for being a man among men.

Oh, as for the gift, it's something I made for you, and was all I was able to accomplish

with my feeble hands (and Mom's help again) and limited waking hours, but if there's anything that may be able to take my place when I'm gone, I figured this was it. Enjoy ;)

Please give Pickle lots of kisses for me. I expect to see you on the other side, but not for a long, long time. Goodbye, and be well, Josh.

Love,

Laurel XOXO

I dragged my sleeve across both eyes and then peeked through my foggy peepers and

saw Pickle perched up on the windowsill, staring over at me. I folded the damp pages, placed them next to me on the porch, and tore open the soft package that accompanied the letter. Inside was a knitted square with rounded edges. A yellow potholder with a bright red heart sewn into the middle. I dropped it in my lap and let my face fall into my hands, laughing and sobbing so robustly that I think Pickle heard me from across the street because he began yapping like a loon. During all this, the nurse arrived, so once she was inside I let myself come apart for a few minutes on the porch, then wiped my face, scooped up the letter and gift, snuck in to kiss Laurel on her forehead, and then made my way home to my twenty-pound best friend, who was still going bananas.

CHAPTER 31

"Hiiii, Josh," they said in unison, as is customary. The church basement smelled of stale coffee and sugar, and a lone fluorescent lightbulb flickered overhead to my left as I straightened myself up in my chair and started speaking.

"I knew I was an alcoholic when I was fifteen. It was a motherfucking Jack Daniels nipper. It just looked so rock and roll, so fun."

Most of them laughed.

"If it weren't for the bellyache I had, I would have drunk twelve more. Taken every last one that hulking senior in the denim jacket had at the soccer game and just pounded 'em. I put down three though, so I was flyin' good," I said, staring into my lap as my forearms rested on my legs. "It's terrifying enough to be an emotional kid at fifteen, in high school of all places—the last damn place you want to give anyone a sense that you're human—but to realize now that you're powerless to stop this liquid scourge from exacerbating it all...shit."

I cleared my throat and repositioned my folding chair.

"I...I have been a drunk for most of my life. That day at the ball field flipped a switch that I've jammed back in the other direction a thousand times, but it never stays. I've created a version of myself, for myself, that's a clever, harmless braggart that likes to have a little too much fun, but that's not a *problem*. Not an addict. Jesus Christ, no. Not one of them. Several years ago, I first began to admit that I drank too much, and did that, 'Hey, yeah, I guess I'm a drunk, but drunks are fun, right?' I wasn't having fun anymore, though.

"I met someone that I loved that died right next to me because of this awful fucking disease. I'd say it was 'her' disease that actually killed her, but it's all part of the same trip. A normie doesn't make a beeline for the woman who's screaming obscenities at the maître d' as she's falling into the Koi pond, right?"

They laughed again.

I hesitated for a few. The rest of them sat patiently, a couple sipping coffee, one holding his left arm with his right while his work boot vibrated up and down underneath his chair. The bright white wall clock's thin red second hand *click-clicked-clicked* as I sat.

"I lost yet another woman that I loved the other day, though for the first time I can say it honestly wasn't because of my disease. What her loss did do, though, is illuminate how vast the destruction of the good in my life has been because of my drinking."

The chin was trembling, and the damn peepers were getting foggy, but I pushed on.

"For the last year, before I met the woman who just passed, I'd been drinking more heavily and steadier than I had in years. I attributed this to guilt and remorse surrounding the death of the other woman from years earlier. How I'd missed what should have been clear signs of a life lived in torment. Some of it was, especially as the anniversary of her passing approached. What I discovered, though, just recently, was that the origin of my pain was, in fact, my mother.

"She suffered at the hands of my violent, angry drunken father for a dozen years before he was finally gone. She saved me from his wrath so many times. She came into my bedroom, often after being struck or pushed down on the floor, hit with a belt, and comforted *me*. Alleviated *my* fears. She taught me about courage, strength, and dignity in ways I only began to understand as an adult. She showed me unconditional love in a home where love could never live.

"I repaid her by becoming a drunk myself and running away," I said before choking up.

I gathered myself and continued. "What I've learned in these last few years is that I'm an alcoholic. Unquestionably. Though what I've also learned is that there's no way I would have ever stayed on this side of the grass without my mother, and several other women that followed. The girl who just passed reminded me so much of her. Her passion, charm, and strength. Her love for her child through anxiety and trauma. Her calm in converging, tumultuous worlds. I've been gifted the love of these amazing women and the only currency I have to repay them in their death is my sobriety. To live a life they'd want for me. It's what I owe them. What I owe myself.

"One day at a time. That's all I've got. Thank you."

CHAPTER 32

T he service was beautiful, and all credit goes to Helen on that one. She orchestrated every detail exactly as Laurel had wished, and it was well attended, followed by a reception at the house. Laurel had a much larger group of folks that loved and cared about her than she'd let on, but that reconciled with her modesty. One fella, rotund and slovenly but otherwise delightful, told me that he'd always wanted to ask Laurel on a date but felt she was out of his league. She was, which of course I didn't tell him, but it wasn't because he looked like manager in a '70s era Las Vegas lounge, but instead because she was out of my league too. She was too good for all of us.

Helen asked if I wanted to say anything at the ceremony, so I got up and spoke to Laurel's kindness, compassion, humor, love of life, and her son, and of course her bravery in fighting her terrible disease. I kept it short, as I wanted those who knew her better than I to have their space. I also didn't want Helen to feel like I was making the moment about me, which I've had a tendency to do in social situations in the past. I'm working on it.

A couple handfuls of people spoke about Laurel and what they loved about her, what they'd miss, and how she touched their lives. I enjoyed hearing their stories, their tributes, but I struggled as I watched Ethan absorbing it all. He was well behaved, never made a peep, and I only noticed him crying briefly, but his face spoke volumes about where his heart and mind were. He was too young to lose his mother. Not that there's ever a good age. I smiled and winked at him while Laurel's friends and former coworkers spoke their kind words, and that kept him from coming apart, along with Helen holding his hand and stroking his head. He's stronger than I would have been at his age. There would be longer, deeper discussions with Ethan—of course—but the day of his mother's service, in my thinking, was to allow him to grieve in his own way. Absorb, process, feel, and react as he saw fit. Pain is personal. It needs to find its way through each of us on its own course, young or old.

Midway through the reception, after letting Helen know, I ducked out and went to another AA meeting, this time in Rutland. It wasn't just a good idea. It was needed. I'd been doing well, considering all that had happened, but no alcoholic is ever "cured." I wanted so badly to chew the cap off a bottle of bourbon at that service, gulp down half the damn thing and just let the lights go out...but then I looked over at Ethan, standing with his grandmother. His face forlorn and his eyes weepy, but he was working it out. There were long days ahead without his mother and an ever-changing path of sorrow for a while. The last thing he needed was some dude across the street screaming at the trees in his underwear, clutching a bottle at 10:30 p.m. on a Tuesday.

After leaving the meeting, I went into town to swing by the hardware store before it closed. I needed an asphalt patch kit. The left front corner of my driveway had cracked after clipping it with the Porsche one too many times. It was already failing, not because I'm an idiot or was hammered or any of the obvious things you're likely thinking. In many ways I *am* an idiot, but that has no bearing on this situation.

When I got into the store, Timmy came over and hugged me. He didn't say anything, though I'm sure he knew about Laurel, because his uncle was at the ceremony. Instead, he held on to me like I hadn't seen him in ten years.

"Thanks for that, buddy. Really needed that today," I told him.

He looked at me and then hugged me again. I damn near lost my shit but kept it tight when I saw Timmy's uncle head over toward us, which sent Tim off.

"Good seeing you," I told him as he walked away.

"Bye, Mister Josh," he said, shuffling to the back of the store, his hand up in the air.

"Evening, Dan," I said. "Thanks for coming by the service. I know it meant a lot to Helen."

"Of course. Laurel will be missed by all of us. She was a good woman," he replied.

His hands remained by his side, though it looked like he almost wanted to reach out and shake my hand, so I said screw it and extended my own. "She was indeed. Thank you."

He hesitated but slid his hand into my mine, clamping down good but not "just out of boot camp" stuff.

"What brings you into the store?" Dan asked.

"Oh right, yeah. Well, if you have it, I need some sort of asphalt patching kit. I have a cut in my driveway at the end. Just wanted to fill it in a little."

"We have patch kits, but they're not great. I'd say you're better off calling Don Justice in town. He does repairs, sealing and all that, but I can show you what we have."

"That would be great. At some point I'll need a refresh, sealing, whatever, but I think I'm fine for now."

"Fair enough," he said, leading me down the aisle to the driveway fixers.

I know what you're thinking. It would be great, I suppose, if that happened, and would feel good, sure, but it would be a lie.

Dan and I didn't hug before I left, say we were sorry for butting heads in the past, and that we should "go out and have a beer" together soon. That's only in the movies.

We also didn't get in each other's shit either, so that's a place to start. He's not an awful guy, just doesn't like half hippies that didn't grow up there is my guess, and that's alright. He has a lot to deal with, caring for Timmy, and I wouldn't jam up his world by being an idiot all the time. I was, however, going to take Timmy for another ride in my car at some point. Maybe Dan would lay me out, or maybe he'd realize it makes Timmy smile like no other person I've ever seen, and he should just let it happen. Whatever it will be, it will be. Que sera, sera, and all that happy horseshit.

I grabbed my driveway goodies, said goodbye to Timmy, who hugged me again and then high-fived me, and was on my way. I had nothing that resembled food in the house, so I picked up a pizza from Luigi's in town, a restaurant owned by the most non-Luigi looking fella I'd ever seen. He was a bowling ball with feet, dressed like a pimp in a music video, and had an accent that sounded Australian. Made a damn fine pie, however. I shoved a slice in my face sitting in the car, burning the roof of my mouth, my lips, chin, and, inexplicably, my right eye. Had to be a projectile grease bullet when I bit in so quickly.

Pickle loved pizza, but a ton of yeast wasn't good for his ears, so I had to be careful with how much I let him munch on. His eyes went full puffer fish when he saw me bring those boxes in though. Despite the burns and the blindness, I fired another piece into my trap while sitting in the car, chewing it more this time. The first piece had also burned my windpipe and esophagus so I was all set with that. You'd figure forty or fiftyish years would be enough time to work through the basics of having a meal without injuries.

As I was reaching into my glove box to grab a few napkins tucked inside, a middle-aged fella and his friend were leaning down over my windshield and waving to me. They looked like they just finished eighteen holes, both in ball caps and plaid shorts, and inexplicably excited.

"Hey, Josh Traxon. How are you, man? I heard you moved into town. I loved you on *Melting Pot*," the larger of the two said.

"Thank you," I mouthed, struggling to wipe the pizza grease from my hands. The other one started taking pictures, and both giggled like tweens watching a YouTube star sign autographs at a county fair.

I started the car, waved, and nodded again, before gingerly pulling away from the curb. What the hell they wanted with pics of a half-assed celebrity drenched in pizza drool was not my business, but it meant something to them I suppose. I wish Laurel could have been here, though, because I missed that eye roll.

I let my mind wander into the too few memories of Laurel, so I almost missed my street, but when I cut the wheel hard and arrived at my busted driveway, Ethan was standing on my front lawn. I waved to him before pulling the car onto the driveway and parked, avoiding the asphalt blemish.

"Hey, pal. What are you doing? Looking for Pickle pup?" I asked him when I exited the car.

He smirked but didn't respond. He was wearing one of his many ball caps, this one a baby blue hue and with a white sailboat on it. His T-shirt said, "Cool Kid" and had a goat wearing sunglasses on it, which kicked ass of course.

"You get all filled up over at your place, or would you want some pizza?" I asked him, grabbing the box, and then slamming the driver's door shut. He shrugged his shoulders.

"You know, usually I get all kinds of crap on my pizza, but today I got just cheese, which I know is your favorite," I said, shaking the box. "I must have known I was going to see you and you'd want some."

He smirked again.

"You ever go see Luigi there, for pizza? Well, shoot, you must have at least a few times, as there's only two pizza places anywhere near here. You like his place?" I asked.

"Ummm, yeah," he answered.

"He's a chubby little fella, wears silly clothes. I like that guy. Makes yummy pizza too."

"His voice is weird."

"You mean his accent? That just means he was born someplace far from here. Do you know where Australia is?" I asked him as I zipped back to the car and reached into the glovebox for the rest of the napkins.

"Far in the north?"

"It's definitely far, but it's south of us, actually. Very warm, lots of critters like snakes and spiders."

Ethan's eyes stretched open.

"You ever have upside-down pizza?" I asked him, plopping the box onto the grass next to the driveway.

He shrugged his shoulders.

"Oh, come on, you've never had upside-down pizza? It's soooooo good, maybe the best ever. You need to try some," I told him, flipping the top of the box open.

"It's gonna drip on everything, and it's just the same pizza flipped over," Ethan suggested, astutely.

283

"Ah, but see that's where you're wrong, my goat-shirted little pal. This is *upside down* pizza, and it's much different. First, we need to sit on the grass, facing each other, so we can see our expressions when we take a bite of the deliciousness," I explained, pulling a slice from the box as I stared down at him. "Then, you fold the slice into a vee before you flip it and take a few bites."

I gobbled three quick bites, chewing manically while making exaggerated slurps, moans, and hums as the cheese and sauce drizzled over my fingers.

"That's ridiculous," Ethan said, and I nearly spit out the pizza.

"Are you saying you don't want any upside-down pizza? Cause Pickle has some leftover beefy looking slop in his bowl that I can get you instead. Not sure if eating it upside down will make it any better though. It's kind of delicious as it is," I said.

Ethan grimaced before pulling a slice from the box, folding it with both hands. Then he flipped it and took three small bites, chewing methodically and carefully, as the toppings ran down onto his thumb. "It's just pizza flipped over," he said with a jammed mouth and sloppy hands.

"Finish chewing, dingleberry," I told him before snickering.

Ethan let his head drop near his folded legs and wanted to laugh but finished swallowing first, and then pointed to his left at the house.

"Holy smokes. Look at that pathetic sight. That dog would know we were eating food without him if we were on the moon," I said, staring at Pickle with his front paws up on the windowsill.

"Maybe *he* likes upside-down pizza. Can we let him out?" Ethan asked.

"Of course, but first you need to admit that upside-down pizza rocks and that I'm a culinary genius."

"What's cuh-lun-airry?"

"It's food, cooking. Like really good food that only I know about, like this," I said, sweeping my hand through the air across the pizza box.

He rolled his eyes. What a smart little bugger this kid was. Just like his momma.

I tossed Ethan a couple napkins that I'd wedged under the box and then hopped up and went to let Pickle out, who was waiting anxiously behind the door. He came barrel-assing across the threshold and over the steps like a bottle rocket with fur, toppling poor Ethan, who started giggling and rolling around with the bulgy-eyed fruitcake. For an instant, Pickle extricated himself from bathing Ethan's face with his slop stick to assess the pizza situation, but he was in a possessed groove, so he went right back to licking, hopping, tumbling, and jolting all over the welcoming little fella. They did this for about ten minutes, so I ate a couple more slices in the conventional direction and watched Helen step out onto her front porch, shooting me a wave. It wasn't impassioned, enthusiastic, or adorable like the ones Laurel would send my way, but it also wasn't that finger, terrifying me in its defiance of physics.

I waved back to her and yelled, "He okay here for a little bit?" She nodded her head before going back inside.

"Pickle give him a break, you nut," I said to the twenty-pound canine that had Ethan pinned on his back, intermittently licking his face when he saw an opening from on top of his chest. Ethan laughed, parrying the tongue blows with his open hands.

I looked in the pizza box and silently deliberated whether I'd have another slice. Then I remembered a button had literally exploded off a pair of my casual pants a week earlier and decided to pass. I had resolved myself to never be more than a 36 waist ever again, after porking up shortly after *Melting Pot* ended, and had held the line beautifully for quite some time. But the

285

absence of alcohol and the addition of stress had slid far too many Ho Ho's into my face of late.

"You want more pizza, buddy? Otherwise, I'm going to tear a corner off for Pickle then bring it inside," I said.

He sat up, with Pickle in hand, and placed him down next to himself. Pickle stood motionless, except for his head, which alternated between me and Ethan, waiting for what was next.

"Yeah, sure," he said, wiping his slobbered face off with his sleeve.

"That little beast can sure slop you up, right?"

"Uh huh."

"Here. I'll let you try a regular piece. No flipping."

He took the slice and chewed off a couple bites while Pickle's head trailed every inch of his movement.

"I was going to have another piece, but my belly is starting to look like a camel's hump," I said, tapping both hands on it like drums.

Ethan kept chewing. Pickle kept following, a string of drool just beginning to stretch from his bottom lip.

"Okay, numb nuts, here you go," I told the dog as I tore him off a corner of one of the slices and tossed it to him. He chewed it like it was taffy, with the piece traveling to all corners of his mouth, covered in drool, half sticking out of one side, then disappearing, then popping out again, and then gone.

"That's one silly dog, right?" I asked Ethan.

He was still working on his slice but shot me half a grin.

"Let me go inside and get some water for you. I may have some lemonade," I said, standing up.

"It's okay, I'm done," he said, reaching for one of the napkins.

"You sure?"

"Yeah."

"Alright, buddy."

He finished wiping his fingers and mouth off and then balled up the napkin and placed it in the cover side of the open box. "Me and mom had picnics in the backyard. In the same spot all the time 'cause it wouldn't get as sunny on my face and burn me."

"Are you getting burned, you think?" I asked, looking up at the waning orange orb in the western sky.

"Um, don't think so."

"Okay.

We can have picnics any time you want, you know. In the sun or out of the sun, whatever you like."

"Yeah."

"We can find lots of cool spots. Out here, in the woods out back, at the park near town. All over. We can leave that spot you had with mom as just your own, you and her."

"But she won't be there," he said, looking down into the grass.

I sighed, and Pickle lay at Ethan's feet, realizing no more pizza was headed his way.

"I know," I said, sliding closer to him and moving the pizza box to the side, which got Pickle reactivated. "No more, Pick. Chill out."

I picked up the box, closed it, and placed it behind us before patting the grass, which brought Pickle back down.

"She won't be with you, you're right. Not sitting there beside you in your spot, but..." I cut myself off, thinking of every cliché someone tells another when someone dies like, "they'll always be there in your heart," or "you have the memories of them," and whatnot, and it just felt silly, even to a little kid.

"I loved your mom. I'm not sure if she told you that, or if she even would have, or if you'd have guessed it, but I loved her. She was funny and kind. She was smart and silly and beautiful, and maybe I didn't know her nearly long enough to feel as strongly as I do, but I got the tickly tummies every time I saw her," I said.

"The tickly tummies?" he asked, looking up at me, his sailboat hat too far down on his forehead.

"Yeah, you know. The tickly tummies. When you go over a big bump in a car too fast or your mom hands you a hot fudge sundae from Frozen Funtown down the road or you open a present on Christmas that you kinda know what it is, but then you see the coloring of the box and you *know* what it is. Those are the tickly tummies."

His eyebrows raised, and a smile stretched over his lips.

"Your mom gave me those every time I saw her. But the funny thing is, I still get them now even when I think about her."

He grappled with the concept, working it out, and came to an understanding of it, at least from what I could reconcile in those short few seconds on his face.

"I still wish I could see her," he said.

"I know. So do I. Sometimes the tickly tummies aren't enough."

But they're all we got.

Or maybe not.

"How about I clean up this mess here, take Pickle inside, and then I'll come by and see if Grandma will let me take you to Frozen Funtown?" I asked him.

"Um, sure."

"Okay, hustle on over there, get your hands washed, and I'll meet you in a few minutes."

Ethan stood up, stroked Pickle's head a few times, and scurried off across the road, at least looking in one direction before he darted over the pavement that rarely had cars on it.

"Both ways, silly," I shouted to him as he ran.

I gathered up the box and napkins and tossed them in the green receptacle outside the garage before letting Pickle into the house and heading out to the shed in back, humming a happy little tune of unknown origin.

Chapter 33

I walked back to Ethan's house, carrying it in a burlap sack that had been left behind by the previous owner, slung over my shoulder, chewing on cashews. I walked around back and placed the parcel near the herb garden that Laurel had often worked on since I'd moved in. I saw Helen peeking through a window at me, and she hurried over to the back door when I waved at her.

"What the heck is that?" she asked.

"Something for Ethan," I answered.

"In a ratty old sack?"

"It's a boy thing. No need to get fidgety," I told her, swallowing the last of the nuts.

She rolled her eyes. "Don't get him all crapped up if you're taking him for ice cream, and as long as you're going, I wouldn't think it would kill you to get me a pint of butter pecan."

"Done. And send the little bugger out if you would."

She called for Ethan, who practically shot out of a cannon from the door. Until he got to the burlap bag.

"What's in there?" he asked.

"Where's the spot you and Mom used to sit for your picnics?"

He looked toward the tree line to the left, adjacent to a yellow shed.

"Over here? Why don't you show me," I told him, slinging the bag over my shoulder again.

He looked up at me and then began walking in that direction, peeking up at me while we traveled, curious about the bag and the plan.

"Right here," he said, pointing to a space in the grass that was worn down, browned a bit.

"Perfect. Is it okay that I'm here? In your spot? If this is private, for just you and Mom, I understand."

"It's okay."

"Alright," I said, placing the bag on the ground, catching my breath. "Well, when I was a little guy, not far from your age, I had this dog. Brown and black like a tree, he was, with super long hair. We named him Timber, 'cause of looking like tree bark and all. I loved that little fella as much as a kid could love a dog, kinda like I do Pickle now, except I'm all grown up and stuff. Anyway, this poor pup of mine died sooner than he should have, like so many that we love do. I was beside myself, crying and carrying on because I missed that dog so much. My mother, well, she didn't know how to get me to stop. So, one day she's out looking for something to place on the spot where we laid Timber to rest, and she finds this here."

I slid the heavy stone from the bag and placed it at Ethan's feet.

"It's a big heart. Is it a rock?" he asked.

"It is, a real heavy one too. My mother found this one day, in the pouring rain, and she said it was because I loved Timber so much that she found it. That it was meant to be discovered because of all that love I had for my little pup."

291

Ethan looked up at me, blinked a couple times.

"If you'll let me, I'd like to leave this stone here, in this spot, where you and your mom used to sit. Something from my mom for your mom. I cleaned it up, and it doesn't need much care except a place to rest itself near someone who loved another so much that it hurts to imagine they're gone."

Ethan looked back up at me and then back down at the stone.

"You don't have to keep it here, Ethan. I want to make sure you know that. This is your spot, and you can have it any way you'd like it to be. I was going to put this behind my house in the garden until I—"

"Would Mom like it to be here?" Ethan interjected, looking up at me, shielding his eyes from the late summer's evening sun.

I felt my lower lip start the wobbles when he asked me that, catching a cloudiness in his eyes when he stared at me.

"I think she would. I think she would be happy knowing this was here, and that you two had something to mark the spot you loved spending time together, where you could come visit any time you wanted," I answered, though my cadence was clunky.

Ethan saw my eyes fog up, and he sat down next to the stone, wiping his own on his sleeve.

We sat there for a spell, as they say. Neither one of us saying anything until a couple barn swallows whizzed by and broke the frozen moment we'd been stuck in.

"Will you, um...do you think sometimes, maybe you and Pickle would come out here and sit with me and the stone, so I'm not alone?" Ethan asked.

It's challenging to speak when your emotions have just been obliterated by a pint-sized human with a heart bigger than an aardvark and misty eyes.

"It would be my pleasure, my honor, to sit with you here any time you like, Ethan," I choked out.

"Maybe the stone will help us not to cry so much, like your mom said."

I laughed, though it was more of a stuttered bellow. My eyes were like two camera lenses slathered in Vaseline. "I don't mind the crying so much. It lets the sadness out so we can let more of the happy back in. There's more room."

Ethan looked up at me, and in that instant, I knew there would never be a reality without him in my life. There were his mother's eyes, her half smile, her curiosity, her kindness, but there was altogether something else that transcended Laurel and was uniquely him. He was the move that I'd never seen in the endgame. He was the quiet calm before opening the bottle. He was the beacon in the long, dark night.

He was the peace.

"We can sit out here and cry until it gets dark, but I think Grandma might sock me in the lip if I don't get her some butter pecan ice cream. You okay if we leave this here and come back and visit again tomorrow?" I asked.

Ethan rubbed his right eye with his fingers and then slid his hand into mine. "Nana would never hit you," he said.

"She might not, but I bet she could beat me up. You think so?" I asked while we walked back around the side of the house, Helen watching us, offering a gentle wave.

"Umm, yeah. She's real strong. One time, Mom and Barry were having a fight, and she chased him out of the house with a wooden spoon."

I stopped dead, nearly doubled over. "She did what?" I yelled, fighting for air.

Ethan started giggling but then continued. "Yeah, she was mad cause he was being mean or something, and she chased him to the driveway with it. Yelling that he was a poop head. Except she didn't say poop."

"Well, I'll be a something or other. That grandma of yours, she's a bag of tricks," I said, watching her watch us leave as we went around the side of the house.

Ethan slid his hand back into mine, and the late August sun surrendered to the darkening skyline. We walked over to my place, grabbed Pickle, plopped him in the back seat of the Porsche, and took him for ice cream too, because he was part of the family.

Yeah, so, I have a family. Well how 'bout that.

Epilogue

How'd I do? I'm no writer, I know that. Some of my songs were halfway decent but scribbling down a few cool lines is no book. With this, I tried to keep you in the moment, write as if things were unfolding in real time and all that, but I'm sure I screwed that up plenty. I wanted it to read like a novel of sorts, because the thought of me just yacking on about my life sounds excruciating. Hopefully, those "third party omniscient" (just Googled that) flashback chapters didn't throw you. Who am I kidding? You're probably all smarter than me.

The constructs of what make a great story are alien to me, so if you'd tossed this whole thing in the crapper ten pages in, I wouldn't have been angry. I'm sending the full manuscript off to this former librarian the nerd accountant recommended, and she's going to "dig into it like an infected wound and find the healthy tissue and cut out the rest." I told her that's cool and all, but if I don't like what's left, then I'm going unfiltered, and that's just the way it is. I'm all for cleaning up my third-grade grammar and adding a few egghead words here and there, but this isn't

Leaves of Grass. It's my life. Interesting at times, it was. Always poetic, it was not.

I wrote this, originally, because I was offered a chunk of cash to do so, and I guess because, like all of us, ego suggests that *someone* will want to hear about our lives. Shit, log onto any social media site right now, and I guarantee one of your numb nut friends just posted a rant three paragraphs long about how nobody can tell them how to live their life and that everyone's going to "need to deal with their choices," blah blah blah—all of us are trying to be heard. The problem is that much of what we're saying is useless noise. Ear and eye clutter that solves no problems, offers few solutions, and is rarely entertaining. I don't think I'm fully exempt from that description either, but I looked over the copy a few times. There are parts I'm pleased with, others less so, but this isn't Hemingway sitting by the ocean tapping at keys. It's me, a guy who has a silly dog and stumbled into some sort of life that a few people found amusing. It had its moments though. I hope you noticed.

Oh, so yeah, I started this book because of the dough, but I finished it because of Sasha, my mother, and of course because of Laurel. With everything I brought with me here from L.A., there's no way I would have made it out the other side, sober and coherent, without her. She collected me, reassembled me, and then she set me free. I owe her at least to not go off the rails again and to love her little boy, which is the easiest damn thing I've ever had to do.

So now what? Well, obviously I have Ethan. To look after, play goofy games with as Pickle darts in between our legs and slobbers all over, and to offer whatever guidance a schmoball like me ever could. I've got a beautiful home in the woods of Vermont that needs the windows to be left open for a month but is otherwise idyllic. There's Barry to help along with his chess game and make sure he goes to some meetings, so all that is a lot on a fella's plate already. I have a pile of cash that I will sort out with Lyle and his pal and figure out how to turn into a bigger pile. Most of that stack will go to Ethan because the T-shirts with goats on them are cool now, but he's going to want some righteous threads at some point. He strikes me as a college guy, so there will be that. He'll probably want to go to Harvard or some shit, so maybe I'll sell the Porsche to Dan Toggins, but he'll have to promise to take Timmy for rides. I have this ridiculous dog in my passenger seat that I love more than I can even understand. I have the cars, for now, one of which I'm driving as I talk into this dictation app on my phone. I have my health, which ain't bad, considering where I've been in days of old and of not so old. I have my sobriety, which isn't old at all, but it's exciting and terrifying, and I'm going to nurture the hell out of it and take it seriously, so I don't end up a sad story like many of my pals over the years, especially ones with large lizards. Oh, and yeah, I have my fame, of course. Can't forget that.

You're no dummy. You've figured it out. This fame thing isn't everything I once believed it was. I'm not saying it doesn't have its perks and that if I walk into a Denny's in Albuquerque and a table full of loons want to take selfies with me that I won't be flattered and all, but it's no longer front-of-mind. I lost three women that I loved in less than ten years and finally acknowledged that more than half my adult life I've been drunk. The adulation from strangers can never change that, and truthfully, I'm glad it can't, because I want to feel this hurt. I want it to be a part of me for a while as I hold it in tandem with some of the recent joy that found its way in. I want to wake up sober for a week at a time, feel the clarity of sound mind, and see what that world looks like. I want to believe that my purpose, if I have such a thing, is something other than what it's always been—selfish and solitary—and rather this self*less*, innate sense of love and empathy that I feel rising after being long dormant.

Maybe Laurel was right, that I found that stone for a reason, though I've resisted believing in such things for most of my life. In first seeing it underneath that snarled grass, in touching it, moving my fingers across its cool, bumpy surface, I connected to something other than myself, and I'm looking forward to where that takes me. Mostly, I'm looking forward to being a grown up for the first time in my life, even if it's in an immature world.

Right now, however, I'm looking forward to taking this trip down to Miami and then shuffling over to New Orleans (did you listen to the song?) with Pickle and Laurel. Yeah, I know it's not really her. I don't rub crystals or read astrology or believe anything that suggests the ashes in the metal can are still connected to the wonderful woman I was lucky enough to be loved by for a while. However, I also acknowledge that what the hell do I know? And just in case, I'm taking some of her ashes to spread into the warm Atlantic and the Gulf because, as beautiful and pristine as that water is, it could only be better served by having some of her in it. And she loved the ocean.

I'm going to miss Ethan, but I told him it's only seven or eight days, and his grandmother wants to take him to see friends in New Hampshire. They have some emu farm or some kinda weird shit, so it works out well. As much as she's started to warm up, I'm sure she could use a break from the Traxon machine that's been cranking at full force for a while, and that wiggly finger must have like four joints in it by now. She and I will find our way. If we don't, well, there will always be Ethan, there will always be Pickle, there will always be chess, and there will always be music. Speaking of which, Marty called me a few days back and said something about a "reunion tour," which sounds excruciating, but who knows. Laurel would probably tell me to do it and write all about it, so maybe you'll hear from me again. Lucky you.

Currently, there's a screaming rear engine roaring behind my head, a happy-as-balls dog with a pushed-in face and bacon slice of a tongue flapping in the breeze, perched on the door sill, and a track by the Counting Crows about to play through twelve speakers. I wish that Laurel was here, sitting next to me with Pickle held tight to her chest, quietly singing along to the melody with lone strands of hair that never stayed tied back scurrying about her cheeks. I wish that I'd had more time with her. I wish that Sasha had better men in her life, including me. I wish I could fully forgive myself for what happened that day. I'm trying. I wish I'd stayed closer to my mother. I wish that Barry wouldn't move his knight right onto the edge of the board every chance he gets. I wish that I could feel the unfiltered joy that Timmy does in what are often our afterthoughts. I wish I were more respectful to that potholder. I wish Pickle could live for as long as his happy little heart wanted to stick around.

I wish I were a better writer. Maybe next time.

Love,

Josh.

THE END

Acknowledgements

"I want to thank all the wonderful Beta Readers that took the time to read my silly little book...Sharon aka "The Wolves," Chris Havener, Rebecca Roberts, Julia Chatfield Levy, Lisa Spencer, Livi Longley, Kerry Eklund, Marisa McCain and of course Lenny. Your time, thoughtful insight, and enjoyment of characters I created was appreciated beyond any words I could ever pen. THANK YOU! Thank you to the editors that helped me get this where it needed to be—Michelle Merrill Gilstrap, Anglea Frazier and Evie Marie. You're the best! Mucho thanks to Treehouse Brewing Company for making the best beer in the world that I often enjoy thoroughly while hammering out some words. Thanks to Stacy Brevard Mays and Hear Our Voice for taking a chance. Thanks to Mom for listening to some of my early chapters and giving me feedback, and for being so brave of late. Thank you to music for existing, otherwise sanity would escape me. I love you all, and sorry to anyone I missed!"

ABOUT THE AUTHOR

Dave is a writer from North Central CT that loves crafting stories about the known and unknown world. He also enjoys music, reading, travel, cars, and adores Pugs (as well as most critters). In past endeavors, he was a music writer that interviewed Van Halen, Blues Traveler, Motorhead, Metallica, Ryan Montbleu, and Big Head Todd & the Monsters, among others.

Most recently, he placed Top 25 in Writer's Digest's annual Personal Essay Contest with his entry, "The Waiting Area," which touched on his rocky but amusing childhood and will be published in Spring 2022.

CPSIA information can be obtained
at www.ICGtesting.com
Printed in the USA
BVHW071222290922
648293BV00001BA/112